THE DEMON CIRCLE

DAN SCHMIDT

LEISURE BOOKS NEW YORK CITY

To my wife Mandi.
All my love, and thanks.

A LEISURE BOOK®

January 2000

Published by

Dorchester Publishing Co., Inc.
276 Fifth Avenue
New York, NY 10001

ISBN 0-8439-4670-9

Printed in the United States of America.

THE DEMON CIRCLE

Chapter One

The chanting curdled his blood with fresh hot terror. At first it struck his ears from a great distance, then slowly washed over him before closing rapidly, a soft dark wave crashing over him from a vast sea of voices, male and female, adult and, even more sickening, children. Voices, he determined, somewhere beyond the last stand of pine trees. His heart was pounding. He was so close but a million miles away from saving all that mattered to him. Fear turned to a writhing nest of snakes in his belly.

Then a man's voice suddenly bellowed above the chanting, "Take their souls into your kingdom, oh, lord and master of all that is flesh and blood, our Prince of the Dark World, lord and master of we, the human race, whose only desire is to worship and serve you!"

Oh, God, no! he heard his mind scream. The sick bastards were going to do it. They were going to butcher them, a human sacrifice for Satan, tear apart his whole world as if they were nothing more than cattle fattened for slaughter.

He hastened his strides, nearly charging up the riding trail, the eerie cadence of their prayers rising to a fever pitch. He drew the .45 Colt from its shoulder holster. But something was suddenly terribly wrong.

He was paralyzed. Oh, dear God, what was this? Why couldn't he move his legs? Why did he feel as if he were suddenly forging into a wind tunnel, but a dark tunnel where there was no wind, just an invisible hammering soundless force? And why couldn't he scream? Alert them to his presence, at least, distract them long enough from their hideous task so he could just start blasting away?

"Take them! We yield their naked flesh to you for your consumption! We rip out their virgin hearts in homage to your eternal glory and undying greatness!"

No! He was too late. Or was he? Why was it so dark all around him in the woods? Ahead, there was the flickering glow of a bonfire, and that should have cast enough light over the clearing where they were prepared to snuff out his world, so that he could see the enemy. But where were they? He heard voices, but he saw no bodies, no black robes and cowls. He had to keep going, will his limbs to move. There. Some dark and flickering shadow, darting into his potential field of fire, then gone in the next moment. With grim determination he moved ahead, but only by a few feet. It felt as if he were slogging through drying cement.

Just one more step and he knew he would be right on top of them. Then he heard a familiar voice, crying out for both their lives to be spared. He froze, searching with wild eyes for these soulless animals, his finger tightening around the trigger. *Bastards! Where are you? Show yourselves!*

Desperate now, he waded into the mist, his heart pounding with primal fear. Then he was plunging into a white mist, heard the crackle of fire, could feel the flames dancing, almost right in his face, only there was no sign of fire. Frantic, he searched the shroud of mist, heard the roaring flames, louder and louder, alive now with animal hunger. Then something parted the fog ahead, winked firelight. And before his mind could register the despair and terror of what he knew was happening, he screamed. But why couldn't he move now? Why couldn't he bring the gun up?

A shrill female scream ripped the mist. The huge hunting knife flew, up and down, then slashing, back and forth. Cold laughter, growls of "Go to him, bitch, go to your master, you little whore!" burrowed into his nauseous sense of impotent rage. He couldn't move—but something was moving him, tugging him in a clawing angry grasp. But, worse, he couldn't even turn his head, or lift his arms to ward off the unseen hands pawing and grabbing at him.

No, he could only stand there, locked in the mist, and watch the great crimson explosions spray, pure red on white, as blood rained over him. He wanted to scream again, but now his mouth was firmly clamped, the sound of his silent shriek of fury and anguish tearing through his mind, an echo chamber of tumbling, endless darkness. Then the grasping and shaking became more intense, demanding, clinging.

Something was boiling out of the mist, clutched in long, white, skeletal fingers, lofted and displayed as if it were a trophy. Something red and dripping . . . and pumping. He knew what it was.

Again the cold laughing voice. "See. I told you. They really had no heart."

"Oh, no! NOOOOOOOO!"

A scream finally erupted from his mouth, an enormous and savage animal bellow, a sound of despair and torture he knew would never end.

"Mark! Mark!"

He heard her voice, familiar, but out there in the darkness. He heard his own cry, echoing all around him in the black confines of space. It was someplace he thought he should recognize but couldn't identify.

Light!

The whiteness pierced his eyes like needles, the tugging and shaking of hands on his shoulders stronger and more desperate with each frozen second. He heard his name called out, over and over in fear.

Mark. Yes, he was Mark Jantzen. His wife's voice. The light, thank God for the light, real light, not the eerie and hazy light of the nightmare.

Slowly reality cleared the fog in his eyes. He found himself upright, soaked in cold sweat. His ragged and long gasps of breathing filled his ears, pulsing angry drumbeats from deep inside his skull. Bile was squeezing into his throat. The wind was his only grasp on reality, which was creeping back, ever so slowly. Yes, the sound of a low and moaning wind, rattling the wooden shutters of their bedroom window.

"Mary," he said, aware of the sweat soaking into his underwear, shivering against the icy cold rivulets running down the back of his neck. "Mary?"

Trembling, he reached for a cigarette. The fog had lifted.

He felt his wife's hands on his shoulders, her touch soft and warm, yet he could feel the anxiety in her fingers. He stood, legs rubbery, dry lips drawing deep on his cigarette. The room. His wife. There in front of him, but they still had some taint of unreality, as the nightmare clung to his memory.

It was getting worse, he knew. So long ago it had happened, but now the memory had come roaring back, invading his sleep with hellish visions. For weeks, it was the same nightmare, over and over, almost every night, until he was nearly afraid to go to sleep. Why now?

"Mary?"

"Mark, I'm here, it's okay, baby. It's okay."

Wooden, he walked to the dresser mirror. There, he stood and stared at his reflection. A hard check, to make sure he was real, alive, back in the present.

"Mark, this is starting to really scare me. Mark. Mark! This past week..."

Her voice trailed off as he stared into the dark brown pools of his eyes. There he stood, mid-forties but looking ten years older. Once thick brown hair, long since gone gray. Look at the face, he thought; it was his but it seemed to belong to another man. What was he now? What was left? Just some ghost of yesterday? The face lean, eyes sunken, deep lines etched in his forehead, around the eyes. Aging fast and hard; worse still, getting a little thick around the middle, but shoulders and chest still solid, the only hint that he was once young and virile.

"Mark...are you listening to me? Have you heard anything I just said?"

He turned. She was sitting on the edge of the bed, drawing on her own cigarette. She had put on her nightgown, flimsy silk that molded a thirty-three-year-old body that was shaped to female perfection in the right places. He focused on her face, the small pert nose, the full lips, the tussled silken mane of dark brown hair. Mary. His wife. Too beautiful, he thought, to endure this grief which had suddenly come flaming back into his life. And somehow more real in the hellish visions of his nightmares than what he knew had happened. But more real than ever. Problems. Serious problems.

Somehow, he found his voice, but words tumbled from some dark corner of his mind. "It...it didn't happen that way."

She heaved a breath. His heart ached for her frustration. The truth, though, was what hurt him the most.

"Mark. Please. You need...I want you to get help."

He hesitated, then nodded, but didn't say anything.

For what help, he thought, could possibly change what had happened? Not even God, he had long ago heard, could change the past.

Jeb Gruber cursed, grabbed his pillow and hurled it into the darkness. His German shepherd, Hercules, had been barking for what seemed like hours, only the dog wasn't in the trailer to receive the brunt of his anger.

He lay in his sweat-soaked sheets, trying to will his dog to stop barking, but knew it was futile. He was going to have to get up, find Hercules and kick him in the tail. "Stop that goddamn barking!" Impossible. Something was up. Damn it, he thought, he had stayed planted in bed during that endless stretch of howling, wanting only to sweat out a long night of whiskey and beer. For what seemed like hours, he tossed and turned, viciously swearing at his dog. Sleeping it off was hopeless. The damn dog just wouldn't stop yapping up a storm.

Snarling, he unfolded his beefy, tattooed, six-five frame and nearly tumbled out of his soiled sheets. Struggling to stand, he reached for the bottle of Jack Daniels, killed a stiff slug, hit the lamp on the nightstand.

He read the clock. Just after four in the morning. What the hell was Hercules so jacked up about? Through the alcohol haze he searched his trailer home. The front door was banging softly on the frame. A low wind was blowing over the prairie, a plaintive moaning, sweeping in from the black desolation and tugging gently at his home. Beyond the door it was, indeed, black as death, but this was south central Oklahoma, a stretch of no-man's-land where he'd chosen to remove himself from the human race. He liked his isolation when he wasn't drilling oil, or working in the sawmills east in the Ouachitas.

Something, though, or someone was really disturbing Herc, and Gruber felt a hot stirring in his belly, a desire to spill blood, that he hadn't known in years. An ex-felon, he knew more than his fair share of trouble, whether it was coming on in his face or creeping up on his backside. This was backside trouble, he determined, sneaky and cowardly, like some punk in the joint sticking a shiv in the kidney when you weren't looking 'cause he didn't have the stones to do it face on. Someone was going to pay for disturbing his night. The townspeople of Newton, even the Indians, knew better than to mess with him. This was his land, clearly marked off, defined. One dirt road led to the county highway more than a mile north; no other way into his turf unless someone hopped the fencing and legged it through the woods. At hundred-yard intervals, he had PRIVATE PROPERTY, NO TRESPASSING signs hanging from fencing which ringed his four acres.

Someone, he figured, wasn't respecting his privacy. He would find out what the hell was going on, and take care of the trespasser his way. He never much cared for Okies anyway, these sleepy cowboys and ranchers who still believed in the American Dream. He cracked a mean grin as he hoped it was an Indian, drunk and wandering onto his property. The whole state was one big Indian refuge. One less Indian, he figured, would make the world a better place.

Shucking on a flannel shirt, shivering against the cold wind blowing into his trailer, he went to the kitchen drawer and pulled out a .357 Magnum he'd bought from a dealer in Texas. He considered taking the Remington pump shotgun, but in the dark a weapon that size would be spotted right away. Shock effect was what he wanted when he blew the trespasser's face off. Yeah, swing the Magnum into view at the last minute, give the bastard his ex-con's grin and blast him straight into hell. It had been a long time since he'd killed a man. That good old predatory hunger was back.

Grabbing a flashlight but intending not to turn it on until he was on top of Hercules, he staggered out of the trailer. The sky was an infinite black void of winking stars and a half-moon. He took a few moments to adjust his eyes to the dark, then focused on that damnable barking. South, he determined, somewhere just inside the edge of woodland that ran a line up the edge of the prairie.

With each long stride toward the towering black sentinels of pine and hickory, the wind, the cold and adrenaline sharpened his senses. He closed on the barking, thumbed back the hammer on the Magnum. The barking took on an angry note, vicious in the impenetrable dark ahead of him. He knew his dog, his only companion in his angry and hate-filled world, and he knew Hercules was poised to attack.

Ears tuned to the slightest noise, a hint of onrushing danger, he caught the sound of brush rustling ahead, then thought he heard a groan from somewhere deep in the woods. His liquor-sodden mind thought it registered the sound of a woman, or maybe a girl, crying out in fear or passion, he wasn't sure. Okay. A couple of kids, humping away on his property? Sweet. He had a real surprise for them if that was the case.

He felt the grin stretch his lips when suddenly a shrill yelp knifed the darkness from deeper inside the woods. He froze as the sound ended with chilling abruptness, and left him locked in cold fear, standing alone and shrouded in the bitter cold and the hard silence. Instinctively he knew without having to see his dog that Hercules was dead. He was certain of it in the next heartbeat when he heard the heavy thud, the horrifying but familiar tearing that was the unmistakable sound of steel ripping flesh apart.

He was cursing the unseen killer of his dog, hearing but not hearing the sudden gust of the gathering wind, before he caught the crunching of brush. The killer was charging him. Gruber was turning to the left, but the sounds seemed to come at him from both sides.

He was snapping on the flashlight, swinging his gun in the direction of a dark shape that rushed him from the bowels of the woods, when he felt the cold steel pierce his side.

Chapter Two

His shell of numbness and anxiety cracked. Gradually he became aware he had been driving aimlessly for almost two hours. His stare dropped, focused on the dial of his watch. It was almost noon. After last night's repeat incident, Mary would be worried sick. And could he blame her? What was happening to him anyway?

In grim reflection, he put the pieces of the morning together. He woke up just after eight, lay in bed for a good thirty, maybe forty minutes, mummified, afraid to get out of bed and face the day after another night of terrifying visions. Finally, anger at himself for clinging to the past roused him enough to get out of bed and shower. Then he found his wife had left a pot of coffee, with a note beside it. "Gone to open the diner. See ya later, baby. Love you." Signed with her usual smear of lipstick, her signature that he was still her world, always the loving and concerned wife. So she had been at their diner since five in the morning, cooking, serving breakfast. Waiting for him to show.

Looking around, trying to get his bearings on an unfamiliar landscape, he braked the Jeep Cherokee to a stop. Where was he? Slowly it dawned on him that he had driven south, away from Newton. Woods loomed to the east, beyond which were granite slopes. He had been driving toward the Ouachita Mountains. He was still in the county, but just barely. What had he been doing? What was he thinking? Was some subconscious impulse driving him to escape? But escape what? Or perhaps he was nursing some dark fear of confronting his wife after she had implored him to get help. Procrastinating? Hiding from the truth? Wishing he could keep that truth secret?

Now he found himself on a narrow dirt road and spotted the NO TRESPASSING sign.

Everything dazzled around him, a shimmering haze of green woods and sun-baked brown prairie. Even his dark sunglasses seemed useless against the harsh sunlight as he squinted behind the shades and scanned the sprawling prairie to the south. The sun blazed with its midsummer fury, a grim reminder that life in this part of Oklahoma was at the whim of Mother Nature, where cattlemen or wheat farmers who couldn't get a bank loan for irrigation were held hostage by the cruel threat of drought.

He sat there, forcing himself to relax in the chill of the air-conditioning blowing over his face.

Snap out of it, he told himself. What was done

was done, what was gone was gone. He had to put it behind him.

But how could he? His second wife of five years... at least she knew the truth. Every last sordid detail. And she forgave him.

She forgave him. God, she was the most beautiful woman in the world, all heart, all passion, all woman for one man. Did he deserve her?

With a slight tremble in his hand, he lit a cigarette, content to squander more time, pull it together, at least until some of the fog lifted.

Time and again it was like that. The nightmares. The waking up, shaking uncontrollably, growling like some rabid animal, even screaming in blind terror. Finally aware that Mary was there to comfort him, but only after sitting stony in her quiet wish that he get professional help. Help, right. Fat chance. Even years after, all he felt was the guilt and sorrow of a dogging sin, a cold fury toward the atrocity. Then the inevitable fight with self-hate. Like now.

He pulled the bottle of bourbon from under the seat and stared at it for a long moment. It was a tough decision, to continue to drink or put it away for good. But he had long since come to some neutral terms with the bottle. It was a thing, after all, and a thing did not control a man. So he was drinking again, breaking his promise to himself that he wouldn't drink before late in the evening. Mary accepted his drinking, and he sometimes silently thanked fate that he had found a drinking woman. But this was Oklahoma, after all. Here, they went to rodeos, farmed, herded cattle, went to church, had rattlesnake festivals, and drank. He was mindful and respectful of his new friends, neighbors and acquaintances, but sometimes caught himself in a moment of cynicism that this wasn't the big city, the fast life. No hidden agendas here, no monstrous crimes, no horrific sins.

Mary was born and had lived all of her life on this prairie land. Tough, hardworking, always compassionate and caring for others, she was his friend, his lover, his companion. She was wife and mother and sister to him.

Whatever. This morning he needed a drink to calm his nerves. He took a deep swallow, let it burn down, warm and soothing, all the way into his belly. It could erase the present, let him drift off, if only for a little while. Of course, Mary would smell the alcohol when he finally showed up at the diner, and she would stand before him in a lingering moment of anxiety and disappointment. Just one more big beautiful swig, just one for the truth.

His Mary knew the truth, all right, and she knew that alcohol had helped bring an end to his police career. Worse, it might have even caused the horrors that—*Stop!* He couldn't think about it. The nightmares weren't fact, but they were close enough. But why now? Why was he suddenly tortured by it all? And his precious, beautiful wife he worshiped more than life itself? How could she be so strong when he was so weak in certain ways? He could wear a mask for the world, for the people of Newton, but she knew him.

Slowly he focused on the trailer home in the distance, aware he was on someone's private property. He saw the woods, south of the lonely shabby home on cinder blocks, skinny pine, unmoving brush, all of it so forlorn and desolate. Indeed, everything looked and felt so still, so silent he felt a stab of paranoia. It was that same gut-wrenching fear of the unknown he'd experienced when he had been the first one through the door with a search warrant or a warrant for a suspect's arrest.

He knew where he was when his gaze fell on the red El Camino in the distance. He didn't personally know the guy who lived there, but he knew enough of Jeb Gruber to know the type, a sullen loner who hated the world, an ill-tempered man with simmering violence inside who had been in more than one drunken brawl in town. Gruber was trouble. Mark Jantzen was a former cop, but he would always be one. He knew people, knew their hearts as only a cop who had seen the worst in men, and women, could know. Jantzen had long since come to terms with life, he believed, clinging to a hope that the world went on only because there were a few good men and women left.

Jantzen was swinging his vehicle around when he spotted the brown Chevy Caprice in his rearview mirror. His heart skipped a beat as he recognized the bulldog face behind the mirrored shades. He braked, waited, knowing this didn't look good, as Sheriff Tod Stephens rolled his cruiser down the dirt road and parked behind Jantzen's Jeep Cherokee, nose to bumper. Jantzen tossed out his smoke and fired up another cigarette, hoping the smoke killed the odor of liquor. Luckily the county was pretty much Baptist, not Mennonite or Nazarene like other parts of Oklahoma. That meant alcohol, pool halls and gin mills were tolerated in Newton. A local killing a couple of shots early in the day might be overlooked by the county sheriff.

They watched each other for a long moment, then Jantzen smiled and waved at the sheriff. Stephens didn't return the gesture.

During the five years Jantzen had lived in Newton he had never seen any crime like he had working as a beat cop and then a homicide detective in Atlanta. Newton, population 376, was a quiet little town of ranchers and wheat farmers. The town itself, maybe all of two dozen buildings, was planted on the edge of the prairie. East were the sawmills, where those men who couldn't afford to own a ranch or secure a bank loan for a farm generally worked. Shopkeepers ran their small businesses in the town, where tourism was virtually nonexistent. People raised families there, went to church with fervent devotion, scraped by on cattle and wheat, the sweat of their brow. Trouble in the form of real crime was foreign to the sheriff and his two deputies, unless they were breaking up a rare bar fight or tossing a drunk in jail.

Still, there was something cold, almost menacing, about Stephens that Jantzen didn't like. He suspected Stephens resented the fact that he was a transplant from back East—one who had married the most beautiful woman Newton or any other county in the state could offer—and the fact that Jantzen was a former policeman. Worse, he'd been a city cop who had known real police work firsthand. Loud and clear, Jantzen had always read the way Stephens had looked at him—suspicious, wary, measuring. Long ago, he decided the sheriff figured Jantzen was a hotshot city cop and he was just a small-town hick with a badge and gun, man pushing fifty, sheriff for life, with a lot to prove and who hadn't proved it yet. Not far from the truth. No, they weren't about to become drinking buddies. In a town where everyone called each other by their first name, Jantzen got the feeling he wasn't exactly on the sheriff's Christmas card mailing list. He was "Jantzen" or "Mr. Jantzen."

Finally the sheriff opened his door but took another long moment before getting out.

"Afternoon there, Mr. Jantzen," the sheriff said in his usual bored drawl. Slowly he moved up on the driver's side on short legs as thick as tree trunks, adjusting his Stetson, then his dark shades. Jantzen watched but made an effort to keep his gaze off the man's hip-holstered Dan Wesson .357 Magnum. Stephens was dressed in brown shirt, khakis and black cowboy boots, sweat stains already spreading around the armpits. The sheriff's cheek was packed with chewing tobacco, and he squished out a long brown stream as he rolled up on Jantzen. The man was showboating.

"Kinda' far from home?"

Jantzen blew smoke, offered what he hoped passed for an easy smile. "I, uh, I got lost."

"Yeah." Stephens leaned against the door frame and looked toward the trailer home. "That right?"

Jantzen drew deep on his smoke, felt the tension knotting in his belly. "I had some things on my mind. Needed a quiet place to do some thinking."

"That a fact? You and Mary having problems?"

Jantzen felt his jaw muscles tighten. He had blundered onto private property but he resented the sheriff's skeptical tone as if he were a suspect under interrogation. And now Stephens made it sound as if he had a right to know personal business about his married life. "No. My wife and I are just fine. I made a wrong turn. I drove in here to turn around and get back on the county highway."

Stephens nodded. "Well, maybe you don't know whose land you just decided to pull off on and suck down a coupla' belts. Yeah, I smell ya, Jantzen."

"Sheriff, come on," Jantzen chuckled, trying to sound casual but fighting down his rising irritation. "Is there a point to this?"

"Yup, there is, now you ask. Jeb Gruber lives here."

"I know all about Gruber, sheriff. An ill-tempered man who likes to get drunk and beat up on people."

"Or worse, he catches you on his property. Mean bastard must be sleepin' off one helluva hangover or he'd be out here looking to tear you a new one. But I figger you could more than likely handle that kinda' situation, you being a hard and streetwise city homicide cop and all."

"Warning received, Sheriff. Now, can I go on my way?"

"Lucky thing I was down this way. The Burtons were at it again. Got a call about a family dispute. Poor guy just lost his ranch. Damn banks. Won't loan a man squat, 'less he has ten thousand head of prime beef. Now Jake just stays drunk and fights with his wife 'round the clock. Kinda' makes me wonder where the world's gone to. Every day seems like they're shuttin' down another oil field or taking away a man's right to make a living off God's land."

Jantzen wanted to say "life's tough all over" but skipped it, knowing it would only inflame the sheriff's resentment.

"Ask you one more question, Mr. Jantzen?"

"What?"

"Gruber's gate. Was it open when you pulled in?"

"It was. Like I said, Sheriff, this was an accident. That all?"

"Sure. Say hi to that beautiful wife of yours for me. Woman makes the best flapjacks around."

"It's all in the buttermilk."

"The hell you say."

"Have a nice day, Sheriff," Jantzen said, backed up, then rolled away. As he headed up the drive, he saw Stephens holding his ground, watching him through his shades in the sideview mirror. Then Stephens gave the Gruber trailer a long stare, seemed to think about approaching the man's home, then decided against it as he walked back to his cruiser.

No, Jantzen didn't care for the man at all, but he didn't want to get on his bad side either.

She couldn't move, couldn't speak or cry out. She couldn't even see or hear at first. What had happened to her? Where was she?

It slowly came back to her, and the shadowy memory of what had happened made her queasy. She struggled for a moment, then realized she was tied up; then she felt the slick, soft, cool nakedness of her younger sister. They were both trussed up, roped together, left alone in the darkness, back to back. Prisoners.

There was something else, too, something she

became aware of through a nauseous fog of pain and creeping horror. Her mind screamed as she realized what had been done to them. She felt it in her, wanted to deny what was happening, but there it was, and it was all too dreadfully, shamefully real.

Something long, thick and hard had filled her between the buttocks, had been shoved up her, left there for her to feel every time she drew a breath. The pressure inside her was excruciating, as if it pierced her stomach. Then she realized that whatever was in her was also locked inside her sister, binding them together in this sick union. If one of them even squirmed an inch, the other felt the hard pole slide up them even deeper. The slightest movement meant more pain, more shame. Acid churned in her stomach. Silently she sobbed. What was this obscenity? What sort of monster could do this to them?

It came back to her in full and shocking and sickening awareness as she heard her sister whimper beside her. She was Julie Fenner, fourteen. She and her sister, Barbara, had been riding yesterday, not more than a half-mile down the trail, within sight of their parents' ranch when they had been attacked, snatched off their horses. She had never even seen their attackers, but recalled at least two very big shadows rushing them from beside the trail. Then something with a sickly sweet odor had been clamped over her mouth...then the warm darkness had descended.

She stared up into the darkness. Above she heard low moaning sounds. Then the discordant, unintelligible noise drifted down over her from above. Footsteps began creaking up there, as if their captors were mentally tuned to both of them waking and stirring. What was that awful chanting? It sounded as if the voices from above were praying. Who had abducted them? How long had they been there? Surely their parents would be frantic by now. Everyone in the county would be out looking for them. Or were they? Did they even know?

Freezing, feeling hate and fear and anger toward whoever had shoved the obscene thing up them, she heard the heavy groaning of wood. The creaking ended. Then she saw a thin knifelike ray of light pierce the darkness around her. More wood creaking, as someone descended steps. The room must be a storm cellar, she decided, like the one her parents had at the ranch, the one beneath their home in the event a twister swept over the prairie.

A roaring twister would be sweet music to her ears compared to the eerie prayers she now heard. With the cellar door left open, it sounded as if an entire chorus washed over her, but she couldn't make out the words. Her heart pounded with fear. She struggled, the obscene object spearing deeper. Groaning against the pain, she heard her own muffled sobbing in her pulsing ears. Silently she prayed this was just a nightmare and she would wake up any second, screaming in her daddy's arms, Dad stroking her hair, holding her tight.

Only it was all too real as she felt the presence of someone beside her. Then a hand was laid on her forehead, a big hand, cold against her skin. She imagined it was how the skin of a lizard might feel.

"Be still, my fair little ones."

The voice was cold, deep. Was he laughing at her? She shivered, repulsed. She knew most of the people of Newton but she didn't recognize the man's voice. She shut her eyes, not even wanting to see the face of her tormentor.

"Sweet and fair, blond and tender. Bet you were Daddy's little girls. Now you are mine, all mine, my little virgins. You're nothing but meat, meat for my grinder."

Oh, God, no, she heard her mind cry, writhing in revulsion as she felt his hands cup her breasts, then slowly stroke her legs. Then she heard the sound of the man's zipper, heard his breathing, heavy, rasping. She felt the burning of tears in her eyes. She felt so ashamed. She heard her mind cry out for her father, for Daddy to come and save her.

"Oh, my fair little ones, this is only a taste. Feel the seed, the hot sweet seed of his life. I am your lord and your master. I will shower you in the real and the only holy seed. Be still. Soon, very soon, you will bow before me. I will give you up to the goddess. Tonight...ah, tonight, you will belong to us. You belong to your lord and master."

She braced herself, even as she felt the bile squirt up her chest. Her sister's squirming and muffled crying intensified as the cold laughter roared into her ears, and Barbara struggled so hard the ropes cut into her bare arms and legs and the object shoved up into her seemed to rip apart her insides.

It was then that she knew the both of them were going to die. It occurred to her that tomorrow was her birthday.

Chapter Three

Rolling down Tyler Street, the main paved road which bisected Newton, Mark Jantzen put on his best work face. But today it was a forced easygoing mask.

It was going to be a long day of faking it.

Wishing he were anywhere but where he was, he watched the smattering of townspeople milling around beneath the awnings of their businesses. They talked, smoked, sipped coffee or drank soda during this time of day when business was even slower than usual. So he smiled, waved to Burt Martin, an old, raw-boned man who had owned the Martin hardware store, the family business for at least three generations that Jantzen knew of.

Slowly he drove on, past the one-room Newton Post Office, the one-story Bank of Newton, the squat Newton Grocery Store, which was about big enough to hold maybe a dozen people comfortably at one time. This was an old town, holding its own against time and the elements, braced to endure the long, cruelly hot summers, the short but bitter winters. Buildings were made of either wood or red brick, everything structured to withstand the elements. Right then, Newton struck Jantzen as a dinosaur wheezing its last breath on the prairie, but lumbering still in the shadows of the frontier days when men were armed with six-shooters and rode horses. That was yesterday, and today it was pickup trucks with gunracks, with a lot of the menfolk still clinging to the cowboy days with their Stetsons and cowboy boots. It was home for him, but sometimes he found it all a little silly.

"How ya' doin', Mark?"

Bob Tamlin, the skinny, crew-cut town barber, smiled beneath his brown Stetson as he waited for Jantzen to roll his Jeep Cherokee past him. Okay, here we go, smile and wave back his how-ya-doin' afternoon best.

Just like that, he lapsed into a dark well of cynicism and sullen anger. Newton looked odd, different, out of all realistic proportions that sun-blazing afternoon. It could have been the bourbon, the aftershock of the nightmares, perhaps a combination of both. But boredom, even discontent, was what he was really beginning to feel. Or maybe he thought himself superior to these easygoing folks who didn't demand or expect much more out of life than an honest day's pay for honest work, three squares and a weekly trip to the white Baptist church, which loomed just east of Miller's lumberyard. Maybe he had put down some roots, tried to be one of them, but was wondering if maybe he hadn't made the biggest damn mistake of his life.

No—the second-biggest mistake of his life.

The first, he reflected, cost him his marriage, and ultimately, he believed, the lives of his first wife and young daughter.

Impulsively, he slammed the steering wheel with a balled fist. Then he looked around, hoping no one had seen the strange outburst of anger, as he slid into a parking slot in front of the diner.

Someone had.

Jantzen found Buddy Simpson walking across the boardwalk of the diner. Peering at him, the tall, lean Simpson walked down the wood steps. His blue eyes were hidden by a narrowed gaze.

As Jantzen killed the engine and opened the door, he found Buddy still staring at him. He wished Simpson would stop looking at him that way.

Buddy Simpson was probably the closest thing Jantzen had to a real friend in Newton. When he first arrived in Newton five years ago, the Cherokee Bluff saloon had been Jantzen's home for some time. Back then, Buddy had just gotten divorced from his wife, lost his job as an oil field worker. Jantzen and Simpson got drunk together, shot a lot of pool until last call, traded some war stories, told lies, yucked it up. Jantzen found out Simpson was a former Marine who had done two tours of duty in Vietnam. A cop and a soldier, it seemed only natural they became friends. Different professions, but each with its code of honor and commitment to duty, to know the meaning of putting it all on the line for country, society, for their fellow soldier or brother officer. Of course, Jantzen had never told the entire truth about his past, skipping the lurid details of what had driven him to call Newton home.

Then came Mary, and marriage, his final toehold to sanity.

"You okay, Mark?"

Jantzen fired up a cigarette and watched Buddy tip back the brim of his Stetson. Buddy had a handlebar mustache, which he often fingered, as he did now.

"Everything's beautiful."

"Coulda' fooled me. Hit that steering wheel hard enough to shake your whole truck. Hey, I'm your pal here. What's eating you?"

Jantzen cleared his throat. "Just thinking, that's all. I was riding around..."

He let it trail off, wishing Buddy would stop staring at him, feeling angry at himself for losing control. He regretted having just opened the door to any extended talk about his personal problems.

"Yeah? Feeling some regrets? Thinking maybe life's a little too slow around here? From the excitement of the big city to this sleepy little dustbowl out in the middle of nowhere. Maybe it's a mistake to keep on livin' here. Maybe you and the Mrs. need a change of scenery." Buddy paused, and Jantzen felt his friend's blue eyes still boring through him.

Jantzen chuckled but it was a mirthless sound. "I won't say you're entirely wrong..."

"Come on, Mark. It's me you're talking to. I was the first person you met when you staggered into the Bluff that night five years ago. Drunk and angrier than hellfire. 'Course, me being the sweetheart I am, Mr. Compassion here and all, I figured you were all right from the first, just angry things didn't work out for you back in Georgia. We talked a lot, a lot of bullshit, grant ya, but we had both lost a lot at the time. Remember those times?"

Jantzen felt his chest tighten. Back then he had lied to Buddy, made the man believe he was only divorced.

"I remember. At least you don't remind me you damn near held my hand until I pulled myself back together."

"I seen a lot in my life, my friend, most of it bad. A lot of bad things that could have, should have, killed whatever faith I had in my fellow man. 'Sides, it was Mary who got you to get your act together. You owe her, not me."

Damned if that wasn't true, he thought.

"Say, I ain't lookin' to pry, but... hell, whatever's buggin' you, Mark, why don't you come to the Bluff a little later? Drink a couple beers, we shoot some pool. Huh, how's that sound? I mean, if it wouldn't be a problem for Mary."

"Might be just what I need." He was thinking maybe he needed a day off from the diner anyway. "Aren't you working, Buddy? First time I've seen you in months. Somebody said you went north for work."

"Hell, no, I ain't workin'. You know me. I took that job near Lake Thunderbird in the spring. Good pay and they only needed me until early summer." He shrugged, showed an easy grin. "House is paid for, I got a little nest egg. Laid enough pipe and drilled enough oil in my day. I owe myself somethin' of a good time, way I figure. So, what do you say? See you later this afternoon at the Bluff?"

"Sure, why not. I'll slide down around three or so."

"Good. I'll have a cold one ready for you. Tell Mary you're in good hands. Not to worry, you ain't gonna' get ugly around me."

Jantzen chuckled, but it sounded anxious in his ears. He knew his wife would reluctantly let him go to the saloon. He would give her the usual assurance he'd stay as sober as possible, make some excuse that he needed a little time to himself. Then he felt a stab of resentment. He was a grown man, he'd bought the diner with his own savings, even if they jointly owned the place on paper. He should be able to have an afternoon to himself if he wanted to. What the hell was wrong with him right then anyway? Why did he feel like he was looking for a problem? What problem? With whom? What did he need, a fight with his wife who only wanted to help him? Since the nightmares started, he was drinking more and barely touching his wife. It wasn't her fault he was so distant, distracted.

Let's go on in, fake it, he told himself as he ambled up the steps and opened the diner door, its cowbell jingling to signal his entrance. He found Mary behind the counter. She had been talking to Pete Murphy, an old rancher whose wife had just died from lung cancer six weeks before.

He glanced around their diner. Right then he felt like a stranger in his own home. It was the first time he could remember thinking just how barren the place looked.

The Newton Diner. It wasn't much in the way of a restaurant—basic wood booths, juke box, long Formica counter—but it was comfortable, clean. Plate-glass window. White-tiled floors. Served everything from basic breakfast to burgers, barbecue and buffalo steak. They hired locals, friends of his wife, to wait tables, cook, keep the place open late at night.

Crossing the room, Jantzen smiled at his wife, returned a few "How ya' doin's" with a nod and forced polite smile. There were all of three customers at the counter. Tim Stallins and Jack Reilly were chomping on burgers, and greeted Jantzen as he rounded the far corner of the counter. Stallins and Reilly were in their mid-thirties, lean, faces weathered from working in the oil fields when they could find work. They both seemed decent enough, but Jantzen never completely trusted them. Once in a while he would catch the sideways glances they threw his wife. Something told him they came here for more than just the food.

"Tim. Jack. How you doin' today, fellas?"

Around mouthfuls of food, they muttered they were just fine. Damn but he was getting tired of these people. Nobody seemed to have much to say, much to do. Life went on in slow and sleepy Newton. Talk about cattle, lack of jobs, wonder how many twisters might blow over the prairie later this summer.

Jantzen kissed his wife on the cheek. Right away, he caught the flicker of concern in her eyes. She knew he'd been drinking.

"Hey," Mary said. She sounded sullen.

"Mary said you weren't feelin' too good, Mark," Murphy said, sipping on his coffee, working on a Camel unfiltered.

"Nothin' that a month in Hawaii with my wife wouldn't fix."

Murphy chuckled. "I hear that."

Small town. Small talk.

"Hear about the Fenner girls, Mark?"

Jantzen stared at the old rancher, read the smoldering anger in the man's eyes. "What?"

"Disappeared."

"Well, not sure they disappeared," Reilly interjected, throwing his perpetually narrowed gaze at Murphy. "They haven't been seen since yesterday."

"They were out ridin', way I heard it," Murphy went on. "Babs and Justin found their horses on the trail. No sign of the girls. Our good Sheriff Stephens and his deputies have been out all morning, combing the county. Don't turn up the girls soon, Stephens already told me he'd be wantin' volunteers to help in a countywide search."

Jantzen stared at the three men. He said nothing for several long moments. "Could be a simple explanation."

Murphy grunted, skeptical. "Like what?"

Jantzen shrugged. "I don't know."

"Yeah. The world's changed, and for the worse," Stallins commented. "Lots of wackos out there."

"Heard they found the horses, not the girls," Murphy repeated.

Jantzen didn't even want to ponder the possibility of a kidnapping in Newton. It would set the town on edge, and it would put Newton on the map. He could see that the trio at the counter wanted to get stirred up about the Fenner girls, let their imaginations run wild.

"Fellas enjoy your lunch," he said, then gently tugged on his wife's arm, steering her toward the back room office. As they neared the swinging doors to the kitchen, he caught a glimpse of his wife's penetrating stare. She was not happy with him.

Quietly Mary Jantzen shut the door to the back office. Outside, the sounds of clattering dishes, rattling pans, french fries sizzling in grease were muted but somehow sounded ominously loud in the stretched silence. She had smelled the liquor on her husband's breath, figured he'd delayed arriving at the diner to do whatever it was he needed to do. Which was brood, alone, nurse all those sudden regrets about the past. Up to a point, she understood, felt deep compassion even, but enough was enough.

She watched as Mark lit a cigarette and settled into a straightback wooden chair in front of the desk.

The office was small. A desk with papers, inventory and bills, scattered around the desktop. A small safe in the corner, a refrigerator with sodas and a six-pack, cold cuts and leftovers. There was a cabinet with a few liquor bottles, a radio in the corner of the room. Locked in a shelf beneath the cabinet was a pump shotgun. She destested the weapon, and knew Mark had a .45 Colt at home, also. He claimed the weapons were necessary; they owned a business, after all, lived pretty far out of town. One never knew what might happen. Reluctantly she indulged his paranoia.

On the desk was a portrait from their wedding day, and she felt compelled for a moment to stare at the picture. Mark was dressed in a white sports shirt, gray slacks and windbreaker and she was wearing a white blouse, Levis, cowboy boots. They were both smiling in the picture, holding each other. A local Baptist minister had married them, one witness, no reception. Like the office and the diner itself, the portrait struck Mary as incredibly simple but clean. It was the way her husband wanted to live. Or so she had believed up to this point.

It was also the way she had always lived her life. She had been born in a small, quiet town, about fifty miles northwest. Her father and mother had owned a ranch, which she sold after their deaths. Dad had died of a heart attack and her mother had shortly followed her father into the grave. Mary Sturbin, now Mary Jantzen, knew something about alcohol. The bottle had killed her mother. Liver failure. Perhaps, she often thought, it was the death of her mother which had drawn her to Mark. Whatever demons had tortured her mother, she would never know. But she knew what had so tormented her husband all these years. She wanted to help, wanted to believe that in some way she could even save her husband from his demons. She had not been able to save, or even help, her mother. She hoped it could be different with a husband she loved with all her heart.

After all, she thought, feeling infected by her

husband's dark and solemn mood, Mark was all she had left. She had had one brother, but he had died twenty years earlier in a riding accident, fallen off and broken his neck. She had always thought it strange that she never had more brothers or sisters, but her mother had confessed to her a long time ago, in a moment of drunken anger and self-pity, that she couldn't bear any more children. Mary never knew why.

"Why do you hate yourself so much, Mark?"

He looked surprised. "What?"

"Why can't you forgive yourself?"

He turned a little in his chair. "What are you talking about?"

"Do you want our marriage, Mark?"

"What?"

"Mark, stop saying 'what,' and stop playing dumb. I may be a simple rancher's daughter who's never been out of this state. I don't have a college degree. I never lived in the big city like you. I don't have all your experiences in life, I certainly have never seen what you've seen or done. But I'm not stupid and I'm no fool. I'm a good woman, who loves you to death." She moved around the desk, fired up her own cigarette. She stared into his brooding eyes as she settled into the chair behind the desk. "I don't deserve this kind of abuse, and I know something about abuse."

"Abuse? I'm abusing you?"

"With your distance, yes. By building a wall and shutting me out. By making me feel as if I'm some sort of leper. You don't have to hit someone to abuse them. You go for the mind and the heart. You intend to hurt someone's soul."

Anger hardened his eyes for a moment. "Mary . . . you're exaggerating. Grossly."

"Am I?"

She watched her husband, and anticipated his next reaction. He rose and went to the liquor cabinet, made himself a stiff drink as that dark look she knew so well lately shadowed his face.

"How can you compare our situation with some cowboy who stayed drunk all the time and beat you senseless as a way to control you?"

"In a way, it's the same thing, Mark. Then there's your contempt, your condescension."

He sucked on his glass of whiskey and peered at her. Softly he shook his head. "What is this?"

"For weeks now, I've seen the way you walk around. The way you treat me, the way you look at people in this diner. With contempt, Mark. Are you tired of our life together? Point-blank—are you sick and tired of life here? Do you want to leave?"

"Mary . . . I love you . . . I worship you."

"If you love me so much, get help."

"It's not that easy," he said, an edge in his voice. "You . . . you . . ."

"I what? Wouldn't understand?"

"I was going to say . . . you couldn't imagine."

She shut her eyes and chose her next words carefully. When she opened her eyes again, she softened her face and voice. "This is not good cop bad cop here, Mark. I know the truth. Mark, you had an affair. You feel as if you abandoned your wife and young daughter at a time when they probably needed you most. They . . . God forgive me for reminding you . . . they were murdered."

He killed his drink, then went and built another

one. "They weren't just murdered, Mary. They were butchered...they were sacrificed. They were... violated in every way...they were part of some...grotesque, monstrous...inhuman ritual... I can't even conceive of. And I saw murder when I was a cop."

She saw he was shaking. It wouldn't do any good, she knew, to tell him to go easy on the drinking. At this point, the day was shot.

"And they never even caught the sick fucks," he snarled through clenched teeth. "Can you blame me for being this way? For wanting justice?"

She paused, sat in heavy silence, then said, "Justice, or vengeance?"

"With animals like that, it's the same thing. Killing them quick and clean would be too damn easy."

"Is that what you want so bad? Is that what torments you? You live to take their lives?"

He stared at his wife for a long time. "You talk about forgiveness, about me forgiving myself. I don't think I can know a moment's peace in this world until I know they're dead."

She closed her eyes, knowing it was futile to make her husband see reason. "I can't go on living like this, Mark. We have a life together. If you're so unhappy...if you can't find peace..."

"What? Then what? Is that an ultimatum?"

"Please. Help me understand. Help me to help you. It's all I'm asking. Is that too much for you? I'm your wife, Mark, I'm not your savior."

He finished his drink, stubbed out his cigarette. For a second his hard and angry stare softened, and she thought she was reaching him. He sucked in a long breath, and all the torture came blazing back into his stare.

"Mary—I need to be out of here. I need some time to myself. Please understand. It has nothing to do with you."

Reluctant, she nodded. "Then go."

He looked at her with regret.

"What is it you want, Mark? You know, you can't redeem all your own sins."

"Answers and closure would be enough," he said, and left the room.

Mary Jantzen slumped back in her chair. She felt her heart sink, a tight sickness clawing at her stomach. Her husband, and their marriage, she feared, were slipping away. She felt like weeping. Instead, she went and made a stiff drink. She had a diner to run, a life to live.

Chapter Four

Even after winning the first two games, he lost interest in shooting pool. Fact was, Mark Jantzen wasn't interested in doing much except drinking to forget.

"Mark, you look like a man who desperately needs a heart-to-heart. You want to tell your buddy here what's eating you up? Mark—look at me. I'm telling you, I'm all ears."

Lifting his head, bent over the table, Jantzen stared at Buddy Simpson for a long moment. Then he glanced around the saloon, debating how to proceed. Yes, he wanted to talk, tell Buddy the truth, or at least most of the truth.

First, he wanted to make certain they were out of earshot. There was another pool table adjacent to their own, and it was vacant. Better still, a juke-box was humming out the soft moaning of country-and-western tunes, not too loud but loud enough to mute any conversation Jantzen and Simpson had.

Despite the music, the drinking, the occasional laughter, the saloon had a tired, almost solemn ambience. It was late in the afternoon and a few of the town's weary and thirsty had bellied up to the bar. Jock Peters was lining up the beers and the shots, the big man somber but only because he was sober. Peters was a muscular, dark-haired man who liked whiskey and gambling, and who ran poker and blackjack games out of the back room on Friday and Saturday nights. Often Peters drank behind the bar, would tie on quite the load, but the Cherokee Bluff was his place, after all. Of mixed descent, Peters had the high cheekbones, coal-black eyes and raven black hair of his Cherokee heritage. Unless Peters was drinking, he was quiet, grim.

There were a few other locals, perched on barstools. They were merely passing acquaintances Jantzen knew by name and occupation. Then he glanced at the two women at the far end of the bar. The petite but big-breasted brunette was Toni Jacklin, a woman who had recently been divorced by a local ranch hand who had run off with another woman. The other woman, a long-legged blonde in blue jeans that looked painted onto her, was Jackie Rawlins. She and her husband, Ben, were his closest neighbors on the northern outskirts of Newton. Both women were the objects of the attention of everyone at the bar, but in a small town where attractive women were scarce, it was to be expected.

Jantzen also caught the way Simpson eyed the women. Again, Jantzen spotted something in his friend's stare as he looked toward the bar, a bleak signal that Jantzen wanted to read as something dark churning in the man's head. There was a sudden burst of laughter from the two women as they drank their beers and male companions lounged near them, ogling the women, yucking it up. Simpson's mouth line tightened.

Indeed, Simpson appeared annoyed or envious of all the attention the women got. It was then Jantzen wondered about the subtle change in his friend. He wasn't sure how much whiskey Simpson had downed before he arrived but there was a definite, even vaguely disturbing, change in the man.

First, Simpson had lost his easygoing drawl, the good-old-boy routine. Then there was something hard, perhaps almost predatory, beneath the surface in the man's eyes. It was as if a shadow had dropped over Simpson's lean and weathered features, a silhouetted shape now barely hiding some cautious anger. Whatever it was, it put an edge through Jantzen, making him wrestle further with his decision to leave himself vulnerable in, at worst, a half-truth. But he knew Simpson, or thought he did. Liquor had always made Simpson more articulate, philosophical, but in a cynical way. Now the man appeared to Jantzen as if he were struggling to hide another person inside himself, as if he were afraid to reveal too much. Or was he too self-involved? Jantzen wondered about himself. Was he reading something into nothing?

"You miss your daughter, is that it, Mark?"

Jantzen looked at Simpson again. Gently he laid the stick on the table, straightened, squared his shoulders. "Yeah. There is something that's bothering me."

"You and Mary having problems?"

"Not exactly. But...yeah. Well, the problem is me."

Jantzen walked to the ledge against the wall. He lit up a smoke, worked on his whiskey and ginger. Obviously, Simpson knew it was serious. He moved and took his own drink, leaning into the ledge.

Jantzen hesitated, then said, "There's something I want to tell you. It's something...something I never told you." He believed that if he told his friend the truth now, it might help bridge the gap between him and his wife whenever he returned home. "My former wife and my daughter—they're both dead."

Simpson's gaze narrowed, a flicker of surprise in his stare. He killed his drink.

Jantzen let his statement sink in. Nervously he worked on his smoke, then finally said, "They were murdered. I'll skip the details."

Simpson let out a long breath. "That's quite a load you've been carrying, my friend. Mind if I ask what happened?"

Jantzen cleared his throat. "I think...in some way I can't define, I've always felt that what happened to them had a lot to do with what happened with me." He drank, smoked, gathered his thoughts. "I suppose...I got tired of policework, fact is I was sick of it, and sickened by it. Could be I was never really cut out for it. I don't know. What

I was really tired of was seeing what people could do to each other, the lies they told, the fact that they could never even admit when they were caught, much less that they were wrong. See the worst in people all day, every day, you come to feel that nothing in life is good or decent. Everyone is a killer, or a potential murderer, or a liar or a thief. Go home, you can't even talk to your wife about it, because she lives in another world, and you tell her about your day, how you see things, she'd tell you you're crazy to even stay on and you know she wouldn't be far from the truth. You go to a party, you sit alone and get drunk because you can't even stand yourself. You build a wall.

"You were in a war, I know you know that... just below the surface of us is an animal, these dark, ugly things that lurk in our hearts. My faith in my fellow men has been put to the test. Most times, I don't think I even like people.

"But what happened to my family, to a good woman and a daughter, the only child I ever had, two people I should have worshiped and adored and honored more than anything in life... well, I let it slip away. No, I drove it away. In some ways, I became an animal, I became what I despised in others."

He worked on his smoke, finished his drink. "What I did or didn't do... it haunts me. I suffer from... guilt at times. Okay. I had an affair on my wife. It was a seedy, hell, it was a sordid thing... I mean I did everything to and with this woman and her women friends a twisted mind could conjure up. My behavior can sicken me to this day. My wife found out, eventually. It caused us to separate, needless to say, divorce impending, my shame about to become public record. But I'll tell you, at the time what hurt the most was that she had...she had the strangest look on her face that day. It was a look of pure contempt for me. She said she hated me, that she didn't even know me, the man she had married, that she regretted, hated the day we ever met. Shortly after...they were murdered."

"And you blame yourself?"

"I suppose I do. I was hardly the husband and father I should have been. I wasn't even all that good a cop. What I mean is that I was borderline dirty. I accepted gratuities from bookies, gratuities, shall we say, from prostitutes. I gambled, I was often drunk on the job, but I was one of those functional maintenance alcholics. I cut people slack who didn't deserve it, and came down on the ones who needed the slack. Too many times I looked the other way when I shouldn't have. I hunted killers, but vice, like gambling, whoring, drug use, to me they were just pleasures. Others indulged, why couldn't I?"

"Atlanta's own Bad Lieutenant?"

"Not quite, but close enough. I tend to see myself as something...of a Judas. I betrayed my dead wife and daughter, and I betrayed myself. I thought I had values, I thought I had principles, I thought I had balls. All I came to see was that I was no better than anybody else. Fact was, I was worse."

"The animal that lurks in all of us, that it?"

"Just because I had a badge, just because I had the law on my side...in some way, it made it even worse. I was shit, I was nothing. I betrayed a code of honor, not to mention I made something dirty that was clean—my marriage."

"The Fallen Angel?"

"You could say that."

Simpson appeared to think about something, not looking at anything directly, then said, "You want I should go and get us a couple more?"

Jantzen nodded, then waited while Simpson went to the bar. As Peters fixed their drinks, Jantzen watched Simpson make curt greetings to the locals, throw his "How ya doin', ladies?" down the bar. It was then that Jantzen clearly spotted the lust in Simpson's eyes as he looked at Mrs. Rawlins. The woman was married, Jantzen knew, and had a teenage daughter. Strange how Simpson just kept staring at her. From a short distance, he thought he read something else in the look. What was that in the man's eyes? Right then Jantzen became uncomfortable with his realization, wondering if he'd just made a mistake, damn near wishing he could take it back. But it was too late.

Simpson came back with a tray of drinks, obviously not wanting to make another trip. He handed Jantzen a drink. "Mary know?"

"Everything. I skipped the details with you, but Mary knows the whole sick truth. She knows they were violated in such a way, murdered in such a way...it wasn't even murder to me. It was something inhuman, something so atrocious, so horrific, I can only imagine that something inhuman could have done what was done to them. I would have rather...they'd been killed quick and clean."

Simpson worked on his drink, deep in thought. "They ever catch them, these murdering animals?"

"That's what makes it even worse. No, they didn't. Maybe a few leads, at first, but they all came to dead ends." He paused, feeling heavy, sipped his drink, took a drag. "Lately... well, after it first happened, knowing what I knew about it, I had nightmares every night. It went on for about a year after, until I thought I was going insane. Then they stopped... I guess some time before I met Mary. I stopped drinking for a while. I even went and saw a priest. Maybe you know him, Father Ben McMartin?"

Simpson nodded. "Of him. Next county up. The only Catholic priest, with the only Catholic parish to be found in a hundred square miles of Baptist, Mennonite and Nazarene countryside."

"I told him what happened."

Simpson grunted. "Did you think seeing a priest would make up for your sins?"

Jantzen put an edge in his voice, feeling a sudden pang of resentment toward his friend's cynical tone. "I did."

"Okay, I'm sorry. Maybe I don't put as much faith in God as you do. Maybe..." He let it trail off, a distant look in his eyes. Then he said, "Look, we're talking right now, man to man, so I feel free to speak my mind likewise. I've seen plenty of that animal inside us you mention, especially in that war. I seen as much if not more murder and suffering than you did when you were a cop. I came to despise the human race. First, that was my way of dealing with it; then I came to see that I was right to feel that way. Nothing wrong with me, it was the world. When I returned here I hid a lot of things—such as my contempt for these people with their small-town ways and their small-town life. In one way, you and I may be alike. You feel superior to all this, just like I do, only I've seen things, I've done things that make me believe in my superiority to the whole human race. Okay, here we are. You want something more, only you don't know what it is. You want to run from the past, only it sticks in your head every day like a branding iron. Why don't you tell me about these nightmares?"

Jantzen looked at Simpson for a moment, wondering about the shift in the man's conversation, where he was headed. Finally, he said, "The past three weeks, I wake up every night with this scream locked in my throat. I lay there in a cold sweat, paralyzed. I remember the nightmares so well, so clear, it's if I was right there, as if it was real. Next day, I walk around in a haze, with this...panic, this tightness in my chest. I feel like I'm about to suffocate. I can't do anything, I don't want to be anywhere. I don't want to do anything..."

"But run? Hide? These nightmares, are they close to what happened?"

There was a moment's coldness in Simpson's voice that made Jantzen hesitate again. No longer did Simpson sound like the concerned friend. He watched him kill another drink. Simpson appeared to struggle to keep himself under control.

"I don't know. I never saw the crime scene. I read the report, I talked every day to the detectives working on the case. Of course, I saw...I had to identify their bodies in the morgue."

"Stayed drunk for days after, I bet. Feeling sorry."

Again that distant gaze fell over Simpson's eyes.

More and more, Jantzen was finding it difficult to read the man.

"You're starting to make me feel like I should've kept my mouth shut," Jantzen said.

"Listen to me, Mark. You did what you did. You messed around on your wife, she found out. So what? You weren't a very good cop, hate yourself for being a drunk, liar and cheat. What would you have me say? A lot of things in my life I could feel sorry about, too. Big deal, right? That you kept this from...well, that was your business. Let me tell you how I see the world, how I see what you see as your big sin of adultery."

Jantzen followed Simpson's hard stare toward the women at the bar. "See that? Look at that, take a good look at that. One's divorced, she rails about her deadbeat ex, how he messed around on her with other women, it was all that guy's fault, what a piece of crap he is. Only I know for a fact she was doing her own fair amount of cheating. There, I'll skip the details on you, but you're such a smart guy, I'm sure you can fill in the blanks. Anyway...moving on, you have the other one, a married woman, with the sweetest little blond daughter I've ever laid eyes on, a real heartbreaking little thing, sure her daddy watches her good. Now, I'm friends with the guy, her husband's a good man. Owns his ranch, has his own cattle, provides a good home, his own little stretch of paradise. Probably all he wants is a little love and respect. Only she's itching for something else."

Jantzen grew more uneasy as he worked on his drink. "Maybe she just wanted to spend a few moments with a girlfriend, share a drink. Sometimes there's a simple explanation."

Simpson scoffed. "Don't be so naive. You know what? I'm beginning to see your problem, friend."

Jantzen felt a deep stab of resentment. He felt slighted, silly at the same time, naked and sucker-punched. "Yeah. And what's that?"

"You want to be a good guy but you can't accept the fact that you're only human. You fail and you hate yourself because you think you should be better, only you're not. Those, my friend, are essentially your own words. Granted, you may have a good woman in Mary, but you can't trust women. For one thing, they're natural born liars, hearts seething with all kinds of stuff. They'll hurt you, they'll desert you."

Jantzen let out a soft whistle. "Hate to tell you this, Buddy, but if I shared that line of thinking I would've checked myself out long ago."

Simpson chuckled, a mean sound. "That's your biggest problem, and you can deny it all you want. So you want to believe in something good and decent. Who cares what you think, who cares what you believe in? I've been around the world, pal, and I've lived to be able to tell you there is nothing good and decent in the world. The young, like the Rawlins woman's girl, they're the only innocents, but that changes soon enough, too. You see, in the end, people bring the worst upon themselves because they deserve it. So if the worst is already coming, why not take what you can get before it comes? Why not live the way your heart tells you you should?"

"You'll have to forgive me if I tell you you're full of shit."

Another mean-sounding chuckle, a sideways glance of contempt. "I don't forgive you or anybody a thing. I don't even need to explain myself. Proof of a lot of what I say is right in front of your eyes. Married woman with a kid, down here around these drooling knuckleheads, lapping up all their attention. She got a few more drinks in her, maybe her husband's pissed her off, you don't think she'd spend some time in a hotel with one of these yahoos?"

"And here I thought I was cynical."

"I'm a realist, pal. The world is going to hell because hell is what it wants. Look around. Look at yourself. The human race has its own agenda. People have made right wrong and wrong right. The light has become the dark, and the dark has become the light."

Jantzen felt stunned by the low voice of controlled fury and hate. He had never seen Simpson so distant, cold, menacing.

"You go on about your life, Mark, trying to be a good guy, go on believing in your wife and your wife's love."

Jantzen felt compelled to fight back. His heart pumping with righteous anger, he told Simpson, "It's all I've got. It's all I want. I think we've talked enough."

Simpson laughed, a strange sound that seemed to bring a look of compassion to his eyes. Or was it forced? He looked at Jantzen for a long moment. Now Jantzen wasn't sure what he was seeing. Friend or foe?

"See, old buddy, see how easy that was? I got you out of your shell. How about that, huh? I just made you admit just what is the most important thing in your life. So you love, honor and cherish your wife. That's noble and I admire you for that. I really do."

Jantzen peered at Simpson. One minute Simpson had been railing at life with a twisted view Jantzen knew he could never hold anywhere close to his heart, and the next minute...what? The old Buddy Simpson? Easygoing and cheerful? Or was Simpson working some game on him? If he was, why?

"You should have been a psychiatrist," Jantzen grunted, a wry glint in his eyes.

"I should have been a lot of things. What I am, old buddy, is a whole lot more than what others see." He cracked a strange grin, then said, "Hey, what say we shoot some pool, unless you have something else you want to talk about?"

Jantzen stared at Simpson, wondering if he would ever feel again that this man was his friend. He wanted to leave, but suddenly felt compelled to stay. Did he have something to prove to his friend? That he could reveal the truth and face it?

Whatever, he didn't feel much better about anything. In fact, he felt worse than before he told Simpson the truth.

"Rack 'em," Jantzen said.

She was chain-smoking, watching the clock. Mark had been gone for a little over three hours but it seemed like days. As uninterested as her husband had been in minding the store, Mary Jantzen was even less concerned about the business. The longer she was alone, apart from her husband, the angrier and more worried she became. Perhaps even resentful.

She sat at the end of the counter by the cash register. A little dinner business was spread around the diner, all of them regulars. They spoke in low voices, glanced her way. Wondering, she was sure, where her husband was.

She wished she could snap her fingers and make their lives return to normal. But how could she fix what he had lived through? Even she couldn't imagine living with his past. When loved ones were murdered, how was that ever forgotten?

Obviously her husband couldn't forget. Perhaps he had shoved the truth, the memories, deep in the back of his mind, but they were still there. When she first met him, drunk all the time, wasting the days, shooting pool at the Cherokee Bluff, she felt a strange attraction for him right off. At first, she thought it was pity, then she decided it was anger. She saw beyond the mask, knew there was more to him than what showed. He was a stranger, drifting into town, angry and troubled, and she had been curious. When he could sober up long enough to find work on one of the ranches in Newton, she slowly came to know him, little by little, day by day. They would share a drink, dinner, talk. Soon they would...

She stopped herself. She was remembering the beginning, the laughter, all the love. Yes, the good old days. Silently, she berated herself. She was thinking those days were gone forever, that Mark had changed, returned to that other man she had first seen, full of torment, dark and brooding. But she knew that wasn't true. She knew the one person who could be the hardest on Mark Jantzen was Mark Jantzen. He would pull through this, come back to her, whole, sane, loving.

She was sighing, grinding out her cigarette when the cowbell rang. She looked up, hoping it was Mark, only she found Sheriff Stephens rolling into the diner. Right away, she sensed something was wrong, reading the sheriff's grim expression behind the dark sunglasses. She felt his stare boring into her, even as he made a few curt greetings to the locals. Slowly he walked toward her, then stopped in front of the cash register.

"Evening, Mary. How you?"

"Just fine, Sheriff." When he fell into grim silence she became uneasy. "How come I get the feeling you're not here to eat?"

"Well, I'm not, Mary. I, uh, I need to talk to your husband."

Alarm bells sounded in her head. "Why do you want to talk to my husband?"

His lips twisted in a fleeting grin. "Just need to talk to the man, that's all. Nothin' to get excited about, Mary."

"Then don't sound so mysterious, Sheriff. If there's a problem with Mark, I should know about it, don't you think? I'm the man's wife."

"Hon, there's no problem. Now, can I talk to him or not?"

Hon. She felt like reaching over the counter and grabbing the man by the throat, both for his condescending tone and his gall.

She had known Tod Stephens most of her adult

life and she never cared much for the man. She had always read Stephens as a bully, hiding behind his badge and gun. More than once he'd proven her right, as she'd seen the sheriff roust one of the locals on a drunk-and-disorderly. But he especially seemed to enjoy a heavy-handed routine when arresting a Cherokee or Cheyenne in the county, jacking arms up behind the back, chuckling as he shoved and manhandled a local Indian. No telling what he did to someone when they were out of sight in his jail cell. There were rumors about beatings, and many of the townspeople feared the sheriff. If he beat on anyone behind closed doors, no one ever came right out and made a fuss about it. But he was a man with a mean streak, pure and simple, wanting to control everything and everyone, his way or no way. No wonder his wife had long since divorced him and left the county, for reasons which Mary was never privy to nor cared about. Since their divorce, though, the sheriff spent a lot of time in the diner with his deputies. She always found his look and tone a little too aggressive, insinuating.

"He's not here."

Stephens let out a breath, exasperated. "Mary, come on, hon, there's no cause for alarm."

"So you say." She decided to tell him, knowing she could question Mark later. "Try the saloon, Sheriff."

He nodded, an oily smile crossing his lips. "Now that wasn't so bad, was it?" He turned, started to walk away, then stopped. "You know, Mary, I always wondered why, all the years you've lived here, we known each other, well, you never call me Tod. Why is that?"

She glanced at her patrons. They were watching the exchange, had surely heard that the sheriff wanted to speak to her husband. If she was worried about Mark before, she now felt a rise of panic. She wanted to answer Stephens with *Because I don't like you,* but instead told him, "You're the sheriff."

He pursed his lips, nodded. "Okay. I gotcha, Mary. 'Preciate the respect. I'll be talkin' to you," he said, and left the diner.

What was going on, she wondered. Something was terribly wrong. Any hope she had of patching up things with her husband, she thought, just went out the door with the sheriff.

Chapter Five

"How all you folks doin' this evenin'?"

"Somethin' to drink, Sheriff?"

"No, thanks, Jock. 'Fraid this is all business."

Jantzen was ready to sink the eight ball in the side pocket when he heard the sheriff's voice, looked up and froze. He found Stephens slowly walking toward him, removing his sunglasses. The sheriff's grim face coupled with his own mean whiskey buzz put an angry edge through Jantzen. Stephens didn't look like he was bringing good news.

"Boys havin' fun? Must be nice, Jantzen. Take the day off, leave your wife runnin' the store while you drink and shoot pool."

Simpson cued his stick. Frowning, he said, "To what do we owe the honor, Tod? You lookin' to take on the winner?"

"This ain't no social call, I can tell you boys that much."

Jantzen stared at Stephens, who was looking right through him with a strange expression. He felt his heart thumping as his paranoia mounted. A heavy silence fell as the jukebox took what felt like an hour before the next song began to play. Jantzen became aware of the curious stares from the bar.

"Your hardworking wife said I could find you here."

"What is it, Sheriff? You want a free meal at the diner for cutting me some slack this morning?"

"Slack time's over, friend. Buddy, maybe you want to excuse us for a minute."

"Sheriff, you don't do melodrama well. Whatever you have to say to me you can say it in front of the both of us."

"Suit yourself. First, you want to tell me exactly why you were out at Jeb Gruber's this morning?"

Warning bells sounded in Jantzen's head. "I already did."

"I know what you told me. But that was before."

Jantzen sank the shot, putting some anger behind the cue ball. The white ball banged off the eight, jumped, hit the table heavy and rolled toward the sheriff. Stephens snatched up the ball.

"I'm talking to you, Jantzen."

Jantzen tossed his stick on the table and squared his shoulders. Jaw clenching, he said, "Before what?"

"What?"

"You said that was before."

"Before I found the man murdered."

Jantzen's heart skipped a beat.

"Whoa," Simpson cut in. "Hold on a second here, Tod. You're not making much sense."

"Yes, he is, Buddy. I already see where this is headed."

Stephens dropped the cue ball on the table. "Do you now?"

"Our good sheriff here is about to accuse me of murder."

"Did I say that, Jantzen? You hear me say that, Buddy?"

"Not yet, but you're itching like a whore in church."

"Oh, ain't you two the comedians. Thing is, I ain't in a joking mood. See, Jantzen, after you left, I thought I might go have a little chat with Jeb, knowin' the man's temper and all. Thought he might've spied you staked out on his property. So I find his door wide open, knock, no answer. Walk in, wantin' to smooth any rough waters. Only the man's not there. Place is cold as hell, stuff blown around 'cause the door's been open all night. You know those prairie winds have no mercy. Car's outside, know the man has to be someplace. Anyway, I take a look around the yard, I don't know, I thought then he might've taken his dog for a walk in the woods." Stephens paused, then said, "The woods is where I found them."

"Them?" Jantzen asked.

"I believe I've asked you a question."

"Look, you want to take me in for questioning, Sheriff, do it. Otherwise I don't have a damn thing to say to you."

"You wanna do it by the book, that'd be fine.

Wanna answer some questions right here and now, we can set it straight without me havin' to embarrass you by draggin' you down to my office. How would that look to your wife?"

"How was he killed?"

"I'm not allowed to say—yet. You bein' a former big-time homicide dick, you should know the SOP. They're still going over the crime scene."

"State Police," Jantzen said.

"They'll handle the investigation. FBI might even come in on this one."

Numb, Jantzen went to his drink. He knew how it looked, but Stephens had it all wrong.

"Sheriff, I don't need to convince you I didn't kill the man. It's no secret he was not well liked. You run a background check on the man, I'm sure he's got a past that's created more than a few grudges. Besides, I never had a problem with Gruber. If I did, I'm sure you would know about it."

"No, I admit, old Jeb was not real well liked. Fact is, the way he was murdered, whoever did it, well, they're either real sick or they had a belly full of hate for him. Killed his dog, same way he was killed."

Jantzen's gaze narrowed. Something ominous in the sheriff's voice and look warned Jantzen that something about the crime scene had unnerved Stephens.

"Couple what I found out there with the fact the Fenner girls are still missing," Stephens went on, "I got a bad gut feeling this town is facin' some serious trouble. Last thing quiet little Newton needs is for the FBI to put this place on the map."

"And I'm the most likely suspect for all this sudden trouble?"

"Let's get something straight, Jantzen. Put the drink down."

Jantzen hesitated, then set his drink down. He looked Stephens dead in the eye as the sheriff walked right up to his face. The smell of tobacco on the man's breath made Jantzen's head swim.

"I don't like you, Jantzen, never have. I read you as something that sees himself a little too good. I see you as a snake that slithered into my town. Ingratiated yourself somehow to the best damn lookin' woman this side of the Rockies. What Mary ever saw in you I'll never know, but I damn near feel sometimes like tellin' that woman she may have made the worst mistake of her life. I know, we're just a bunch of dumb cowboys and hillbillies. You think you're better than us 'cause you came here with a few dollars in your pocket and carved out a cozy little nest for yourself."

"I think your perception of things, Sheriff, is not only a little warped but tainted with envy and a hard-on for my wife."

"You shut your filthy hole! You smug bastard, you listen to me. I find out you had somethin' to do with Gruber's murder I'll hang you myself. Fact, I'll make it my life's mission."

"I think you should have your facts straight first, Tod," Simpson said, "before you go off half-cocked here. Some evidence would help, too. Way I read you, the last thing you want is to have to apologize to Mark."

Stephens snorted, stepped away from Jantzen and addressed Simpson. "They'll be drinkin' cold beer in hell before I do that. And the rest of the time you chum around with your boy here, it's 'Sheriff' or 'Sheriff Stephens' to you, Simpson. We clear?"

"Crystal," Simpson growled.

"That all, Sheriff?" Jantzen said.

"For now."

Jantzen cut a wry grin. "But don't leave town?"

Chuckling, Stephens slipped on his shades. "Boys excuse me, I got a murder to help solve."

As Jantzen watched Stephens lumber back to the bar, the depth of the sheriff's hatred for him sank in. And now there was a murder in quiet Newton. Plus two girls missing.

Stephens addressed the barflies. "Folks, listen up. Might as well know, you'll find out soon enough. Jeb Gruber was murdered."

Jock Peters shook his head. Was that a smile Jantzen saw on the barkeep's lips? "Not surprised. Man was about as popular as a tarantula."

"He was a tarantula," Jackie Rawlins said. "Literally crawl all over me sometimes."

Someone chuckled.

"You may find it all amusing, folks, but I don't take murder lightly. Had you people seen what I seen, I gotta believe you wouldn't be laughing."

"What happened?" Peters asked.

"Not really at liberty to say, Jock." He paused, looking over at Jantzen and Simpson. "Well, I guess I can bend policy. I'm sure the buzz will spread soon enough."

Stephens searched their faces. Jantzen felt his chest tighten as Stephens angled his body, glanced at him.

"Jeb Gruber was gutted. His heart was ripped out of his chest. Whoever did it did the same sick thing to his dog."

The women gasped. Horrified, the other patrons stared at Stephens.

And Mark Jantzen felt his legs turn to rubber. It was all he could do to keep a poker face, stay standing.

"Didn't mean to sour everybody's fun. Folks enjoy. But be careful, people, there's a killer around here, that much is certain. Not just an ordinary killer, neither. A psychopath, someone who likes killing."

Stunned, Jantzen watched Stephens leave the saloon. He felt terribly alone, and very afraid. His mind reeled with a hundred questions. He couldn't help but feel locked in a nightmare.

"I don't believe this. Stephens suspects you of killing the man?"

Mark Jantzen sat in the passenger side of his wife's Chevy pickup. He had decided to leave his vehicle in town. With Stephens on the warpath, the last thing he wanted was to be arrested for driving under the influence. It would mean a long night in jail, more insinuations, embarrassing questions. Unless, of course, Mary came down and bailed him out.

As he drew on his cigarette, he felt Mary's stare bore into the side of his head. She drove the truck down the main county highway. God, but it was dark out here in remote prairie country, he thought. Look skyward, and the moon and stars seemed to almost sit right on the land. Black as death out there, he decided. Somehow it fit.

"Not in so many words. It's no secret the man doesn't care much for me. Sees me as this villain who rode into his town and stole the best-looking woman in the state. Factor in some professional jealousy on his part, me being the former big-city cop versus small-town Sheriff Barney Hillbilly... well, you've got the picture."

"Why would he even imply you might have something to do with the murder?"

Finally he dredged up the resolve, told his wife about his morning encounter with Stephens on Gruber's land.

"Oh, wonderful, Mark. You know how that looks to him?"

"I know how it looks, but how it looks isn't the way it is. But there's something else, Mary, that really disturbs me." He looked at his wife with all the torture he had felt the past few weeks. "First, Stephens tells me he can't divulge any details about the murder. That's routine. Then, after grilling me in front of everyone in the bar, he's leaving, right? Next thing I know he's announcing to everyone exactly how Gruber and Gruber's dog were murdered."

"All the while looking your way, I suppose."

"More or less. But when I heard how the man was murdered...Mary, you're going to think this is crazy. I know I've put you through hell lately. But something...something has been happening around here...and it's coming back, full cycle. Sort of...in my face. I can't explain, it's just this sick sinking gut feeling. Gruber...Mary, the man had his heart ripped out."

He found her staring at him with a sick expression.

"That's right. His heart was ripped out."

"So...what are you saying?"

"I don't know."

"Mark, I know what you're thinking."

"You do?"

"It's...it's just a weird and sick coincidence."

"How can I be sure?"

They were looking at each other when something suddenly darted across the road.

Jantzen spotted the shape, thought he recognized the figure as a man but couldn't be sure. A glimpse of a face, white as a cue ball. A fleeting figure, eyes as black as coal, reptilian in the cold lifelessness of the flashing glare of light. A shaved white skull? He saw teeth bared, white on white, grinning, on the fly, taunting, ugly in the stark white shroud of light. There and gone.

He shouted, "Watch out!"

He heard his wife cry out in alarm. She hit the brakes, threw the wheel hard to the left. A moment later, the truck was spinning, then righted itself but bounced hard into a ditch. Before he knew it, he saw the tree loom up in the headlights. Jantzen braced himself for impact.

The tall man with the shaved head hit the field laughing.

He glanced back over his shoulder. Across the road, the truck came to a jerky stop. It was just short of crashing head on into the tree. The two in the truck would have certainly died from the collision. He was disappointed their souls had not gone to the Master, but the night was young.

The night was good. The darkness, the silence of the prairie filled him with a warm sweetness. The only problem with the night was he knew he would stand out, a warning beacon in the darkness. Cursed, indeed, but blessed with knowledge, not to mention power.

He looked at the whiteness of his skin. It was not an albino color, but it was close enough. His skin was so white it seemed transparent sometimes, bones shining through, stark, jagged.

Repulsive.

The world must pay. The world did not even know what it wanted, what it even needed. He, the servant to the Master, would show the way. Desire was eternal, after all. Hate was love, and love was hate. They, those beyond their circle of immortality, mere mortals clinging to the fantasy of a better world, would never know. But they would understand. Tap the human heart's want, and they became enslaved.

He forged across the field. The others were waiting near the woods. Sweet fulfillment of desire was just ahead. The couple who lived on the ranch were young, married in the eyes of their God. No children, but he already had two young innocents. And they thought their love was pure. Already he was turning it to the sweet and true purity of hate.

And he had just defied death. Defiance of death, he knew, fed the spirit. He had seen the truck coming, waited until the last possible moment before racing across the road. He had glimpsed the shock and terror on their faces.

Shock. Terror. They fed his soul. He had dangled their lives over the abyss. He had plucked them back. They would keep.

He saw the others in the distance. They were robed, black figures hugging the tree line, waiting, calling to him.

He had called himself Judas.

Judas Pilate.

Indeed, the lambs were ready, but it wouldn't happen tonight. For one thing, the young girls nurtured his spirit. He was not prepared to give them up.

It was always like that. Find, hold, clutch, for pleasure and self, then destroy because pleasure, like life, could not be sustained. Only pain, only death was everlasting.

He wondered when they would have to move on. He liked this town. It was remote and isolated. Perfect.

And there were others feeding the core source of the group's spirit. They were growing stronger every day. Already they had recruited. Soon, very soon, it would all begin.

The world would see what it truly wanted.

"Are you okay, baby?"

He found his wife shaken but unharmed. She nodded and said, "I'm fine."

Relieved, he searched the road. Then in the distance he saw whoever had charged across their path. The figure clung to his memory but the details in his mind were vaporous, already fading. What was that he saw across the field? Were they shadows of people gathered near the woods?

Then he saw the darkened shape of the ranch home in the distance. He got his bearings and knew Tom Delmarvin lived there with his young bride. Given the events of the day, Jantzen wanted to find out if the young couple was home. And safe.

Jantzen opened his door. In the distance he already saw the shadows fading into the woods.

"Hey!" he yelled, crossing the highway.

"Mark! What are you doing? Where are you going?"

"Stay there."

Jantzen ran onto the field. His attention was fixed on the shadows in the distance. He intended to confront whoever had nearly caused them to get killed.

Then they vanished.

Chapter Six

A dog was barking, a throaty and distant growl that snapped Jantzen out of his angry search.

"Mark, what are you doing? Come back here!"

"Hey, what's going on?"

Jantzen stopped cold in his tracks. Whatever, whoever he thought he had seen was gone. Now Mary was racing up behind him. And a blaze of light spilled from the Delmarvin home, the ranch owner alerted to their intrusion on his property. Suddenly a flashlight flared to life, hit Jantzen in the face. He squinted away from the harsh glare.

"Mark? Is that you? Mary? What in the blue blazes are you doing out here?"

Jantzen recognized Tom Delmarvin's voice. Moments later, Delmarvin appeared, parting the darkness around Jantzen with his roving flashlight.

"What's going on, Mark?"

"It's okay, Tom," Mary said, catching her breath. "We almost had a bad accident."

"Anybody hurt?"

"We're fine," Mary said. "Just shaken up a little."

"What happened?"

"Someone ran in front of our truck," Jantzen explained. "I saw him cut across your field, headed toward the woods. I would have sworn I saw a group of people waiting there for him."

Jantzen was done talking. He wanted to find the daredevil, certain the man had intentionally run in their path. But why?

"Who was it?" he heard Delmarvin call out. "Did you recognize him?"

"Tom, let me see that flashlight."

Swiftly Jantzen went to Delmarvin. He saw the anxiety and confusion in the young man's dark eyes. Delmarvin was medium height, lean as a bullwhip, his short brown hair mussed after what Jantzen was certain was a rude awakening. Like Jantzen, Delmarvin was city-bred, having moved to Newton from Dallas less than a year before with his twenty-five-year old bride. Occasionally he and Mary had dinner with Tom and Judy Delmarvin. Jantzen liked the young man, who was honest, polite, wanted nothing more than to raise some cattle and run his own ranch which an inheritance from his father had provided. Jantzen had even helped the couple build their home, with the aid of other townsmen who knew construction work.

Jantzen took the flashlight. With long sweeps of the light, he searched the woods. Nothing, not even a fleeting shadow.

"There's nobody out there," Delmarvin said.

"I'm telling you I saw somebody. He came this way. Right, Mary?"

"I'm not sure. It could have been a deer, it could have been anything. I didn't see anyone."

Jantzen strode to the edge of the woods. In the distance he could still hear Delmarvin's German shepherd barking. From that direction, he made out the voice of Judy Delmarvin as she called for her husband.

"Mark, please, if there was somebody there, they're gone now. Come on, I don't want to alarm Judy."

Jantzen felt futility settle in but he kept raking the woods with the beam. How could they have slipped away so quickly? Or had he imagined seeing figures near the woods? Maybe too much adrenaline after the near miss had made him see something that wasn't there? Finally he gave up the search. Still, he was sure someone was in the woods, believed he could feel him, them, whoever, in the darkness. Maybe even watching them, he imagined, waiting until he left.

"I'm sorry, Tom," Jantzen said, handing the young rancher back his flashlight. "False alarm, I guess."

"You sure someone came onto our property?"

Mary answered the question for her husband, sounding exasperated. "No, he can't be sure."

Jantzen looked at Delmarvin's tanned, hawkish features. Working outdoors and with his hands had chiseled the young man's face and body. Shirtless, with only his pajama bottoms on, Delmarvin showed corded muscles in the shoulders and chest.

"Listen, why don't you two come on inside? I can fix you some coffee," Delmarvin said. "If you're hungry, we'll make you some sandwiches. Sounds like you two had a close call."

Judy Delmarvin, a robe wrapped tight around her, walked up behind her husband, asked what was wrong.

As Mary and Tom Delmarvin explained, Jantzen found himself growing annoyed that nobody believed he had actually seen the man. A tall, bald man, he believed. Only now it was a flickering image in his head.

He listened to his wife decline the invitation, saying it was getting late.

"Okay, some other time then," Tom said. "Say, we haven't gotten together in a while. Maybe dinner some night soon?"

In a way, Jantzen was irritated with Delmarvin shrugging off his claim about an intruder so easily. Was the young man naive? They lived out in the middle of nowhere, the closest neighbor maybe three miles away, and yet he acted as if he didn't have a care in the world.

He listened to the nervous apology from his wife, heard Mary offer them breakfast at the diner.

"Might do that, Mary," Tom said. "I have to go into town for supplies tomorrow."

Thinking about the circumstances of Gruber's murder, the disappearance of the Fenner girls, the young newlyweds' isolation, Jantzen figured he needed to talk to Delmarvin. Now was not a good time, sensing Mary was getting more put out with his behavior.

"Come by the diner in the morning, both of you.

Breakfast is on me," Jantzen said. "I insist. Anyway—I didn't mean to alarm you."

"That's okay," Tom Delmarvin said. "Good to know my neighbors care enough to check up on us. We're pretty much alone out here. Appreciate your concern, Mark."

They all said good night to each other. Walking back to the highway, Jantzen ignored his wife's penetrating stare. Silently, they hopped into the truck. It was the kind of tight silence that told Jantzen he was in for a long night.

"You need to get some sleep, Mark."

She pulled out onto the highway. She looked angry.

"You're probably right," he grunted.

Sleep was the last thing he wanted.

"It is your own death you seek."

He was awake suddenly, rolling over, turning on the light. What was that voice? What was the face he'd seen in the dream? Eyes as black as coal, face as white as a sheet, staring at him, then gone.

Swinging his legs over the edge of the bed, Jantzen rubbed his face. She was awake; he could feel her eyes boring into the back of his head. Slowly he turned, found Mary's face, framed in the outer periphery of the light from the nightstand.

"Go back to sleep, baby," he said.

At least he wasn't shaking, sweating. He was grateful there had been no nightmare. Still, the voice had sounded so real, so clear in his mind... the face. Was it the same face he had seen tonight on the highway?

"I can't take this anymore, Mark."

Groaning, he rubbed his face. "So don't."

"What does that mean?"

"Go back to sleep."

"What is wrong with you?"

He looked at his wife, and indeed wondered just what was wrong with himself. "You honestly didn't see a man run in front of us tonight?"

"Is that what this is about? Listen to how angry you sound. No, I didn't get a chance to see anything, I was too busy trying to keep us alive after you screamed at me. Yes, I believe something did run in front of us; what, I don't know."

He sank into himself. "Something bad is happening, Mary."

"No doubt. It's called our marriage slipping away."

"I'm talking about Gruber's murder. I'm talking about those two little missing girls. I think...I think what ripped my life apart so long ago is here. I'm afraid it's going to happen again."

She looked stunned. "You're losing it."

"Am I? I don't know, maybe I am. Maybe it's like you said, just some weird coincidence."

He turned away from her and sat in heavy silence. He heard his wife sigh, felt her drop back on the pillow. Finally he turned off the light, lay down, shut his eyes, but didn't think he would fall asleep anytime soon. If at all.

Suddenly he was more afraid than ever of tomorrow. He wasn't sure why, but he suspected his whole life was about to become a living hell.

Jantzen read the article in the *Newton Gazette* about Gruber's murder. It wasn't much of a report, no suspects, no motives, but he knew the police wouldn't freely give out information. He knew the writer, Jason Collins. The paper was right in town, all of a staff of four. Later he intended to go talk to Collins. Since yesterday, the old detective instincts had been coming back. Suddenly that morning, he had a sense of purpose. It felt good to be alive again. He showed the article to Tom and Judy Delmarvin.

They were sitting in a booth in the far corner of the diner. Mary was in the kitchen, preparing the four of them breakfast.

"Thanks for taking me up on my invite," Jantzen told the couple. "I only showed you that because...well, it might explain what you might think was bizarre behavior on my part."

They read the article, turned grim.

"Didn't know the man, but I knew of him," Tom said. "Not terribly likable, from what I've heard, but still, for anyone to be murdered...What does this have to do with last night?"

"Tom, do you own a gun?"

He watched surprise fall over the couple's expressions.

"You can feel free to tell me it's none of my business."

"That's all right." Tom Delmarvin sipped his coffee, glancing at his wife. "No, I don't own a gun. Not even a hunting rifle, not even an alarm system in our home. You saying I should have a gun?"

Judy said, "You don't think you're overreacting after last night, do you?"

He wanted to do this while his wife was out of earshot. "Look, I can see that married life has been real sweet for the both of you. I'd like to see it go on that way."

For a moment the concern on Judy Delmarvin's face faded as she smiled at her husband and squeezed his hand. "Tom's a wonderful husband. I couldn't ask for a better man."

Jantzen was happy for them, a smile dancing over his lips as Tom returned his wife's smile. Seeing how in love the couple were, it took him back to his early years with Mary. Not that he'd lost any love for his wife, but things seem to change over the course of day-to-day living. Bills to pay. A wife and husband come to really know each other. Passion may even cool at times as a certain degree of comfort settles in. Still, Jantzen had to admit Tom had married quite the beauty. Judy Delmarvin was petite but all woman in the right places. Her blond mane fell like dazzling sunshine to her white blouse. She had the face of an angel, blue eyes sparkling with love and contentment.

"I showed you two that article about Gruber's murder," Jantzen said, "just to let you know that life can be ugly. I was a cop, remember."

Tom Delmarvin cleared his throat, his expression serious, thoughtful. "Mark, after my father died I took over his business for a while. Finally sold it. The real reason being I was tired of living in fear in the big city. Judy and I made a joint decision to move away from Dallas, trade in the big city for quiet, small-town life. No crime. No drugs. No murders. No fear of your neighbors. I remember we moved here after spending some time in the county, then we bought that piece of land. You and some of the others in this town helped us build our home from the ground up. It's something I'll never forget. It wasn't about money or business of any kind, it was just people helping other people. Do you understand where I'm going with this?"

Jantzen nodded. "You found a slice of heaven, I understand, and you want to keep it way, peaceful and clean. Have you heard about the Fenner girls?"

"We have," Judy Delmarvin said, grim. "We're friends with their parents. They're worried sick."

"My whole point, Judy. Crime doesn't always confine itself to the big city. Allow me to be blunt, but I think I know a little something about the dark side of life. I really think you need more to protect yourselves and your home than your dog."

The young man clenched his jaw for a moment. "Mark, I could almost say you don't think I can take care of myself and my wife. I'll tell you, if I didn't see you as the older brother I never had, I might take offense to that."

"I didn't mean any offense. I just want you to be careful. If you ever need me, just pick up the phone." There was an awkward silence as the young couple stared at each other. Jantzen hoped at least he had given them something to think about. He scooped up the paper. "Okay, enough of that. Let me go help Mary get our breakfast."

Excusing himself, he went back into the kitchen. There he found Mary heaping four plates with scrambled eggs, six-ounce steaks, toast, sausage and hash browns. When she looked up from the grill, Jantzen smiled at his wife. It was the first time in days he had actually felt good about something. Mary peered at him.

"What's with you?"

"Just coming back here to help my beautiful wife with breakfast. Didn't mean to goldbrick."

She handed him two plates. "What are you up to?"

Jantzen chuckled. "Nothing. I can't say I love you just to hear myself say it?"

She smiled, still dubious. She kissed him on the lips, then said, "I gather you've had a nice little chat with our young lovebirds. What? Were you remembering how we were?"

"Were, are, and will be."

Wryly she said, "For an ex-cop you're not very good at conning someone."

"My wife, forever the cynic."

"Your wife, forever the woman who only wants her husband."

She turned serious. He read her frustration, became painfully aware he'd neglected her lately, in every way. He wanted to say he'd make it up to her, but actions speak louder. Even as that thought formed in his head, he felt guilty. Already he was looking for the appropriate excuse to leave the diner for a while. He needed answers about Jeb Gruber's murder. Already he had a mental shopping list of whom he would interview, and he would start at the *Newton Gazette.*

She smiled and kissed him again. "Whatever the reason for your mood, hold it. I like the man I'm seeing now."

Jantzen's moment of hope vanished. He doubted she would understand his need to depart the diner later.

Chapter Seven

Walking up the stoop to the small, red-brick building that housed the *Newton Gazette,* Jantzen was thinking his wife never failed to amaze him. Before leaving the diner he had decided against excuses or deceit. When he told his wife the truth, she had merely nodded and shown him what he wanted to believe was an understanding smile. She said if Sheriff Stephens was hell-bent on soiling his name, then he should go on a mission to get any information about the Gruber murder that might help defend him against the sheriff's ugly insinuations. Both her intuition and intimate, almost eerily psychic awareness of him rejuvenated some desire for his wife that he had lost during the past few weeks. Indeed, his wife seemed to know his agenda before he did. She was behind him, though, and that was all that mattered.

Inside the *Newton Gazette,* Jantzen saw Jason Collins look up from his computer terminal. Through a cloud of cigarette smoke, Collins squinted from behind his spectacles. The low hum of an ancient rattling window air-conditioner filled the silence.

"Mark. What brings you here?"

For a moment, Jantzen thought he heard suspicion, or caution, in the elderly newsman's voice.

"Mind if I pull up a chair, Jason?"

Jantzen waited for a response as the man seemed to ponder something. Jason Collins was about sixty, he figured, but the gray-skinned, emaciated man behind the wooden, paper-littered desk looked eighty years old to Jantzen. He knew the man was married to a big, heavyset woman named Thelma, a farmer's daughter, that his two sons had long since fled Newton to live in the big cities to the north. Beyond that, he didn't know much about Collins, maybe sharing a few drinks and a couple of laughs over the years. Collins knew he had been a cop. Now something warned Jantzen that Collins already knew he was there to ask questions.

"Help yourself," Collins said, nodding at a wooden chair with a green cushion. The furniture looked every bit as old, if not older, than the newspaperman.

The newsroom was so small, with only two desks, two old Smith Corona typewriters and two phones, Jantzen felt as if he was right on top of Collins as he settled into a chair that creaked under his weight. Like the rest of the town, the newspaper seemed stuck in a time long since gone and forgotten. The printing press, he figured, was probably an antique in the back room, one of those rolling presses that groaned and strained as it chugged out the paper. Then he caught himself before he lapsed into self-righteous cynicism. Collins struck him as a sad, lonely old man who had probably at one time had dreams of turning the *Newton Gazette* into a paper that reached throughout the state and put him in the public eye as a respected journalist. In fact, Jantzen recalled that Collins had mentioned that had been his dream at one time. Jantzen almost felt sorry for him. Funny how a man's dreams can die.

Collins hacked around his cigarette, then smoothed back the stringy tufts of white hair on the side of his bald, liver-spotted scalp.

"I read the paper this morning, Jason."

The newsman smoked. Grinning, he showed badly nicotine-stained teeth. "So let's cut to the chase. You're here about the Gruber murder. You want some facts."

"I don't want to waste your time, but maybe you've heard our good sheriff has made some ugly insinuations about me. My problem is maybe Stephens may even try to spread a little poison around here about me being his prime suspect in the murder."

"Talk of the town, sort of." He scowled, grunted. "Yeah, Stephens has been running his mouth, the usual bluster from a man who doesn't have much upstairs and too much time on his hands to let an overactive imagination get the best of him. But people around here don't latch onto rumor like a dog with a bone. Everyone knows Stephens doesn't like you."

When the newspaperman paused, smoking like a dragon, Jantzen sensed the man was disturbed. Collins seemed to make a point of looking away from him.

"What is it, Jason?"

"Mark, I'll be up front with you. This morning, the sheriff stopped by. Stephens told me you might come by here, ask a bunch of questions about the murder, pick my brains, you know, play cop on the snooping reporter. He told me to say nothing to you, not even a whisper as to any hunch I might have."

"Really? Don't you find that a little strange?"

"Yes and no. Far as I'm concerned, the sheriff can kiss my liver-spotted be-hind. I'll talk to who I damn well please. Here I am, sitting on top of the biggest story to ever hit this town outside some twisters that raise hell around here. I got a gruesome murder and two missing girls. I got Pete and Jake out trying to get a statement from Colonel Ben Wiley of the State Police. You know the drill. No one's talking. That tells me they know there's trouble here in the county that hasn't ended. Now the FBI has come on, we got suits all over the county in fleets of unmarkeds. I find suddenly I don't need to be getting the national news off the UPI and AP wires. I've got days ahead of me where I'm not writing about the rodeo, the rattlesnake festivals, don't need to bother to cover all the local events. All that's taken a backseat. Today, I'm a real reporter who can go out there and ask some hard questions."

"Mind if I smoke?"

"Don't be so damn polite, Jantzen, you hear me hacking up my lungs? I been smokin' these unfiltered sonsofbitches for forty years. Either smoking or whiskey is going to kill me, but we all die of something. You got questions, then ask me. But I'll tell you right now, you know as much as I do, which is next to nothing."

Jantzen smiled at the man's cranky honesty and fired up a cigarette. "How did you find out about the murder?"

"Bad news is the only kind of news in this or any small town and it travels faster than the speed of light. Deputy Jenkins couldn't keep it under his hat."

"Didn't see the crime scene?"

"Didn't get close. Wouldn't let us."

"Do you know the hearts of Gruber and his dog were apparently ripped out?"

"Rumor. I know Stephens has a big mouth. He made that announcement at the Bluff. Big shot, man can only play at being the law."

"So you're saying the good sheriff is grandstanding to scare folks around here?"

"Can't say for sure. All I know is Gruber was a bully, a loner, a drifter, most likely has a bad past he brought with him to Newton and it probably followed him here. I'm trying to get some background on the man, but so far me and my two-man staff have hit a stone wall. All I know is the cops and the Feds aren't talking, but they're interviewing any and everyone in the county."

"No one's talked to me."

"Yet. I'm sure they'll get around to you."

"So you see my problem?"

"Crystal clear. I'm sure Stephens has dumped his suspicions on Colonel Wiley. I don't have a damn thing that's concrete about the murder. What's more, I've been told not to write the first word about the Fenner girls, too. That came straight from Wiley."

Jantzen smoked. It all smacked of something sinister. But was it his gut instinct, or paranoia, or simply the torment over the memory of what had happened to him that was driving him to seek out the truth of the murder?

"The alarm bells have already sounded, Jason. Everyone knows about the Fenner girls. What's your hunch?"

"There's a sicko or sickos somewhere out there. Those little girls were clearly snatched."

"Same individual or individuals who murdered Gruber and ripped his heart out, you think?"

"Anything is possible. Mark, you've got this look about you."

"Unlike the dear, departed Jeb Gruber, I'd like to believe I have nothing to hide." He stabbed out his smoke in an ashtray that was overflowing with crushed butts. "But you're right. Newton has problems."

"I take it that's police experience talking?"

"That and bad gut instinct. Have you heard of any outsiders, strangers who have moved into the county?"

Collins shook his head. "Not that I've heard of. This is a big state, though."

Jantzen stood. "If you learn anything..."

"I'll stay in touch."

Jantzen grunted. "You don't care much for Stephens slinging mud my way, that it?"

"Part of it. I like your wife, you married a good woman."

"And you don't want to see her hurt?"

"I figure she learned her lesson after the bum she was with before you."

"There are those who might say she simply picked up where she left off."

"They don't know people like I do, or the ones making all those assumptions about you—well, in my mind, they've got their own agenda. If I thought you were a bad man, I wouldn't be sitting here talking to you."

Jantzen smiled, nodding his head. "Thanks for your time, Jason. I'll see you around."

"Take care."

Outside, Jantzen began playing back his conversation with Collins, his heart pumping with righteous anger toward Stephens. Then he froze.

The window of the unmarked cruiser was already rolling down. He'd never met the man, but Jantzen had a sinking feeling in his gut who was behind the mirrored shades.

"Mark Jantzen?"

"Let me guess. You're Colonel Wiley of the State Police."

The clean-shaved, squared-jaw man nodded. "Why don't you hop in, Mr. Jantzen. We'll take a little drive, catch some scenery."

Slowly Jantzen went around to the passenger side. He gave the sun-baked buildings of Newton a hard search. He could feel the stares from the shadows beneath the awnings drilling into him.

Sure enough, some of the locals who owned businesses were silently watching him get into the cruiser. He had a nagging suspicion that he was about to become something of a pariah in his adopted town.

For fifteen minutes, Jantzen rode in silence with the colonel. He watched the flat prairie countryside roll past them. Here and there, a ranch house and meandering cattle popped up. When he couldn't stand the silence any longer, feeling his nerves, he said, "Mind if I smoke?"

"Yes."

"All right, Colonel. I take it it was no mere coincidence you just happened by the *Newton Gazette*."

"Was I following you? Not exactly. But I figured we needed to talk."

"Let me guess," Jantzen said, an edge in his voice. "I'm a suspect in the murder of Jeb Gruber and his canine."

The soft chuckle from Wiley surprised Jantzen. He actually thought the colonel cast him a friendly look.

"No, you're in the clear. Okay, here we are. I've been interviewing your friends and neighbors, not about you but about any strangers they may have seen pass through town lately, or anybody who might have had a grudge enough to murder Jeb Gruber. I've got a list of about five men, two of whom are married and whose wives were messing around with Gruber."

"I'm off the hook?"

"You were never on it. For one thing, I know all

about the professional jealousy between yourself and Sheriff Stephens."

"Not on my part."

"No, not on your part. Stephens has it in for you, why, I don't know, don't care."

"He tell you I was on Gruber's property? Call me a trespasser, the same day the man was found?"

"And then some. I already ran a background check on you, Jantzen. I know everything, at least all I need to know about you. Know about your wife and daughter. I suspect you left Atlanta hoping to find a new home and a new life here in Newton."

Jantzen sat in silence. He knew the colonel was only doing his job.

Jantzen decided to hit the colonel pointblank. "Are there any cults in this county, Colonel?"

"You mean like they had down in Waco?"

"Maybe. Or the kind of cults that sacrifice animals... or young girls."

Colonel Wiley turned his head. Jantzen felt the man's stare bore into him.

"What kind of question is that? What are you saying?"

"It's a simple question, Colonel. One day a town is squeaky clean by all outward appearances. Could be someplace in northern Wisconsin, Idaho, wherever in sleepy, small-town USA. Next day you find out on the evening news an entire town is part of a paramilitary group that's looking to storm the White House gates, or is raping and cannibalizing young children, or is running around burning down churches. Unfortunately, it happens all too often. Now, you claim to know my background, doing your job, maybe trying to clear my name. If that's the case, I appreciate it. Man to man, cop to cop, like that. Now, do you know my wife and daughter were murdered as human sacrifices by a Satanic cult? That they were found, naked and mutilated, and with their hearts ripped out?"

"I checked. I know the case is still open."

"Unsolved and unsolvable."

Wiley gave Jantzen a hard look. "What are you saying, Jantzen? That this county has a bunch of psychopathic Satan worshipers on the loose?"

"Just keep an open mind, Colonel. Tell me, is it true Gruber's heart was ripped out?"

"I can't talk about that."

"Can't or won't? You're talking to a former homicide detective, Colonel."

"I will neither deny nor confirm your question."

"Were there any symbols around the corpse? Such as a pentagram, maybe a crucifix stuck in the ground, upside down, right above Gruber's head?"

Even with the shades on, Jantzen was certain he saw something flicker in the colonel's eyes.

"You know better than to ask those kinds of questions. You know I can't and won't tell you a thing. Listen to me, don't get all riled up about this. Whatever you went through back in Atlanta, it doesn't have anything to do with our investigation."

"Why am I not convinced?"

"I'm not here to convince you of anything."

A moment of silence, then Jantzen said, "Something tells me you didn't just spin me around half the county to let me know my good name is in the clear."

Wiley slowed the cruiser, checked his rearview. The east-bound lane was clear and the colonel swung the cruiser into a U-turn. Obviously the discussion was over.

"I didn't. Lawman to lawman, I had a feeling you'd start your own investigation, of sorts."

"And this is where you tell me to let you and the FBI handle it?"

"You got it. It's police business. You're no longer a homicide detective."

Jantzen just sat there in silence. So the colonel finally got to the bottom line. Butt out, keep his nose clean.

Looking away from Wiley, Jantzen decided not to pursue any more talk. Wiley had his mind made up, but so did Jantzen. There was more to the ongoing investigation of the Gruber murder than Wiley or the Feds cared to divulge to anybody. Jantzen believed he had struck some nerve in the colonel. Colonel Wiley was hiding something.

They ate the dinner they had prepared together. It was simple enough, steak smothered with sauteed onions and mushrooms, red potatoes, salad. With a bottle of red wine between them on the dining room table, Jantzen looked at his wife and smiled into her eyes. He had already told her about his day with Collins, then Colonel Wiley. Right then he realized just how much he owed this woman, how much she had put up with lately. He felt an incredible warmth toward his wife, a stirring he had not felt in weeks. He became painfully aware of just how much he missed her love.

"Thank you, baby."

Mary sipped her wine, her expression soft. "For what? I only wanted you to do what you felt was necessary. I can see the change in your mood. You're with me, not off in the past, beating yourself up. I'm happy that someone with real authority like this Colonel Wiley believes you didn't kill Gruber." She smiled with a sweetness Jantzen hadn't seen on her face for weeks.

"You're right, Mary. I feel whole again." It was only a partial truth, but at least he felt free of suspicion in the murder. "I am with you. I would never want to be apart in any way from you. You're my life, Mary. You're everything to me. You are the most beautiful, the most precious gift I have ever known."

"No one has or ever will love you, Mark, like I do."

"I know that, I always have. Any problems we've ever had, and ever may have, we love each other enough to work them out."

She held his stare. He saw her eyes start to mist with tears. Her smile was genuine, full of relief and joy.

"Mark, I love you. And I've missed you. I've missed the man I came to know and love and respect so much. We've had a wonderful evening, just being here with each other." She fell silent, her gaze warming. "I need you. I really need you now."

Smiling, he stood and picked up the bottle of wine. "Get your glass, let's go to bed."

He took the first black-painted chalice. They were roped to stakes driven into the ground. Young, creamy flesh, perfect in every way, cowered beneath him. Low chanting of "Praise the Prince of Darkness, take their souls into your kingdom," filled his ears, sweet, oh, so sweet music.

This was his ritual, they were his followers. The night belonged to them. They were deep in the woods, every corner of the prairie beyond already searched. Even then four of his clan, armed with revolvers or shotguns, guarded the trails in every direction. Any intruder would be shot on sight.

Indeed, the night belonged to the Sweet Master of Death and Darkness.

"Be still, little ones." He saw the terror bulging in their eyes. Their ivory flesh quivered in the flickering glow of firelight. "Fire, oh, wonderful warm fire, touch me tonight, uplift my soul."

He listened to their sobbing, muffled by the red rubber balls stuffed into their mouths, covered with duct tape. He felt himself stiffening beneath his black robe. Images of what the women in the clan had done to the little girls flamed into his mind. They had been initiated into the pleasures of the fleshly world, but they were still virgins in his mind. They would never know a lover outside of himself or the men in the clan. They would never have husbands, never give birth. They belonged to him, body and soul, in life and in death.

Sweet bliss. Short life, long death.

Slowly he let the chalice tip over, spilling the warm and sticky white fluid over their faces, the seed of life the women had earlier pumped from the men. They writhed, shut their eyes, cried.

He laughed at their horror.

Over the years, how many young ones had he offered, in body and soul, to the Master?

Over the centuries, how many had his clan, his heritage, which was the real and the only Alpha and Omega, sacrificed? How much flesh, so much of it untainted by animal lust, had been devoured by his ancestors?

Ten thousand? Twenty thousand?

A million?

How many lands had they crossed? How many cultures had they known and consumed, or at least infiltrated in their own ways? It was all written, both questions and answers, in the chronicles of the clan, handed down through the family over the ages. Details of rituals. How to perform the ceremonies. How to sacrifice, move on, fade away, vanish like vapor in the wind. Indeed, what to do, what to use, who to use, who to reach out to and draw into the fold.

He lifted a hand and they fell silent. When they were all kneeling at a safe distance around the girls in a perfect circle, broken only by the crucifix impaled upside-down in the ground, he took the knife and plunged it into the first victim's chest.

Chapter Eight

At first, Tom Delmarvin thought he was dreaming, wondering why nothing felt or looked real. Slowly he became aware he was awake, that his eyes had been open for a few moments, as he lay in bed, staring up into the inky blackness. Why did he feel so strange? Why did something suddenly feel so terribly wrong?

Only a little while earlier—he checked the illuminated dial on the nightstand clock, which read two-thirty in the morning—he had fallen into a deep sleep after making love to his wife. Briefly he recalled they had shared a night of wine in the living room, talking about the future, getting nostalgic over the first time they had met in high school. Everything so warm, sweet, tender. But why did it feel as if it had happened so long ago, if, indeed, it had happened at all?

He felt their presence invaded, that something was moving around their bed. It seemed to be circling, closing.

Then he realized he was afraid, but couldn't understood why or what he should fear.

They weren't alone, he believed, and felt rising panic. He was sure it wasn't just his imagination.

He shivered. It was cold in their bedroom, and he was sure something or someone else was there in the house. And why did the darkness feel as if it held some force around him that made him believe—or wish—he was still asleep? From some great distance, it seemed, he heard the wind. Like the low moan of an animal, the wind seemed to cry softly through the house. The front or the back door or both were open, but why?

Panic kept welling in his belly, shooting up his chest, into his throat until he felt he was suffocating. It was no dream, he was all too wide awake. He checked his wife. Outlined in the shafts of moonlight that shone against the window, Judy lay curled up on her side, a smile of contentment on her face. He searched the darkness around them, certain he had heard movement or voices out in the living room.

What was that he saw in the doorway? Was it light flickering from the living room? Terrified, he quietly rolled out of bed. If someone had broken in, why wasn't Russ barking?

He was rising from the bed, his wife groaning as his movement stirred her—when terror paralyzed him.

They swept into the bedroom, dark figures shrouded in black but with gleaming white faces that didn't appear human. Before he could warn Judy or defend himself, they descended on him like a pack of wild animals. They smelled coppery, like blood. Bile squirted up his throat as his mind registered other vile odors. What were these things? They were human, but there was some fury, coldness, hatred in their eyes that made them look—what? Demonic?

Instinctively he started flailing, striking flesh, but arms with incredible strength seized him as soon as he fought back. He fell to the floor, a crushing weight on top of him. There was light, dim, distant. Shadows danced all around the room. He looked over, calling out to his wife, who was screaming, thrashing. He saw her naked form dragged away from the bed.

He couldn't believe what was happening, what he was seeing. All around him, figures in black robes filled the room. He heard his mind scream, struggling to break free of their grasp. He had heard about witch covens, Satanists, occasionally on the news, but that was a world beyond his comprehension.

"Judy!" he cried out, then caught a whiff of some pungent odor. His scream was muffled; then he realized they had clamped a rag over his mouth. A sharp, stinging sensation bit his nose; then a warm, sweet darkness filled his head.

Within seconds, a veil of total blackness descended over his eyes.

He blacked out, but felt terror still clinging to him, his awareness tumbling into a black void where he heard only his voice screaming in outrage for his wife.

* * *

It was a full bladder that woke Jantzen up.

He lay there, feeling a strange calm he hadn't known in some time. Beside him, snuggled close, he could feel Mary's smooth and silky nakedness, her moist flesh, cool now after their passion. Sated, savoring the memory, he listened to her quiet snores. He couldn't remember the last time he felt so good. It wasn't just their lovemaking, it was that his wife had touched his soul, with both words and thoughtful, caring insight into what he was, all he had been, what he could be. She knew his fears, his desires, his sickness—and she was still there. In a way, he felt selfish to know that he was always in her thoughts.

He didn't want to move, lose the warm, floating feeling of serenity and peace. The night had been beautiful. The last of the candlelight was only now fading.

Careful not to rouse her, he slipped out of bed. He looked back at his wife, cherishing the memory of their love that night. She had touched a part of his soul he had begun to fear was dead at worst, dying at best. Where there had been no joy for him in the simplest act, she had given him back hope. Her weeks of patient understanding, waiting for her husband to come back to her in every way, had been his true reward. God, he had been so lost in himself, he reflected, torturing himself over the self-pity and loathing of the belief that he had lived a wasted life. Now, tonight, he felt resurrected.

Somewhat.

Without reason, he felt a stir of primal fear in his gut. He looked at the clock beside the bed. It was two-thirty-five in the morning. Why did he care what time it was? Why was something feeling all wrong all of a sudden? Why was the tension, the anxiety, the paranoia coming on?

He went to the window and pulled back the curtain. He felt some need to reassure himself that he was there, that it was all real, that he was alive, in his home with his beautiful wife. Beyond their bedroom window, the flat prairie stretched away like some infinite expanse of nothingness. Whatever he had grasped that evening with his wife was threatening to flee him. Far in the distance, bathed in the glow of moon and starlight, he made out the dark humps of the eastern hills. It was so quiet, so still out there, as it was in the house.

He thought he had been dreaming, but he couldn't be sure of what. It had been good to sleep so deeply, so content, just drifting away in a dark, peaceful void, a warm, dreamless sleep he only wanted to return to.

Then he started thinking of the Delmarvins. He wanted to believe he was feeling an irrational fear for the safety of the couple. But a ghostly vision of the figure on the road leapt into his mind. He recalled just a fleeting glimpse of the face. He was sure he had seen something malevolent in the eyes, the whole picture of the figure's senseless dashing in front of their truck, a jigsaw portrait of insanity.

He had an impulse to call Tom, even though it was the middle of the night. He couldn't pin down the source of his paranoia and mounting agitation, but he felt that something ugly, evil was out there in the county.

He let the drape fall back over the window. He

decided against calling the Delmarvins, realizing how foolish he would look. Still, he decided to drop in on the Delmarvins tomorrow morning. Make some excuse, check up on them, perhaps invite them over for dinner tomorrow night. He was worried about them in some instinctive yet seemingly irrational way he couldn't pin down.

A few minutes later, after relieving himself, he was back in bed. He wished for the calm peace of his marriage to return.

All he felt was a nagging fear he couldn't understand.

Rage cleared the fog in his eyes, the bubbling nausea in his belly. Tom Delmarvin didn't know who or what these people were, but he sensed something evil about them.

From the cold hardwood floor, he turned his head. They had Judy stretched out on the floor, just beyond the couch. She cried, fought, but they kept her pinned down, these black-robed creatures. In his mind, they weren't even human, as their eyes kept flashing in his sight with some warped light of savagery.

Whatever they had done to him, he fought the stiffness, the nausea. He was grimly determined to fight to save his wife, even if it meant his own life. He was no hero, but death was preferable than living the rest of his life without her in shame and degradation.

Looking up, he found three pairs of those lifeless eyes fixed on the outstretched body of his wife. It sounded as if they were praying.

Enough! With determination fueled by rage and

terror, he exploded off the floor. Every ounce of angry resolve was thrown into a series of wild punches. He saw their heads snap sideways, heard the crunch of bone.

"Grab him!" a voice bellowed. Dark-clad shapes were rushing him, but he was fighting for his and Judy's lives. He kicked, punched, clawed, kneed flesh and bone. Grunts and curses filled his ears. He was close, so close to reaching his wife, when a giant figure appeared to arise from the floor beyond the couch.

Some angry force slammed him in the back.

"Hold his arms!"

He felt himself hammered to the floor, felt their combined weight on his arms and legs. Above he saw the black eyes set like coals in the stark white face, the bald head appearing to glisten white as snow in the wavering light of a kerosene lantern.

"Let my wife go, damn you!"

A cold chuckle came from the face above him. "We are already the damned. Have you no idea who we are, young man?"

Terrified, he saw the blade flash into his stare.

"We are who was, who is and who always will be!"

Tom Delmarvin knew he was already a dead man, even before the cold edge of the steel sliced across his wrist. His only hope, his last desperate thought, as he felt the warm stickiness rush over his hand, was that they would kill his wife quickly and painlessly.

The tall, shaved head man led his clan across the prairie. Beyond the woods, the vans were waiting with their change of clothes. Outside the home, they had used a hose to rinse off the blood and other bodily fluids and secretions from the earlier sacrifice. Now he shivered in the cold wind that moaned over the prairie, his robe soaked with the cleansing water.

It had been easy to break into their home. First they had lured the dog to the side door, then shot a tranquilizing dart into the animal. One of them now lugged the German shepherd's limp body. The dog's disappearance would only add confusion and mystery when the dead were found. On the surface it would appear a murder-suicide. The young man had put up quite the fight, until he'd been put under for a while by the chloroform. He gave the young man high marks for the courage and tenacity he had displayed. It made their sacrifice that much sweeter.

Tonight they had been the Dreamwalkers. It was so written in the Book. Centuries of ritual, of steadfast prayer, the summoning of spirits from the Dark World, of knowing when, where and in whom to instill the fear of the unknown, still worked as magically as it had a thousand years ago for the Elders. In theory, the idea was simple enough. Use whatever fear already lurked in the corner of the heart. Prevail upon that fear by creating circumstances, such as the first sacrifice of the brute and his dog, and men will succumb to their fear. Throughout history all of the great ones who had served the Master faithfully understood that basic concept that assured power and dominion.

He led them into the woods.

What had happened tonight was only the beginning.

* * *

"Thank you, baby."

Jantzen watched his wife turn his way. She smiled as she drove them toward town.

It was early morning, a new day, the first time he remembered them driving to work together in weeks.

"For what?"

Innocent, but already knowing what he meant.

"For the love."

"Thank you."

He reached over, squeezed her hand.

"I'm the luckiest man alive, Mary."

They rode in the calm quiet of two lovers who had rediscovered each other. It was a good day, Jantzen thought, to be alive.

A few minutes later he felt his mood darken. Ahead the Delmarvins' home came into view. He searched the land, the barn beyond their home. Usually a few head of cattle were grazing, Tom riding around on his horse. Jantzen saw no animals, no Tom.

"Tom must be sleeping late this morning," he commented. "Do me a favor, Mary. Pull in."

Dubious, she stared at him. "Mark, come on, we just saw them yesterday. I'd feel like we were intruding, the nosy neighbors."

"Indulge me. We don't have any plans tonight, why don't we invite them over for dinner?"

She seemed to consider something, sighed, then slowed the truck.

As she swung onto the gravel drive, Jantzen searched the low-lying ranch house. Something was wrong.

"Mark, I feel kind of silly about this."

"Hon, please."

"You're getting that strange look again."

When she stopped by Tom's Chevy Blazer, Jantzen hopped out. He looked around the front yard. Tom Delmarvin was a man of routine. He kept Russ's bowls of food and water near the drive, let the dog roam freely around the property. With a quick look in that direction, he saw both bowls were empty. Russ should have been barking.

Perhaps there was some logical explanation why the place, the air itself around the home, was so quiet, so still, but Jantzen couldn't think of one. He bounded up the stoop, rapped on the windowpane of the front door. As Mary called his name, he looked over his shoulder, found her standing her ground by the truck.

No one answered the door. He moved to the window, peered inside.

And he saw them, stretched out on the floor of the living room. Unmoving, with blood pooled around their bodies. He knew they were dead.

"What's wrong, Mark?"

"Stay there!" he called back, but knew his grim expression had alarmed his wife into following him.

His heart pounding with terror, he burst through the front door. He wasn't prepared for what he found.

The world spun as he stared at the great washes of crimson, the blood-spattered walls and couch. *Dear God in heaven!* He didn't even recognized the slashed body of Judy Delmarvin, couldn't even fathom her as something human, until he spotted the patch of pubic hair.

Parlayzed, he stood rooted at the edge of the living room. Time froze, a sound of utter silence ringing in his ears until it was shattered by Mary's scream.

Chapter Nine

Mary Jantzen was slumped against her truck. What she had seen inside the home—she couldn't think of it anymore as someplace where a young married couple had lived and loved and planned for a future together—was a scene she would never forget. It was something that would fill her sleep with nightmares.

How long had she been outside now? At first she had been sick and sickened, then horrified and shocked, then enraged at the senselessness of it all. Now she was drained, numb, lifeless. She felt like nothing more than a sack of bones, barely able to stand.

"Are you going to be all right, Mrs. Jantzen?"

It was one of the state troopers. Uniformed state policemen, with maybe a half-dozen men in dark suits and sunglasses who had identified themselves as FBI, were either in the house or all over the property. They had been there for several hours but it felt like days to her. They had already spoken to her briefly, when she wasn't vomiting. They had asked questions that she resented. Did either she or Mark touch anything? How did they know the Delmarvins? How long? Why did they decide to stop here? As if they were suspects. All she could wonder was how someone could have done what they did to Tom and Judy. Her mind reeled with horror, images, twisted and flashing, living in her head. So much blood. The expressions on their faces, contorted, waxen masks, it seemed. Lying in their blood, naked.

"Mrs. Jantzen?"

"Y-yes, I'm fine."

She was shivering.

"You're shaking, ma'am. Would you like me to find you a jacket?"

She wrapped her arms around herself. "No, that's all right. Where's my husband?"

"He's out back, ma'am, with Colonel Wiley. Anything I can get you?"

She shook her head, watched him peer at her; then the trooper walked away.

Alone, watching the police moving about her, all these cold, grim-faced men, she began to see Mark in a new way, even if she understood him less. She now knew how many scenes like the one inside he had witnessed when he'd been a detective. How could he look at so much death over the years, see what atrocities people could inflict on each other, and stay sane? Perhaps that was one reason why he had quit the police force. Maybe he just didn't have the stomach for it.

Where was he anyway? She didn't want to stand there by herself, shooting her nervous gaze all around at the suits and the uniforms, the ambulance that had pulled up moments ago, now parked in the drive and reminding her that two people who only yesterday were alive and in love were now dead.

No, butchered. All that blood. She had seen them only yesterday. How could she ever remember them as...something chopped up, hacked and slashed to pieces?

Finally, she saw Mark appear as he walked across the field from the direction of the barn. He looked shaken, and as he drew close she saw his hands were trembling as he lit a cigarette. He was fighting to control himself, his eyes full of grief, anger, fear.

Tears burst from her eyes. She collapsed into her husband's arms. She just wanted to be held, needed Mark to hold her tight, tell her it was all a sick joke, an ugly misunderstanding. That they were still alive. It was just a nightmare, like the ones he suffered from, and soon she would wake up.

"I'll drive, baby."

So it was real. Dear God, she thought, it had really happened. Suddenly she couldn't stop sobbing. Numb, she let herself be led into the truck and settled into her seat. She was wiping away the tears when she heard tires grabbing at the gravel drive beside her. Turning, she saw the bulldog face of Sheriff Stephens in his cruiser. She read the anger on the man's face, caught her husband staring, locking eyes with the sheriff. The silence around her became deafening.

Mark hopped in and fired up the engine. Finally, blessedly, they were turning around, driving away. She watched what she began to think of as a slaughterhouse fade in the rearview mirror. She didn't think she'd ever be the same again.

"Why?" she cried. "Who... who could do that to two such beautiful people?"

Her question, her anguish, seemed to hover in the silence between them.

Again she looked into the rearview. Just beyond the spool of dust in the truck's wake, she made out the fading, squat figure of the sheriff. Stephens stood there like a statue, watching them leave. What was he thinking, she wondered. Were they suspects in the sheriff's mind?

A nagging dread told her they would know soon enough.

The silence seemed to hold their fear like a palpable force. Eyes fixed straight ahead, Mark Jantzen kept driving, searching his mind for anything to say to comfort his wife, anything to snap some life back into her. He listened to the engine, which seemed to roar in his ears. He hated the silence between them, but he understood.

What he had seen sickened and enraged him. Two young people had been butchered like cattle.

Not even he could remember ever seeing so horrific a murder scene, and he thought he had seen it all. It was something he wished Mary had not seen.

She had lost her innocence somehow, he feared. It took him back to a time and a place he had long since forgotten.

Like Mary, he had gotten sick the first time he had witnessed the end results of violent death. He had been a patrolman, responding to a domestic disturbance call. What he found was a man who had stuck a .44 Magnum in his mouth and blown off half his head, after he had shot his estranged wife to death. Up close, in real life, a bullet traveling at 1,200 fps or better can shred human flesh like it was nothing more than paper. It was nothing like he had expected. He still remembered how the suicide victim's partially decapitated head looked. Back then, he saw it in his dreams for months. Skullbone and brains had burst like a ripe melon, spattered the wall in a gory spray, sticking there like some bizarre abstract painting. Gristle hung down over gleaming exposed jawbone. The estranged wife had taken a .44 slug right between the eyes. In death, her three-quarters blown-off head had mirrored, maybe even mocked, her husband's death.

And he remembered how he had vomited at the scene.

After that, there was a change. He felt contaminated in some way every time he arrived at a crime scene. In time, he managed a numb state between morbid humor and a slow-burning rage toward the human race. Perhaps now he was so deeply affected because he had known and liked Tom and Judy Delmarvin. They had been real, breathing, flesh-and-blood people to him.

Now they were just ugly memories. Visions of

Judy's hacked-up body, her face slashed to ribbons, the death blow probably the gaping yawn in her throat, so deep it exposed her neckbone, would cling to future nightmares.

"Mary, do you want me to take you home?"

She took several moments to respond. When she finally looked at him he saw the pain and horror in her eyes.

"I don't know. I'm not sure. Why were you with the police for so long?"

"It's routine. We were the first ones on . . . who discovered . . ." He struggled to find the right words, realizing it was his wife he was talking to, careful not to fall into police jargon. "We're not suspects."

"I never said—God, I never thought we were. But the way they asked questions. . . ."

"I know. It's just routine."

Wiley, he recalled, then Special Agent Thomkins of the FBI had asked him some pretty hardball questions. It was not so much what they asked, but their tone of voice. He understood. Even they had been affected by the brutality of the murders, and they wanted closure. What he wouldn't tell Mary was what he thought of the crime scene. He had urged her to stay outside, go get him a rag from the glove box of the truck while he phoned the State Police. He had searched the living room. Furniture was askew, indicating a struggle. Then there was the large hunting knife, what he had to assume was the murder weapon, clutched in Tom's hand. Blood patterns seemed confined to the immediate areas around the bodies, but it all looked and felt staged. It appeared that Tom had died from a deep slash across his wrist. On the surface, it looked like a possible murder-suicide, but Jantzen knew that would never wash in a million years. For one thing, there were several sets of bloody footprints leading toward the kitchen. Then there was the sheer fact he knew the couple. Factor in the murder of Jeb Gruber…

He played back part of his conversation with Special Agent Thomkins.

"You touch anything, Jantzen?"

"I was a cop."

"Still doesn't answer my question, sir."

"No. You want to know what I think?"

"Not really."

"You've got a serial killer or killers camped out in either this county or somewhere close, maybe in one of the next counties. I'd look for strangers, I'd be talking to any and everyone who has lived in this county all of their lives and ask them if they've seen anyone they don't know. You people have a problem, trouble the likes of which you've never seen, and it's not about to go away."

"Mark, I asked you something."

He snapped back to the moment. "I'm sorry. What did you say?"

"I'm scared. I asked you what do we do? How do we live? Three murders. Do we just live in fear?"

"No. We go to work."

"Like it never happened?"

He lit a cigarette. At least she was talking.

"No, Mary."

She was looking at him strangely, as if she suddenly understood something about him.

"How could someone do something so horrible?" she asked, her voice nearly a choked whisper.

He had no answer. He shook his head.

"They were so young, so full of life, so full of love for each other."

It struck him that was exactly why they were murdered. They had been stalked, observed, chosen, he suspected. But why? By whom? He knew what it may look like, but there was no way what he saw could be written off as a murder-suicide.

Two hours later Mark Jantzen found out how wrong he was.

Understandably, the morning had dragged. They had arrived late at the diner. Finding Tim and Martha Hurkins, the couple who helped them run the diner, they had told them why they were late. The Hurkins were shocked. Jantzen had no answers for all their questions.

As the regulars rolled in for a late breakfast or an early lunch, the diner was abuzz with grim questions, the air heavy with sadness and anger and fear.

News of the killings spread like wildfire. Word that Mark and Mary Jantzen had discovered the bodies drew the curious from miles around. At one point, it seemed half the town arrived at the diner, asked questions for which Jantzen had no answers, then left.

Burt Martin and Bob Tamlin didn't eat but drank one cup of coffee after another as they asked Jantzen questions. He grew tired, exasperated with all the inquiries.

Jantzen heard the weariness and irritation in his own voice. "I don't know, fellas. I don't know what happened. I'd rather not feed the rumor mill, if you don't mind."

Jantzen noticed that Mary kept to the kitchen while he served the food and drinks.

"I can't believe this," Tamlin the barber said. "They were the nicest young people—you don't see young kids like that, so full of love for each other, anymore. They were kind, decent, respectful."

"I hope they catch the sonsofbitches who done that," Martin growled around his coffee. "What the hell's this world coming to anyway? You aren't even safe in your hometown. You aren't safe anywhere."

Standing behind the counter in his apron, Jantzen observed the strange, quiet attitudes of Tim Stallins and Jack Reilly. As usual they ate burgers and fries, but they were unusually silent that morning. He thought he spotted a wry glint in Reilly's eyes as the man glanced over at Martin and Tamlin.

"It's the beginning of the end," Reilly said.

"The what?" Martin groused.

"He said it's the beginning of the end, old man," Stallins said.

Martin turned angry. "Who you callin' old man, sonny?"

Whether it was the news of the killings creating tension or something else, Jantzen read a situation about to get out of hand.

"Whoa, whoa, fellas. Hey, hey. What's wrong with you? Jack, Tim, you two hung over or something?"

Was that a smirk he saw on Reilly's face? Both

Reilly's and Stallins's gazes narrowed, and something dark appeared to shadow their expressions.

"The two of you act like you don't give a damn the Delmarvins were murdered," Tamlin said. "Sit there shoveling food in your traps like this is just another frigging day."

"Murdered?" Stallins said. "You know for a fact they were murdered?"

"Listen to what Mark said, what he saw. What other conclusion can you come to?" Martin rasped.

"You two boys need to find steady jobs instead of hanging out here all day or over at the saloon," Tamlin grumbled.

"Idle hands are the devil's workshop?" Reilly said, and chuckled.

A hard silence hung. Jantzen peered at Reilly and Stallins. What the hell was with them anyway? He'd always thought they were a little odd, but today he was sensing something cold, unfeeling about them, saw some change in their expressions but couldn't pin down what it was. If he didn't know better, he would almost swear they savored the gory details about the gruesome killings.

Suddenly Sheriff Stephens appeared. Silently Jantzen groaned as all eyes turned to the sheriff.

"We heard about the Delmarvins, Sheriff," Tamlin said. "Some of us don't mind telling you, we'd like to know what the hell's going on in this town."

Stephens clenched his jaw as he stepped toward the counter. Looking at Jantzen from behind his shades, he said, "Just couldn't wait to start a panic, could you, Jantzen?"

"Damn, Tod," Martin said, "if it wasn't Mark, we all would have found out soon enough. Just so happened Mark and Mary found the...found them."

"Yeah. Just so happened."

"Is this where you tell me we need to have a little talk, Sheriff?" Jantzen said.

"Nope."

"I sure hope you're not going to tell me what I think you might want to tell me."

"Which is?"

"Skip it." The word "suspect" clung to Jantzen's mind. "I'll wait to hear from Colonel Wiley."

"Don't need to."

Jantzen peered at Stephens, sensing he was headed somewhere in his usual bad dramatic way. "What's that?"

Stephens pulled a handheld radio from his belt. "See this? Colonel Wiley gave me this. One each to both of my deputies. We're all patched in to the same frequency, I'm not to be away from this, even if I go to the can. Me, I've got to file my own report since this is my county. From what I saw at that ranch, I'm writing a report that goes down as murder-suicide."

Jantzen stared at Stephens. He heard the gasps from around the diner. Jantzen's anger faded to confusion.

"You're kidding me, Stephens."

"No, I'm not." Suddenly the handheld crackled with a voice Jantzen recognized as belonging to Deputy Bob Jenkins.

"Yeah, Bob, what is it?"

"Uh, Sheriff, I'm afraid we need you."

A pause. Jantzen could hear the anxiety in the deputy's voice.

"Speak up, son."

"Uh, Sheriff, you know where the old Donner home is?"

"Yeah, near the county line just north of the old oil field, east of the reservation."

"Uh, Sheriff, they, uh, well, it was some kids apparently...they found the Fenner girls."

Sheriff Stephens looked around the diner, his expression dark.

And Jantzen felt the silence thicken, wrapping him in a suffocating shroud. With everyone there already knowing about the Delmarvins, Jantzen smelled the new fear in the air. They all looked braced for the worst possible news.

"And?"

Jenkins hesitated on the other end. "I just think...you'd just better get here, Sheriff. They're...they're dead."

"I'm on the way," Stephens said, clearly stunned, and severed the connection.

Shock and disbelief hung in the diner as the sheriff fled the place for his cruiser.

Already Mark Jantzen was moving for the door, digging in his pocket for the keys to the truck. Whatever he thought he'd heard in the deputy's voice, he knew this second crime scene was as bad as, if not worse than, what he'd found at the Delmarvin ranch. Somehow, he would see it for himself.

Chapter Ten

Jantzen had to know. But even if he could sneak or burst onto the crime scene, he wondered if he *should* see the manner in which the victims had died. And there was no doubt in his mind the Fenner girls were dead.

Beneath a blazing sun, the hazy prairie countryside, with its meandering cattle and ranchers on horseback, swept by in the corners of his eyes, a white but frozen blur beyond his tunnel vision. About a quarter-mile ahead he locked in on the sheriff's cruiser. They were heading north. He figured the county line wasn't that much farther, as he passed the unmoving pumps of the depleted Cameron oil field.

So far, Stephens hadn't spotted him on his tail. But Jantzen didn't care if Stephens saw him and pulled him over. He could bull his way past the sheriff and hit the scene on the fly.

For if he found what he suspected he would at the crime scene...

Recalling the slaughter at the Delmarvin ranch, he found himself tumbling into the dark days of the aftershock of the murders of his wife and daughter. Whoever had butchered the young couple had enjoyed it, just as whoever had murdered his own family had taken pleasure in the brutality of the killings. Both had been overkill, but the Delmarvin killings had been made to appear like a murder-suicide. Why?

It all took him back to a time he so desperately wanted to forget but couldn't.

Years ago, he had thought he could seek out his own trail to the killers. When the detectives working the case came up with no leads, Jantzen, on a hunch, had gone into a store in Atlanta that sold occult paraphernalia. Everything from tarot cards to Ouiji boards to Satanic bibles had been for sale. Browsing, he opened a Satanic bible. He had been trying to fathom the minds of the killers, figure out their motivations. To defeat an enemy, he believed he must have some knowledge of that enemy.

What he read had sickened him. The basic philosophy was indulge the senses, fulfill your every desire, even if it is rape and murder. The author said that Satan wanted as sacrifice all souls, but he particularly wanted the blood of the pure and innocent, the virgin. Joy should be strife, order should be chaos, love was simply primal aggression for the acting out of desire for the flesh. Basically, right was actually wrong, and wrong was right. The true lord and master of the universe, of man, of all that was on earth, was the righteous one who, along with his devoted legion, was kicked out of heaven by an angry and jealous God. If a man coveted his neighbor's wife, what wrong was there in that desire? If a man needed money, go take it, any way he could. Never turn the other cheek, always strike first. In short, it went against everything Jantzen had been raised to believe in as a Catholic. Revolted, he had put the book down.

What had disgusted him, though, was that in some ways he was not too unlike some of the sick values he had read about. Had he not always pursued his own wants and needs and put them first and foremost? He told himself there really was no comparison between what he read and what he was. Even so, he had filed away the name of the author, tracked the location of the man through his publisher, intent on finding and questioning him. But it turned out that Blackwell—the pseudonym for one John Peters of Seattle—had died from a drug overdose two months before the murders of Jantzen's wife and daughter.

It wasn't long after that that the official investigation hit a stone wall. He was told by the detectives that whoever had killed his family was probably a drifter, long gone, and the only hope of catching him was if he killed again.

He told himself events of yesteryear had nothing to do with the present—or did they? Anything was possible. If what had happened today was somehow linked to what had happened then... how could he know? There was only one way to find out.

He saw the line of State Police cruisers in the distance. It was a standard cordoning off of the area. Clearly they wanted to keep anyone unofficial from even getting a peek at the crime scene. Northwest, Jantzen saw the uniforms and the suits of the FBI combing, inspecting the edge of the woods beyond the old Donner home.

The white, two-story farmhouse had belonged to an elderly couple, both of whom had long since passed away. A son, he believed he once heard, had inherited the home but no one lived there on a permanent basis. Once, maybe twice a year, Paul Donner, a middle-aged bachelor who resided in Tulsa, would stay for a month or so. Jantzen didn't know Donner personally but he had seen the man in town, all of maybe three times in five years. Briefly he thought it strange that though he had lived in Newton for so long, he really knew very little about the people, the town history, their ways. It was as if he kept everyone mere acquaintances.

Jantzen saw that the police and the Feds were looking around the house also. He didn't see any ambulance, any figures who appeared to be forensics techs in or around the house. The crime scene, he believed, was somewhere north, in the woods, judging by the number of cruisers and uniformed troopers in that direction.

He thought quick. Turning off onto a dirt road that was partly blocked from their view by a line of trees, Jantzen parked. It was risky all around. If he even got as much as a glance at the crime scene, he would incur the wrath of Wiley and the Feds. It was a chance he would take.

One look, even if it was a few seconds, was all he

needed. He hopped out of the truck, his heart pounding, sweat already rolling off his brow.

Jantzen feared what he would find.

Swiftly he moved in from the west. Jantzen had circled wide of the Donner house, chewed up at least thirty minutes angling far away, keeping out of sight from any watching eyes. He stayed hunched, used the rolling terrain, the trees, the brush as cover, watching them on the move.

Finally, hugging the tree line, he pinpointed a flurry of activity in the woods just north of the old farmhouse. He spotted the forensics people scouring an area that looked to be a small clearing beyond a stand of trees. Uniformed troopers were either on the radios in their cruisers, which were parked on a narrow dirt trail beside the clearing, or they watched for unwelcome visitors. Luckily they kept grim watch to the east.

Cautious, quiet, finding there were no troopers covering the angle of his approach, Jantzen spotted two pairs of naked legs in the distance. The rest of his view was obscured by gloved forensics techs.

His heart hammered in his chest. This was the moment of truth. There was no other way than to just walk right up to it.

From somewhere he caught a retching sound. Somehow, somewhere in his tunnel vision, he became aware of a fair amount of attention being paid to a trooper who was vomiting out his guts near a cruiser. Suddenly Jantzen felt lightheaded, everything so bright and alive but somehow unreal. Except for the sweat he tasted on his lips, his mouth was dry, his throat tightening as if clenched by an unseen hand.

He walked into the clearing, angled himself into position to get a better look—and there he saw his worst fear come screaming out of the past.

"Jantzen? What the hell are you doing here?"

"Somebody get him out of here!"

It was a fleeting glimpse but it was all he needed. He was vaguely aware of Wiley and Stephens and Special Agent Thomkins shouting.

Jantzen stood rooted to a spot that wasn't more than twelve feet away from *it*.

It.

Over and over his mind raged with *it*. Something that was inhuman, or nonhuman, something so monstrous, so ugly it contaminated every living thing under the sun.

His heart sank. Bile squirted into his throat. Then cold rage knotted his guts. He found it obscene that they could be allowed to lay there like that.

There they lay, in full, awful view, the death of innocence, once so alive, so young, so beautiful, so full of life and promise and hope. So cherished.

Now—*it*.

With troopers and forensics people standing, aware of his intrusion, shuffling and moving, he took it all in but wished to God he had never seen it.

What was left of the Fenner girls was drenched in slick crimson. What he found was exactly the same crime scene he had read in the detectives' report so long ago.

From the black circle painted around the victims, broken only at the twelve o'clock position where an upside-down crucifix had been planted in the earth...to the gaping, dark holes in the chests of the girls where their hearts had been cut out.

"I want that man taken away from here and detained until I get to him!"

From a great distance, Colonel Wiley's angry voice struck Jantzen's ears. Numb, he felt the rough hands on his shoulders, pulling him away from a hazy world that was spinning in his eyes.

It had been perhaps thirty minutes since Jantzen had been marched to a spot near the edge of the woods. He had been watched by a state policeman, felt the trooper's gaze boring into him every few minutes. He could no longer clearly see the crime scene. He wanted a cigarette, a drink.

He wanted to...what? Track down and kill with his bare hands the monsters who had not only murdered the Fenner girls but butchered them? Yes. God damn it, yes!

A hundred questions with no clear answers tore through his mind. All the signs were there that the killers were part of some Satanic cult, but that was the only thing that was clear to Jantzen. Something instinctively wanted to fit, but he couldn't quite grab it, not without evidence, not without facts, a face, a motive.

Was it the same killers who had escaped punishment for their crimes against his family?

His own pain, shame and failure settled like a great, burdensome stone on his shoulders. Was he being haunted? Stalked? Or was it something else?

His mind reeled. He could not pin down the source—of anything.

Something, though, did strike him just then about his life, some burning pain in the heart. It was all part of a bigger equation, perhaps even the core of his own torment, the missing piece to the puzzle, something he wanted to grab but that always eluded him, a wisp of smoke, vapor in the wind. Dear God, he realized, that anger and fear had kept him going all of his life. What sort of way was that to live?

You small, smug, angry bastard, he thought. It was all in front of his face, and still he denied it. Or tried to. He had been running all of his life, and now he was being asked to stop running.

So he had been raised, the only offspring, by a divorced, sometimes employed, alcoholic father who had never remarried. So he had been angry toward a mother he felt had abandoned him. So he practically raised himself, worked through high school, a loner, determined and driven, and put himself through the Academy. Made his own way, on his own, by himself. The world could kindly kiss his ass. All that came to nothing, ashes in the mouth. Or was there hope?

In some selfish way, all the jagged, torturing pieces of his existence—it was not really living—fit. And those sharp edges tore at him all the time, trying to make him see, or be something more than what he was.

Problem was, he still wasn't sure exactly what he was supposed to be.

Whatever was happening now, it was a reminder of how much he had failed in the past. Or was it all just some ugly, bizarre coincidence? He didn't think so. "Something" so evil, so monstrous was out there, somewhere, that he knew he had to face it down or he would be lost forever. Worse, he would lose his soul.

The sight of an angry Colonel Wiley and Agent Thomkins snapped Jantzen out of his solemn reflection.

"That will be all, Paulsen," Wiley told the trooper, who nodded and walked away.

"What the hell are you trying to prove, Jantzen?" Wiley growled.

Jantzen looked at both the colonel and Thomkins. If they were at all shaken up by what they had seen, they didn't show it.

"I have to tell you, Stephens wants nothing more than to run you in. I had to practically hold the man back!" Wiley said.

"On what charge? I just blundered onto a crime scene."

"This is no joking matter, Mr. Jantzen," Thomkins said.

"Anyone see me laughing?"

"Why did you come here?" Wiley asked.

"Because I had to know, that's why."

Thomkins cleared his throat. The FBI man's soft, nondescript features were moist with sweat. "Know what?"

"You want to tell him, Colonel, or should I? I could make a quick phone call to Atlanta PD and have the report sent to Agent Thomkins."

Wiley hesitated, glanced at the frown on Thomkins's face. The look of confusion on the FBI man was the first sign of emotion Jantzen had seen from him. Wiley gave Thomkins a quick summary of the murders of Jantzen's wife and daughter, a little too cold and blunt, but the agent seemed to understand something.

"So you think what happened to your family and the victims here was done by the same person or persons?" Thomkins said.

"You won't find their hearts," Jantzen told them. "Those girls were sought out for a specific reason."

Wiley and Thomkins glanced at each other.

Thomkins asked, "What reason might that be?"

"They were pure and innocent, they were virgins. Just for one thing, you'll find they were raped and sodomized."

"What the...are you trying to be sick?" Wiley growled.

"They were sacrificed as part of some unholy offering to the devil. Your suspects are part of a Satanic cult; they aren't from anywhere near here. They'll move on, and unless you do something quick, the likelihood that you'll catch them is next to zero. The murder weapon was most likely a large—"

"All right, Jantzen," Wiley said, "we've got the point."

"And we don't need your interference," Thomkins added.

"You need my help."

"That's where you're wrong," Thomkins said. "Further, if you leave here and start telling everybody what you saw, I will think of something to charge you with."

"What do you think is going to happen when the parents of those girls are told, when they have to identify their daughters? A storm like no twister that every hit this state is going to rip through Newton."

Thomkins fell silent.

"Right," Jantzen said. "I assume I'm free to go, now that I've been warned."

"Don't go playing Inspector Jantzen on this one. Are we clear?" Wiley said.

Jantzen said nothing. He turned and slowly walked across the field toward his truck. Looking back he found Wiley and Thomkins staring after him.

Whether they cared to admit it or not, Jantzen knew that both the colonel and Thomkins believed a reign of terror was about to descend on small-town Newton.

Population 371.

Mark Jantzen was an angry man. And more afraid than he'd ever been in his life.

Chapter Eleven

Jantzen wanted a drink, even though he knew he shouldn't, not the way he was feeling. Hell with it, he told himself. What he had seen, what he felt, needed relief or he thought he might go crazy. Lost in himself, he was angry at the world. He tried to make sense out of the senselessness of the murders, find something rational in the irrational, horrible way in which five people had been butchered, but he already knew there was no explanation, not even a shred of sanity. Usually murder had a motive—greed, jealousy, rage. Not here. This was killing for the sheer pleasure of killing. All he knew was that something—he couldn't even think of the perpetrators of the murders as human—was out there, at large, stalking, selecting its next victims.

A monster, some evil he couldn't even begin to

understand, walked among them. And it wasn't going away.

As he walked into the Cherokee Bluff, he was bogged down with indecision, weighted with pain and fear. He wanted answers, but knew he wouldn't get them from Wiley or Thomkins. He wanted in on the hunt for the killers, but they had made it clear they wanted him to butt out.

Worse, he wasn't even sure he could talk to his wife about the grisly sight of the murdered girls, but figured he should be the first to tell her. And do what? Try and comfort her?

He was alone in a world that had suddenly turned insane.

All he could really do was sit on the sidelines, watch and wait for another killing. And he knew there would be more killing. That was the grim reality. Violence fed on itself. It was like a snowball, rolling downhill, gathering momentum, strength, size until it became a raging, unstoppable force. It wouldn't stop until there was an avalanche. He had an overpowering desire to shout in the middle of Tyler Street at any and everyone he could find. Newton was in serious trouble, and the trouble had only begun.

Standing at the end of the bar, Jantzen searched the faces of the six male patrons, perched on stools. They stared back, greeted him, nodded. For some reason, the saloon had an ugly ambience, cold and lifeless. Then he decided it was just him—perhaps. He almost walked out, knowing he should be with Mary, offer some explanation, lame as it might sound, as to why he suddenly bolted from the diner. Briefly he wondered just how much more his wife could take.

"Howdy, Mark," Jock Peters said, moving down the bar to him. "You look like you need one bad, my friend."

"Whiskey, make it a double."

He searched the faces of the patrons. Grizzled, hard faces, some weathered from working outdoors in the oil fields or as ranch hands, others just dark shadows, solemn faces hunched over beer. For some reason, even though he knew them, the regulars who always came in at that time, they were faceless, nameless entities. Why did life appear so hazy, so...contaminated?

"Jantzen, you look like you seen a ghost."

Jack Barker, a burly, bearded trucker.

When Peters served his drink, Jantzen asked, "Jock, have you seen anybody in here lately you don't know? I mean, like someone who may just be passing through town?"

The barkeep's gaze narrowed. He shook his head. "Can't say I have." He turned grim. "We all heard about the Delmarvins. Terrible. Something like that makes you wonder what the hell the world's coming to."

Was it his imagination, or did Jantzen detect some coldness in Peters's voice?

Again Jantzen scoured the men's expressions. Why did he suddenly feel so terribly alone, as if he didn't know these people, didn't want to get anywhere close to them? They should have been talking about the murders, scared to death, angry, wanting swift justice. Instead they drank, smoked, went on, business as usual.

"You think a drifter killed the Delmarvins and that jerk Gruber?"

Stan Garrett, the mailman for the county. Jantzen stared at Garrett, tried to find some life in the man's hawkish features, but would have sworn he saw only indifference.

Jantzen killed his drink.

"Another one, Mark?"

He thought about it, nodded. "One more."

He needed to get out of there; he had a sudden puzzling urge to flee from these people. But why? Perhaps it was what he had seen. Perhaps it was the first time he was actually looking at these people he knew only by name and a few passing words. Something felt wrong, terribly wrong. He felt as if the world were about to spin off its axis and hurl him into space.

"Mark, don't mind me saying, but you're acting kinda strange," Garrett said.

"I was a cop, Stan. Let's just say I have a suspicious mind."

"You think whoever killed the Delmarvins is a local?" Peters asked.

"I don't know."

He paid the tab. He felt their stares. The jukebox was silent, and he became uncomfortably aware of just how strange his behavior must seem.

He left the bar, wanting only to be with Mary. He hoped she wasn't angry with him.

She was furious.

He waited for his wife to unload on him as she slammed the office door. He didn't know how to tell her about the latest murders. He had been searching for the right words since leaving the saloon, but there was no way to soften the blow.

"Where have you been? You've been drinking, that much I know. What is wrong with you? How much more of this am I supposed to take?"

He told her point-blank about the murders of the Fenner girls.

The silence between them became so heavy Jantzen didn't think he could move. He looked at Mary, wishing to God he could tell her that everything was going to be all right, that the killers would be found and captured. That life would go on, and the memories of what they had seen that day would fade, and tomorrow everything would be normal, quiet, routine.

But Jantzen was terrified—for himself, his wife, the whole town. He read Mary's disbelief, but the look changed into a distant and haunted stare. Slowly her jaw went slack, her mouth hanging open like some grotesque parody of a jack-o'-lantern.

"I don't believe...I can't...why is this happening? What...is going on?"

Sensing she was about to collapse, Jantzen took his wife into his arms. He held her tight. She wept.

"I want us to leave, Mary."

She pulled back, puzzled, brushing tears off her cheeks. "What?"

"We need to leave this place. I don't care where we go, but I'm telling you...something...something is here and it's looking to eat all of us alive."

"You're not serious. We just pack and move?"

"Not move, just a...a long vacation."

She wiped more tears off her face. "Why?"

"I can't say why. I just know that whatever's happening, it's only just started."

Grim, she lit a cigarette. Something hardened her eyes that alarmed Jantzen. She seemed to think long and hard, choosing her next words carefully. "Mark, I need to go home. I need to be alone for a while."

He felt a stab of panic. "What are you saying?"

She looked as if she had something dramatic or awful to tell him, then seemed to decide against it. It was in her eyes, her voice, a need to get away as she said, "Will you close up? We'll...we'll talk later."

Stunned, he watched her practically run out of the office. Right then he was sure she wanted to leave him.

Later that night, Mark Jantzen watched his wife pack a suitcase.

"Mary, will you talk to me? What's going on?"

"I have to get away from here for a while." She kept folding clothes, neatly laying them in the suitcase.

"Will you look at me?"

With a heavy, pained look she turned and faced her husband.

"You haven't even told me where you're going."

"I called a girlfriend. She lives in Tulsa. I'll leave you the phone number."

"This is crazy. First, you tell me I'm the one who always runs when things get tough, now you're running."

"I'm not running, Mark. It really isn't even you. Understand, I've lived quiet and simple all of my life. I like peace and tranquillity and some sense of order and structure. Now...now people we've known are being murdered, plus the sheriff implies that you're somehow involved—"

"Forget Stephens. You know why he's doing that."

"That isn't the point. Whatever it is you're going through, I'm giving you just as much time to get through it as I'm giving myself."

"We need 'space,' is that it?"

"Mark, please don't be sarcastic."

"This is crazy."

"No, it isn't. I've been thinking about it for a couple of days. I try to reach out to you, and you stay locked up in yourself. Now, with everything that's happened...I'm afraid that it's only going to get worse. Everything. I shouldn't have to fight for my husband. I give you everything, and lately I've gotten nothing back. All I'm asking for is a little time to think, sort it out, and hope you can pull it together. Try to understand. Every day I don't know what you're going to do anymore. I'm even beginning to wonder who you really are. You leave the diner, twice now, no explanation, no 'excuse me but I really have something important to do,' no nothing. You go get drunk, or go chasing off...after this thing that's obsessing you."

He stared at her, stunned. Up to that point, he hadn't been aware just how angry she was with him. He didn't know what to say to change her mind. Perhaps, he decided, it was best she get away for a while. At least until the killers were caught. Maybe then some sanity would return to their lives in Newton.

Finally he nodded. "Okay. Maybe you're right. How long will you be gone?"

"A few days." She touched his face. "Mark, I still love you, I still believe in our marriage. But if you don't get help, if you can't find peace with yourself somehow..."

She let it trail off.

"I'll walk you out," he said.

He watched her slip on her jacket, his heart growing heavier by the moment. Taking her suitcase, he walked with her into the living room. All of a sudden he felt as if they were strangers, that they didn't even belong in this home where they had lived for five years. He appreciated her honesty, but he couldn't help but feel angry that he was being abandoned by his wife. With each step toward the door he felt older, more tired, more used up. In a million years, he would have never dreamed it possible his wife would feel the need to get away from him. But it had happened before. Was there some sick pattern in his behavior? Was he missing something? Did he purposely want to drive away the only thing in life he loved?

When they reached her truck, he took her in his arms. The night felt colder than usual, looked dark, bleak.

He told her, "I love you, Mary. Come home soon."

She kissed him. "I'll call you."

He couldn't take his eyes off her, imagined the earth was opening up and swallowing him. She got into her truck and fired up the engine. When she hit the headlights, he met her gaze, her eyes full of loneliness, pain. She waved good-bye, then drove off down the dirt trail that led to the highway.

The sound of her truck's engine faded, but it echoed in his ears, straining his senses, his heart thumping like a jackhammer. He desperately wished it was a bad joke, or that she was testing him. Perhaps he should have begged her to stay.

Her truck vanished in the night.

It was then that he heard another engine growling to life. He searched the highway. In the distance, just beyond their field, he saw headlights flare on. It was a van, pulling off the shoulder of the road. Some dark instinct churned in his belly as he watched the van drive off. He was certain that their home was being watched. And why wouldn't he believe that, given the events of the past few days? He almost decided to chase the van down, afraid for his wife, but he knew she would go in the opposite direction to take the Interstate.

For a full minute at least, he didn't move. He only listened to the wind whistle across the field. The wind seemed to carve right through him, gathering ominous strength.

He was more alone than he had ever been in his life. It danced through his mind that this was perhaps what he really always wanted.

From the passenger seat of the van, the tall, bald man said, "That's an interesting story."

"It's the truth. It's easy enough to check."

He listened to the voice of the Other. It was fascinating, this change that came over the Others, he thought, when they finally made the decision to come into the fold. The eyes, even the face and the voice, would change. Once the conversion process started, it became an inside job from the soul.

Always something cold and dark and rumbling would settle into the voice if they prayed, took the blood oath, which involved drinking the blood of a sacrificial lamb, eating a human heart. Feeding them the right amount of peyote also helped.

"You know, I've been seeing you off and on for three weeks and I don't even know your names."

The bald man looked at his disciple, John, who took his gaze off the highway for a moment.

"This is John and I'm Michael," the bald man told the Other. He could feel the man's energy in the deep shadows behind them, hungry for action, to unleash his own desires. From what he could gather, the other had uncontrollable lust for the flesh.

"It looked as if the wife was leaving him."

"They've been having problems," he heard the Other say.

"You said he was a policeman from Atlanta. And that his wife and daughter were offered?"

"You keep questioning me like you don't believe me. Yes, that's what I told you."

Michael thought back. It was a long time ago, and there had been so many since then. He could remember each ritual as a sacred moment unto itself, but after so many offerings they seemed to all meld into one. Faces and places almost became unimportant. It was the act itself, doing it, then doing it again.

"Could he be a problem?"

The Other said, "Perhaps. Knowing what I know about him, he won't rest until he gets answers."

"A driven man, obsessive most likely. Ambition is good. But in this case... if he starts his own unofficial investigation, shall we say, asking questions, getting people around here in an uproar... well, he might have to be dealt with. Perhaps... if it comes to it..."

"Comes to what?"

"Never mind. Let me ask you, what is it you seek from us?"

The Other said, "A new way. I know men, Michael, and the first time I saw you in that bar outside Oklahoma City, I read something in your eyes that had seen, known and devoured souls. To me, that's what life is all about. The devouring."

"Then you have some understanding."

"I want more."

"Which is what, precisely?"

"I want to vent my aggression, unload myself."

"Is there anyone in particular?"

"There are two women."

"Why would you need us?"

The Other hesitated, then said, "Because I like your philosophy. 'Do unto others before they do unto you.' You've reached others who confided in me after your blessing."

"You're a grown man, and yet you still feel the need for some connection to something real. You need a family, and perhaps we are the family you seek."

"I've thought about it."

"Are you willing to leave behind everything you know and come with us?"

"If it's power you offer, yes."

"Power, yes, and then some. From what we've talked about, I know you know the feeling of power you get when you take a human life." Slowly he turned, looked at the Other's face as he scratched a match and lit a cigarette. Swathed in the glow of the firelight for a brief second, Michael peered at the hungry blue eyes, the lean, chiseled face. Yes, he thought, the Other was perhaps ready. It didn't matter what led them to this point. All that mattered was the gathering of souls, in order for him to make the legion stronger.

"All right, Buddy Simpson, tell me, just what will you do for the Master?"

Chapter Twelve

Mark Jantzen figured the first day would be the toughest, and he was right. He arrived at five in the morning—fairly well rested, not too badly hung over—to open the diner. No nightmares, a few drinks alone, watching television. Perhaps his mood had brightened when his wife had called to let him know she had arrived safely. Their talk had been short, bittersweet. He told her he truly understood. Everything would be all right when she returned. Have fun, get some rest, visit. What surprised him was that not only did she say she missed him, but that she was praying for him. He hadn't heard something like that since he'd been in Catholic grade school. He hadn't seen the inside of a church since his first marriage. And he certainly tried to never think about God.

Until lately. Until a crisis arose. More and more

these days, he had begun to think of Father Ben McMartin. So long ago, the priest had helped him put some things into perspective. That was yesterday. Or was it?

Deal with the day, he told himself. She hadn't left him, she was just regrouping. And praying for him. Had he married a closet saint?

Whatever would happen, he still couldn't believe Mary was gone, even if for a few days. But a solemn acceptance settled in, sort of like when a man has a broken leg and comes to terms with being incapacitated.

At first he went through the motions, listless, somewhat angry, making coffee, setting up the donut displays, all the usual routine. Then he grew bored, restless, agitated. A thousand and one things seemed to be happening in his life lately and none of it made the least damn bit of sense.

Fifteen minutes later he had his first drink of the day, Wild Turkey up, to the brim.

Shortly after six the Hurkins arrived, and the first thing they asked was where was Mary. Any reason, any excuse would sound bad at best, suspicious at worst. He decided a half truth was in order.

"Well, with all that's happened," he told them, filling the first of what he suspected would be many cups of coffee, firing up what he knew would be the first of countless cigarettes as he stood behind the counter, "she's terrified. In fact, she's scared out of her mind. We talked about it. She needed to get away, so she's staying with a girlfriend in Tulsa."

"Can't say I blame her," Martha Hurkins said.

"I can't understand what's happening around here," Tim said. "You can smell the fear in the air, even this early in the morning with folks just waking up. Town's quiet as a... forgive me, but quiet as a graveyard."

Maybe it was because he was lonely without Mary, but Jantzen became aware of how much he liked this couple all of a sudden. Martha was lean, long-legged, with short red hair and green eyes, her face long, her jaw a little too big, nose small. Her eyes always beamed with a carefree joy he envied. On the other hand, Tim was short and stocky but with a lean face, a big aquiline nose, brown eyes that often looked troubled. In their early forties, childless, they were something of a stark contrast in appearance, but they were both friendly, cheerful and helpful to a fault. They owned some cattle but nothing that would keep them employed on their own. They were longtime friends of Mary, and she had been the one who suggested they offer the couple work in their diner. Depending on business, Jantzen paid them out of pocket, 150 a week each for four days, plus Martha worked the counter and the floor for tips.

"Must be hard on you, Mark. You and Mary are never apart," Martha commented.

He wondered if she smelled the liquor on his breath. "She'll be back in a few days. Thing is, until they find out who killed five people around here and catch them, I'm almost glad she's away."

"You were a policeman, Mark." Tim Hurkins turned grim. "What's your hunch?"

Jantzen sipped his coffee, worked on his cigarette. "I can't say. It's just all happened so fast, the killings were so brutal—there's a madman or madmen out there. Someone who enjoys what they're doing, as sick as that sounds, I know. I would stay alert, lock your doors at night, get the most vicious dog you can find—like a pit bull with rabies—and maybe buy a gun. Least until the police or the FBI get to the bottom of it."

He saw their mood darken, knew the best cure to keep everyone's thoughts from spiraling down was to get to work. He hoped for a busy morning.

He got it.

By nine o'clock the diner was jammed. Jantzen and Martha worked the counter and the floor, took the orders, poured the coffee, ran the food. Kitchenward, the grill and fryer were packed to capacity. Dishes stacked up quickly, threatening to topple, but there was no time unless it was stolen from a customer.

And, indeed, Jantzen could smell the fear. He got the impression that no one in Newton wanted to be alone, that everyone needed to band together, to find strength and reassurance in the numbers of the pack. By ten there was a standing line at the door.

Silently, at times cursing to himself, playing host, waiter, busboy, dishwasher, cashier, Janzten ran in a sort of controlled frenzy, zipping past people waving empty coffee cups, calling his name. He'd get to them when he got to them. It was his place, they could kiss his ass. His wife was usually there anyway, but she was gone, and what the hell was that really all about anyway? First, he wasn't used to working this hard. For another—and it was something he rediscovered about himself but came to despise, knowing it was wrong—he figured those he waited on should, in fact, be waiting on him. Arrogance, he wondered, or was it something else?

Frequently he was forced to go to the back sink to wash the sweat off his face. It was proving a tough day already, but he had no idea how Newton—and the small-town diner he ran with his wife—was about to be put on the map.

The regulars lined the counter, making it doubly aggravating for Jantzen and Martha. Martin and Murphy, Tamlin, and Stallins and Reilly, hunched over, smoking, drinking coffee. Even the hardcore Cherokee Bluff crowd, including Jock Peters and his girlfriend, wandered in for breakfast, the barflies looking hung over, haggard, surly. Almost everyone was polite enough, meaning they didn't start barking for their food within two minutes. Still, there was an understandable tension in the air. All around him, the diner buzzed with talk about the killings, all manner of wild speculation hitting Jantzen's ears as he dropped off plates, refilled coffee.

"Heard we got Satanists living in Newton."

"That's bull. We'd know about devil-worshiping weirdos if that were true. No secrets in this town. Everybody knows everybody's business."

"Maybe there's some doomsday cult we don't know about, like they had down in Waco."

"The poor parents of those girls."

"What the Fenners must be going through..."

"...can only imagine..."

"...and pray..."

"Whoever did it, well, I'm a Christian man, but

may God strike them dead and see them burn in hell."

"Should we send flowers?"

A maddening swirl of voices in his head. Keep his mind on the business. Who wanted what, needed what. Check right? Food ready? Extra this, extra that, don't want the yolk runny or it goes back. *Is that right? Just leave twenty percent tip, I got people here to pay.* He used to be a cop, dammit, now he was a waiter. Blood pressure pounding in his ears, everyone wanting, demanding, needing, a bunch of animals.

"Well, you know that Donner kid was always a little weird, if you ask me."

"What's that got to do with anything, Bob? He had good folks, may they rest in peace."

"Understand he rented the house to a guy about six months ago. No one knows who he is, don't even think anybody saw him but from a distance, late in the evening, but I heard a few other strangers ended up moving in a few months back. Stayed in the house the whole time."

"Those poor Delmarvin kids," He heard the widow Gracie Thomas tell one of her elderly blue-haired lady friends. "They were so sweet. What's wrong with people these days?"

"Heard you were the first to find those kids, Mark."

Another widower, Julie Parker. "Yes, ma'am. I can't even put into words what I saw. We're just sick about it, Mary and I."

He moved on, uncomfortable with their scrutiny, the chance they might ask more questions. At that point they were just customers, money in his pocket, but they seemed like faceless, shouting mannequins.

"Can I git some coffee over here!"

Jantzen's mind raced as he zipped around the floor. It was the first time he'd heard that the Donner home had renters. And it was the site of the Fenner murders. He was sure some clue had been found at the old home.

"What about that coffee?"

Jantzen rolled up to the old geezer, a retired ranch foreman, Jeb Dooley. *Coffee—I'll give you coffee*. Service with a scowl, he poured the codger's cup. He was glad when he was back behind the counter, but he was far from being in the clear.

"Where's Mary, Mark?" Tamlin asked, chomping down on a nine-ounce sirloin. "She sick?"

He saw Reilly and Stallins perk up, look his way with sudden interest. Jantzen told Tamlin and the others in earshot the same thing he'd told the Hurkins.

Reilly snickered. His buddy muttered something in his ear.

Jantzen put a hard look on the two men. He wasn't in the mood for their crap. "I say something funny, Jack? Tim, you got something to say, feel free to speak up."

Stallins buried his face in his burger. Jantzen was pretty sure he'd heard some comment about his wife leaving him. His blood boiled.

Reilly took the bun off his burger. "Nothin' funny about nothin'. Ask for medium rare and this thing is so done I could throw it across the room, hit somebody in the head and kill 'em."

Stallins had to get into the act. "Mary never gets our food wrong."

Jantzen had the urge to reach across the counter and slap both of them. He put some ice in his voice and said, "Well, Mary isn't here. You're dealing with me. And the next time either one of you has something to say about my wife, take your lips out of the other's ear and say it to me. Are we clear?"

Jantzen had everyone's attention at the counter.

"Sounds like you're looking for a problem, Jantzen," Reilly growled. "All I want is for my burger to get cooked the way I wanted."

"You asking or telling me to recook it?"

Tamlin butted in, the peacemaker. "Hold on, Mark. Slow down here. What's gotten into you lately? You been wound up so tight, you're gonna burst a gasket. All the man wants is another burger."

Jantzen felt his gaze narrow, his teeth clench. "I know what he wants, Bob."

The tension thickened as Jantzen walked up, leaned down and picked up Reilly's plate. "Medium rare, you said?"

"Yeah."

"Good enough. I'll even hold the spit."

The morning grueled on. Jantzen got Reilly's burger right. They left exact change, of course, not the five-spot they normally left his wife.

It was pushing noon when Jantzen spotted the caravan of television newspeople pulling up outside his diner. Within minutes, with reporters and cameramen disgorging from a dozen or so vans, a crowd of locals had gathered.

He wasn't sure why, but he became angry. Through the plate glass window, he read the different lettering from various television stations. They had come like a tornado, roaring in out of nowhere. They came from Oklahoma City, Tulsa, even as far away as Dallas. He heard the muttering of questions from the thinning crowd in the diner.

Newton was about to become a freak show.

He watched as a pretty blond reporter, mike in hand, began walking straight for his diner with a cameraman on her high heels.

Jantzen felt the blood pressure shoot straight into his ears.

As ugly as life already was in Newton, it was about to get uglier.

A few moments later, she was through the door, giving instructions to the cameraman.

Today Mark Jantzen was just a waiter with his whole future in doubt, his marriage in danger, and he was in the mood to kick some major ass.

Chapter Thirteen

Jantzen was about to blow up but the lady reporter told the cameraman to wait outside. Eagerness turned to disappointment on his young, bland face, but he left the diner. She looked around, and Jantzen felt the whole place going quiet. Somehow he held his temper in check, then decided that if she wanted to talk, he might just have something to say to her. At first she seemed to shrink inside her white blouse and dark slacks as she became aware of the intense scrutiny of strangers. Then an air of cool professionalism hardened her face. She was about to speak but Jantzen beat her to it.

"Can I help you, ma'am?" Jantzen said, moving across the diner.

"Do you own this diner, sir?"

"I do."

"My name is Penny Timms, I'm from—"

"I read the logo. I don't watch much news, but I'm sure you're a big star up in Tulsa."

She was taken aback by his sarcasm, frowned, but kept her composure. "Well...what's your name, if you don't mind me asking?"

"Jantzen, Mark."

Obviously still stinging from his encounter with Jantzen earlier, Reilly called out, "He used to be a cop, Miz Timms. You're here to ask questions about the murders, he's the man to talk to."

Jantzen gritted his teeth and threw Reilly a look over his shoulder.

The reporter's eyes lit with interest. "Really?"

"You're here to ask questions," Jantzen said to her, "about things none of us can really answer. All we know is five people are dead and families are left in ruins."

"I'm here to report the news, Mr. Jantzen. That involves asking questions, even painful ones."

"Look, I don't know how anybody else feels, but I resent a bunch of reporters invading what they see as quiet, small-town America gone berserk."

"Sir—"

"You want to eat here, that's fine. As for me letting you use my place of business as backdrop for what you might want to turn into a carnival sideshow, that's out. All I want to see, all anyone in this town wants, is the killer or killers caught and brought to justice, and for life to get back to normal around here." He heard the murmurs of assent around him.

"Can I ask you a few questions, at least?"

"No. Who are the killers, do I think?"

"Well, not exactly—"

"A Satanic cult has descended on Newton." He wasn't sure why he blurted that out—perhaps it was impulse. Then again, he suspected she would latch onto that, try and run with it, ask questions of Stephens, maybe Colonel Wiley. "I'm being serious, and you can feel free to quote me. I was a cop, a homicide detective, in fact. I saw one of the crime scenes, I've had some experience in this area. Anyway, that's what the rumor is, that's what the sheriff and the police think—it's a devil-worshiping cult," he lied. But he wanted to do something, anything to shake people up, alert them that something far more than just brutal and cold-blooded murder had happened.

It already started. He heard the buzz behind him. Questions were flung at his back. The law knew something the town didn't and were holding out? A slow-burning fuse of outrage was lit.

And Jantzen saw the reporter's eyes glint with sudden interest. She had her potential sensational story.

"Is that what you think, Mr. Jantzen?"

He decided to keep the ball rolling. "Yes. I saw the crime scene where the Fenner girls were found, I saw some things I will not elaborate on. And, yes, I believe these murders are the work of some devil-worshiping cult."

"Will you describe the crime scene?"

"I can see you're persistent, but I know that comes with the job. No, I'd better not. I'm not real popular with our town sheriff. Now, if you'll excuse me, I've got people to feed. Anybody here wants to talk to you, I'd ask you to kindly do it outside."

He walked away but he'd created the whirlwind he wanted. Good enough. From psychological profiles of serial killers, he knew they reveled in a sick sort of glorification of their deeds. Failures in life, those types of individuals clamored for fame and recognition. Somehow, he suspected the monsters who had committed these murders were a little different from the standard profile of a serial killer. Either way, he hoped the killers watched the evening news. If he could flush them out somehow, he didn't mind being the bait.

And he was sure Penny Timms would find something to report—rumor, if nothing else, tearing like a twister through small-town USA, a people at first shocked, now living in terror.

From behind the counter, he saw she was leaving. A swirl of questions hit his ears, but he ignored every one. Whatever he had just done, he feared he may have created a problem for himself with the official law.

Later in the afternoon, Jantzen found out just how much flak he had brought down on himself.

He was sipping coffee laced with bourbon, perched on a stool at the counter, when he saw Colonel Wiley's cruiser slide to a jerky stop out front.

Jantzen was all alone in the diner. When business died after lunch, no one ventured in. He gave the Hurkins the rest of the day off. His intent was to close early and go home and watch the evening news. He had cable and knew he could get the Tulsa channel.

The news teams had left only about thirty minutes before. From what he viewed as the safe cocoon of his diner, he had observed the different news teams setting up their cameras, interviewing a few of the locals. He was curious as to how they would report the story. Fact or wild rumor? But what facts? He didn't think Colonel Wiley would give them anything to inflame paranoid imaginations, other than five people had been brutally murdered, no motives, no suspects. Ongoing investigation, like that.

Right away he read the anger on Wiley's face as the colonel barged through the door. For long moments, Wiley just stood there, finally removed his shades and looked around the empty diner. Strangely enough, the sheriff had not blown into Jantzen's place to rail at him about what he'd told the lady reporter. Briefly Jantzen wondered why the sheriff had not made an appearance, unless he didn't know about his short interview with Penny Timms.

Jantzen sipped his coffee. "Colonel, you look pissed. You the bearer of more bad news?"

"You got some real balls on you, mister. And pissed is the understatement of the century, so spare me your sarcasm. I got a call from your lady reporter friend at the barracks who burned my ear about your little stunt. Damn you, Jantzen! What the hell is wrong with you anyway?"

"I expected Stephens to be the man to chew me out."

"Apparently your sheriff's too busy making an ass of himself with those reporters. I call him to tell him not to say a word to the media, and he's just given this Penny Timms and everybody else with a mike and camera statements he has no business giving."

Jantzen's gaze narrowed. "That right? You mean Stephens has his fifteen minutes of fame?"

"He's making noise, blowing smoke, talking like he's some kind of big shot all of a sudden, got the crime of the century in Newton and how he's the man to bring in the bad guys."

"Our Sheriff Columbo."

Slowly, Wiley walked across the diner. "First, what the hell is the meaning of you telling that reporter we have a Satanic cult behind these murders?"

"Because it's the truth, and we both know you suspect as much."

"Only thing I know is you're making yourself a major pain in the ass. I can't bust you for having a big mouth or I would."

"Look, Wiley, the newspeople are gone, we're alone. No Stephens, no FBI, we can cut the crap. What have you found out?"

Wiley seemed to think long and hard about something. Jantzen believed he was reaching the man, and prodded, "Colonel, talk to me. You know my past, you know I know that something more than just a series of murders is happening. And that it's going to happen again. Donner let the suspects stay at his place, didn't he?" He got no answer, but he knew Wiley was holding back. "All I need to do is drive out there and find a yellow line across his front porch."

"Jantzen, Paul Donner's dead."

"What?"

"I shouldn't be telling you any of this, because my ass would be in the frying pan with the FBI."

"What you tell me will stay right here."

"It better, or I'll make your life a living hell."

"It already is."

Wiley seemed to consider going on, but drew a deep breath, blew it out loudly, squared his shoulders. The colonel looked grim as he said, "There were some rather strange items in Donner's home."

"Such as."

"Don't push it."

"Maybe a Satanic bible, a pentagram drawn on the floor, forensics gathering evidence that maybe the Fenner girls were held there against their will. Maybe even some truly obscene sexual paraphernalia that was used on those girls. You'll find those girls were raped, repeatedly. It's part of their sick ritual. Something about the sacredness of the seed of the devil's followers, cleansing fire. Some unholy baptism of the virgin. I read that somewhere. In a Satanic bible that scared me to death. You're dealing with some sick and extremely dangerous people, and I even hesitate to call them people."

"You seem to know a lot, Jantzen."

"I know enough."

"You actually suspect it's the same people who killed your family, don't you?"

"Now who's picking whose brains? Beyond a shadow of a doubt, no, I can't say it is. You said Donner is dead? How?"

Anger grew in Wiley's eyes. "You want answers,

so do I. Okay. We tracked Donner down to his place in Tulsa. He was found hanging from the rafter of his condo."

"Looks like suicide, right?"

"On the surface."

"And?"

"That's all I'm going to tell you. I really came here to warn you..."

"Or to tell me you think I was right."

"Whatever. Don't say another word to the media, to anybody, not even your wife about what you suspect. Only reason we had this little talk was because you used to be a cop and I don't need you snooping around on your own, creating a panic, which you already have, by the way. Just keep your nose out of this."

"So you feed me enough to try and keep me at bay. Fat chance. Colonel, if I find out it is the same people, I'll do whatever it takes to see justice is done."

"Jantzen, we will not have another discussion like this, I hope. And if you go playing vigilante, I'll throw the book at you."

"You know this town has a problem that's not about to go away."

"Yes, I do."

Jantzen knew the Q and A was over. He softened his expression and said, "Looks like you've had a long day, Colonel. You want me to fix you something to eat or drink?"

"Thanks, but no. Now, if you'll excuse me and kindly keep your mouth shut from here on, I've got some damage control to take care of."

When Wiley departed, Jantzen sat there stone-still. Donner was dead, but he was sure it wasn't suicide. Donner had been into something way over his head. Jantzen had heard mention that Donner was a little strange, but to involve himself in a Satanic cult? Far as Jantzen knew, the man had been a loner when he'd stopped back in his hometown, no friends, no ties to the Newton community. With what he'd seen so far, Jantzen was beginning to believe more and more that anything was possible. Perhaps even that certain individuals thought they could sell their souls to the devil in exchange for the fulfillment of some worldly desire.

Pieces of a warped picture were trying to fit, but the latest news about Donner raised more questions than answers. For one thing, outsiders had obviously moved into a town where everyone knew each other by name, where strangers were noticed. So why had no one made any noise about strangers living in the Donner home?

And if the killers were still at large, in or just outside county limits, why had no one alerted the police to anyone they found suspicious? Surely the whole county would be swept by the FBI, everyone living in Newton interviewed, asked the questions Jantzen would about strangers or suspicious activity. Surely someone had seen or noticed something out of the ordinary.

It was suddenly beyond suspicious in his mind. He began to think that someone knew something they weren't revealing.

He decided to go home and catch the Tulsa news.

* * *

Jantzen sipped a beer, slumped on the living room couch, the television struck by low, gloomy light from the lamp beside him.

It was the top news segment, and Penny Timms had center stage. Standing in the middle of Tyler Street, the blond reporter came off as suitably grim as she gave her report. He listened to her as she stated the small town of Newton, a town of mostly farmers and ranchers, had been besieged in the past two days by a rash of brutal murders.

He tuned her out as she rattled on. It was pretty much what he expected, the reporter having gotten a statement from the State Police, no motives and no suspects. She followed up with the interviews of a few locals who answered her questions, Burt Martin and Bob Tamlin, a few others saying they were afraid, nothing like this has ever happened in Newton. It was terrible, it was a tragedy.

Jantzen listened with one ear until the scene shifted to the sheriff's office. At first Stephens sounded eager to talk on camera, but a slow change fell over his face, like a shadow rolling forth over the sheriff's features from behind.

"Ma'am, this is the worst imaginable sort of tragedy. This has always been a quiet and God-fearing town." Eagerness faded, changing to something Jantzen couldn't pin down. "Good people live here, Miz Timms, hardworking and honest people who want only to raise families and live in peace. And this horror...bodies hacked and shredded beyond recognition, pure savage butchery...animals, monsters did this...well, there are no words to express our sorrow and anger for the lives that have been so viciously snuffed out. I've been sher-

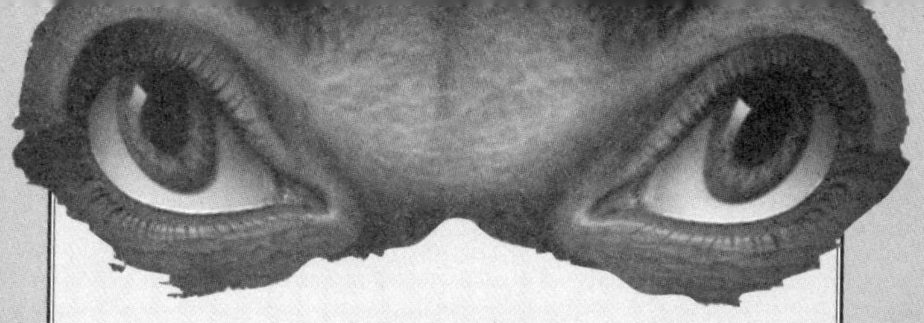

iff here for twenty-six years, ma'am, and I ain't never seen nothing like this."

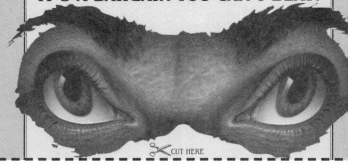

"Do you have any leads, any clues, Sheriff Stephens, as to who the perpetrators might be?"

Jantzen knew Stephens didn't have a clue. The sheriff looked right into the camera, playing to it. Or was he? Something kept disturbing Jantzen about the sheriff's expression, his tone of voice. The man looked and sounded cold, lifeless. He issued words of grief and confusion, but there was almost a quiet underlying note of...what? Pride? Usually he knew Stephens as full of bluster, anger inside him rolling out like thunder.

"My office is working together with the State Police and the FBI, ma'am. Trust me, we'll catch these people. This may be a small town, but me and my people know how to do our job, and if whoever did this is out there listening, you will be caught and punished to the full letter of the law."

Penny Timms thanked the sheriff, but she looked at him strangely before she faced the camera. Was it all an act on the sheriff's part? It all felt wrong somehow. It was as if he had been looking at a chameleon changing colors.

Again the scene shifted. This time Jantzen saw Penny Timms standing right in front of his diner. He figured she'd done this take when he'd been washing dishes, cleaning the grill.

"The man who owns this diner along with his wife, I'm told, is a former policeman. Earlier I had a chance to visit with him and he told me something very strange indeed, very frightening. He told me he believes a Satanic cult is behind the killings. Now, of course, that is merely speculation at this time, but all I can say is that this small and once quiet town of ranchers and farmers is now living in a state of pure terror. And everyone here is all too aware that the killer or killers of their friends and neighbors is still at large. Will this small town ever again be the same after the horror they have known here?"

Jantzen worked on his beer as she finished her report. He didn't need or want to hear any more. He had sounded the alarm, if nothing else, and the lady had played right into his hands.

Taking the remote, he snapped off the picture. Surrounded by silence, he became aware of just how big, cold and empty the house was without Mary.

He picked up the phone and dialed the number. He felt his pulse throb in his temples. Four rings later an unfamiliar female voice said, "Hello?"

He identified himself and asked to speak to Mary. Moments later, he heard her say his name.

"Hi." He tried to put some energy into his voice, to not sound like he was dying without her. "How you doing?"

"Just fine."

Why did she sound so glum? "You don't sound so fine. What's the matter?"

"Judy and I just finished watching the news, Mark. Congratulations. You're a veritable celebrity now. I'm glad at least she didn't blurt our names out."

"She barged in, Mary. Wanted her big story. All I did was warn people in this town they need to stay on guard."

"You used her."

"And?"

"Is this what you want? You want to keep on clutching to this obsession and drive me away in the process?"

"It's no obsession anymore. I think even Colonel Wiley believes what I believe. He came and talked to me today. Apparently the lady reporter told him what I thought."

"And now everyone in town thinks you're crazy."

"Do they? Who cares what they think? It's what I know and may know that matters. And what matters is that no one is safe until this is all put to rest."

There was a heavy pause on the other end. For a moment, Jantzen thought his wife had dropped the phone. "Mary?"

"I'm here. God, Mark, I'm sitting here, hoping, praying this all goes away or that it's put to rest. But you don't even see how insane this is making you. It scares me."

"I didn't call to get into it with you."

"Then why did you call?"

"To tell you I miss you. When are...you coming home?"

"I don't know. We can talk again in a couple of days."

It was as if he'd been punched in the stomach. He wanted to pursue it, but dropped it, knowing any sort of imploring would only lead to an argument.

"All right, babe. Stay in touch. And if it will make you happy, I won't talk to any more reporters."

"More sarcasm. What will make me happy is for you to come to peace with all of this and try to restore our marriage."

"I..." He almost admitted he couldn't come to the peace she so desperately wanted him to find. "I love you. Take care, Mary."

When she said good-bye, there was no "I miss you," or "I love you" like he wanted to hear. Just the dial tone sounded, like a klaxon in his ear.

After hanging up, he sat in the silence, wondering what tomorrow would bring.

Chapter Fourteen

Day two without Mary began at just after three in the morning.

It was the nightmare that clawed Jantzen from a restless sleep.

Snakes, a sea of writhing, angry, lunging serpents.

He bolted upright, his cry of alarm choked off with sheer willpower. Were they right on top of him, in the room, sliding across the floor, surrounding the bed? Winding up beneath the sheets? There was no sound, no tambourine-like rattle. He kicked his legs out, hurled up the blanket. Nothing but his legs. His breathing slowed. He could feel his heart pounding in his ears.

Memory and motive swirled in his mind, then seemed locked in the air around him, a living force. He knew why it felt that way, or so he believed.

Earlier he had told himself he would fight the nightmares, will them to go away, or at worst hold them back with grim determination. If he had those lifelike visions of horror and brutality and felt himself want to come screaming back to reality, he would summon up all resolve to feel and appear normal when awakening. He realized then that he had been attempting to do that for his wife, to prove he had it under control.

He tasted the fear on his lips. And he realized that his experiment in willpower had failed.

Wiping the sweat off his brow, he searched the impenetrable darkness of the empty bedroom. Listening for any strange sounds in the house, he pulled the .45 Colt ACP from under his pillow. The house felt eerily still, quiet. He could remember only one other time in his life when he was so agonizingly aware of his aloneness. And so very much afraid.

Sliding out of bed, thinking how cold the sheets felt, his undershirt plastered to his torso with sweat, Jantzen fanned the gloom with the stainless steel handgun. The Government Model MK IV held seven rounds in the magazine, but he already had one slug up the spout, the gun cocked and locked. Any home invaders, any shadows moving in the house, would find a lethal surprise waiting for them. No longer would he take any chances.

He didn't want his wife or himself to end up like the Delmarvins.

How he would handle the gun situation when Mary returned he wasn't sure. But he would try to talk reason into her, and he doubted she would think him unduly paranoid. Of course, for the sake of safety, he wouldn't keep the gun cocked and locked under the pillow when she came home. With a sudden angry flash he thought, *If she came home.*

He had to believe she would.

He took the flashlight from the nightstand. Snapping on the light, he raked the beam around the room. Empty. He ran the beam across the floor. He might have been dreaming of snakes, but once in a while he knew of ranchers who had found a rattler had slithered into their home. He searched every corner of the room. No snakes.

But was there something or someone else in the house?

Out in the remote areas of the county, nearly everyone owned a dog. But last year Mary's Great Dane, Mike, had died from old age. He wished now they had gotten another dog, preferably a Doberman or a pit bull.

Shadowy images of the nightmare clung to his memory as he walked out of the bedroom. There had been hundreds, maybe even thousands of vipers, coiling and slithering around him, fangs dripping with venom. He was outstretched on a dirt floor, unable to move, limbs heavy as concrete slabs. From somewhere beyond the sea of vipers he thought he had heard long bellows of cold laughter. And he thought he had seen a giant man with a bald head and black eyes, hovering a great distance above him.

Was it the man on the road, the darting shadow in the night with the death wish?

He heard a rustling noise, a scraping sound, but it could have been the wind blowing a tree branch against the roof.

Moving in a crouch, gun poised, he went into the kitchen. Nothing.

A low wind howled around the house, the wind sounding far louder than it really was because of the deafening silence around him.

Within minutes he had checked the guestroom, the garage, all doors and windows, and found them securely locked.

He jumped when the phone rang. Who the hell would be calling at that hour? Was it Mary? Worried about him? Checking up to see how he was making it without her?

Fear knotted an iceball in his guts. With the light hitting the cordless phone, the solitary illuminated object looked especially obscene as the images of the nightmare clung to Jantzen's memory. He moved woodenly and picked up the phone.

Cradling the phone to his ear, he didn't say a word for long moments. He knew someone was on the other end.

"Who is this?" he growled.

No answer.

"Who the hell is this?"

Click. The dial tone buzzed in his ear. He became angry, then even more afraid. If Mary had been there, she would have been crazy with fear, he knew. Either someone was playing games or he was being watched, or worse.

Alone in the darkness, he began to feel like a weak animal about to be preyed upon by a larger and more vicious predator.

But he would not go down without a fight.

He set the phone down, then sat on the couch. They were listed in the phone book. It could have been anybody on the other end, but who? He knew it was no crank call; there was meant to be some threatening message in the silence of the caller.

It worked. Fear had him wide awake, and he didn't want to return to sleep.

The snakes had seemed so real, so damned alive, one writhing mass of glistening scales and gleaming fangs.

He snapped off the flashlight. Something, someone was out there, close and watching their home. Every instinct from years of bad experience screamed at him, warning him that he—no, he and his wife—had yet to see the worst.

For the next few hours he watched the dark hole that led into the kitchen.

He saw the sun rise.

Tired, agitated, Jantzen was on edge as he drove toward town. Ranch houses and barns and stables blurred by, cattle wandering listlessly across the sun-baked fields, the woods in the distance bleak and barren. Everything felt and looked lifeless. It was strange how he encountered no traffic on the main county highway, saw no ranchers on horseback. It was as if everyone had shut themselves in their homes, pulled up the drawbridge. Or maybe this was a day of mourning.

It dawned on him that funeral arrangements had to be made for five dead people. All of them would be morbid, closed-casket affairs. His life the past few days had been so full of turmoil he hadn't even bothered to extend his sympathies to the Fenners. He needed to inquire in town about the funeral arrangements. Josh Stankin was the local mortician, but he ran his business on the northern outskirts of Newton. Jantzen would make a call later to Stankin. If nothing else, he would send the Fenners flowers, and attend the funeral mass and burial.

Unlike the husband his wife so desperately wished for, he was becoming more paranoid, more afraid, and more obsessed with finding out the truth behind the killings, the identities of the murderers. Now he even had the .45 locked in the glove box. It was risky, but he was licensed. Any drinking would be done at home for the immediate future. He didn't need to give Stephens the least excuse to pull him over.

He didn't find a living soul until he got to the diner. Even the lumberyard had been strangely inactive lately. But the Newton sawmill was miles southeast, thanks to a long-standing noise ordinance imposed by the three-man city council. Lumber was trucked in maybe every two weeks from the sawmill and stacked at the edge of town. Jantzen noticed the four parked flatbeds in the yard. He could tell they hadn't been moved in days. Any orders for lumber were taken by the two yardmen, Hurley and Gibbons, who could call out for a local driver if necessary. There wasn't much building done in the county, but sometimes a large order would go out to surrounding counties.

Earlier he had called the Hurkins, told them to open up, that he would be late. He found a few vehicles parked out front, recognized the older-model cars and trucks of the regulars, including Reilly and Stallins. After yesterday, he was beginning to wish those two would eat at Jim Milton's grocery store, which also doubled as a deli, all of three tables. One vehicle was the sheriff's cruiser. Jantzen felt his blood race.

As Jantzen parked, he saw the sheriff walk out of the diner, as if Stephens had been waiting for him to arrive. Jantzen braced himself for a rude greeting.

But the sheriff went straight for his cruiser. Strangely, the sheriff just watched Jantzen, the man's dark shades mirroring the glare of the sun. Jantzen stayed behind the wheel. It seemed as if Stephens was walking in slow motion, trying to unnerve the man he disliked so much with a hard eyeballing. Jantzen sensed something else about the man's attitude, the hard set to his features. But what exactly? Why the silent stare-down?

Finally Jantzen stepped out of his truck. Why did the world feel so strange, out of proportion that morning? Why was Stephens acting so weird?

The whole time the sheriff opened the door to his cruiser, settled behind the wheel and fired up the engine, he never took his mirrored stare off Jantzen.

Jantzen had an urge to charge up to the cruiser and confront Stephens. Instead he held his ground, wondered briefly over his inability to move. It was like the nightmare, where he felt mired in sucking mud.

Finally Stephens backed out, swung around and slowly rolled toward his office at the other end of town. But Jantzen found the man still watching him in the sideview mirror.

Once inside the diner, Jantzen went straight for the counter. He saw Murphy, Tamlin and Burt Martin lined up side by side drinking coffee. Then he spotted Reilly and Stallins. Both men were hunched over their usual meal, but they were sitting in the far corner booth, alone. They appeared grim, didn't bother to look up or even glance at Jantzen.

"What the hell's going on around here?" Jantzen asked, more casually than he felt, as he walked up beside Tim. Martha was refilling coffee all around.

"Well, we were just talking about all the funeral arrangements, or rather the lack of them," Murphy blurted out, and Jantzen knew the old-timer was oblivious to his own dark mood. Still curious, Jantzen listened.

"Seems relatives of all... well, the victims," Martin said, "have come to claim the remains."

"Turns out Gruber had a brother from down near Dallas," Tamlin said.

"Everyone's been calling Josh," Martin went on, "trying to find out about the arrangements, you know, funeral mass, burial."

Tamlin said, "I don't think there will be any viewing wherever they take the bodies. I even heard the Fenners aren't receiving visitors, unless it's the police."

Martin filled his coffee with a long stream of sugar from the glass bottle. "No one really cares about Gruber, though his brother claimed the remains."

"Good riddance," Tamlin said, drawing deep on his cigarette. "But it turns out the Fenners are taking their... girls up north—Kansas, where the grandparents live."

"What about the Delmarvins?" Jantzen asked, pouring himself a cup of coffee.

"Her parents came to take them back to Dallas," Martin said.

For some reason, Jantzen found it all strange, but then again maybe it wasn't. Maybe the idea of burying the victims in the town where they had been murdered repulsed the next of kin.

Jantzen changed the subject, nodded at Reilly and Stallins. "What's with them?"

Martha Hurkins shrugged. "I couldn't tell you." She lowered her voice to a near whisper. "They came in here, haven't said two words except to order the usual."

"Maybe they're too good for us old men," Martin groused.

"Okay, it all makes sense now," Jantzen said, a sardonic edge to his voice. "Now, can someone tell me what the sheriff wanted and why he was acting so strange?"

Blank looks settled on the faces of the Hurkins and the men at the counter.

"He didn't say much either," Tim Hurkins said. "Just ate some eggs and bacon and left. We tried to talk to him, polite, not too nosy, y'know, wanting to know about all that's happened, but he said he couldn't talk about the investigation."

"Kinda odd, huh, after he ran his mouth for that lady reporter," Tamlin said. "I mean, one minute he's damn near telling all of us what the bodies looked like, then he clams up. Maybe the FBI had a hard word or two for him."

"Maybe," Jantzen said, his voice going distant. There was some reason Stephens had shown up and given everyone the intimidating silent treatment. Odd. Even bizarre, he thought, recalling the dark look on the sheriff's face.

"I think all these killings have disturbed people around here more than they want to admit," Murphy said. "I've lived here all my life, never seen or heard anything like it. Now...well, forgive me, Mark, I mean you saw the Fenner girls and all...but that talk of a bunch of Satanists has everyone real spooked."

"I should have never said that, Pete." Jantzen sipped his coffee. "I can't prove anything, I was just talking from past experience. I'd just as soon forget about it. Did we do any business this morning?"

"Not like yesterday," Martha said. "I don't know why, but yesterday was the kind of crowd you only see in here after Sunday service."

Sunday service. He thought of the county minister, John Standford. He wondered what Standford thought about recent events, but his thoughts wandered to Father Ben McMartin instead. He felt more inclined to seek out the Catholic priest than the opinions and advice of the Baptist minister, a man he had never said more than six words to the whole time he had lived in Newton. Mary was a regular at his Sunday service, but she always attended alone.

Jantzen made a decision and he would tend to it shortly. It was time to get help, and the only person, beyond his wife, who could give him that was the priest. When he had so desperately needed answers and insight, Father McMartin had been there.

Yes, he was long overdue, even as stubbornly as he resisted the idea of outside help. Then again, who was he doing it for? At that point, perhaps it didn't matter.

"Get the check over here?"

Reilly's gruff voice interrupted his thoughts. "Allow me, Martha," Jantzen said as he took the check from her. Tension thickened as he walked from behind the counter. He noticed the same coldness on their faces as he'd seen yesterday. Only today the two men had the same lifelessness in their eyes that he had seen when Stephens had been on the news.

Right then, like a slap in the face, it hit Jantzen that what he saw was the same look he had come to know so well on the faces and in the eyes of hardened career criminals. Call them sociopaths, psychopaths, legally insane, whatever. But Jantzen knew when he was looking at someone who only cared about what he or she wanted or could get. If the eyes were the windows to the soul, then Jantzen read both Reilly and Stallins as seeing the world full of others who were just obstacles in the way of their wants.

They didn't look up as Jantzen dropped the check on the table. "Was it something I said, gentlemen?"

There was no change in their expressions as they dug some crumpled singles and change. Obviously they were going to also stiff Martha.

"Look, you come in here, you demand service, you show everyone in my place of business what a huge chip on your shoulders you two have. Now, I don't care that you don't tip me, but Martha's another story."

Reilly turned his head up. There was a look of simmering rage in Reilly's eyes that sent a chill down Jantzen's spine.

"We're almost out of money these days," Reilly said.

"So get a job."

"We don't need a job," Stallins said.

"We've got things figured out," Reilly told Jantzen.

Jantzen felt his shoulders tense as they stood. These two were becoming a definite and potentially serious problem. They lived together, south, near the county line, in a trailer home. Beyond that, he realized then he didn't know much about them. Right then, he knew there was something mean in their eyes, something shadowy, even insidious in their voices and expressions. He wondered if they had been friends of Jeb Gruber. Suddenly he noticed they smelled of dried sweat, mingled with some sweet fragrance he didn't recognize. Their faces were scraggly with several days' growth of bristles. Their eyes appeared dead to Jantzen.

When they brushed past him, Jantzen said, "Have a nice day."

As they left, Jantzen heard Stallins mutter, "Fuck you."

"Those two are trouble. I don't know what's with them these days," Tamlin growled.

"I don't know what's wrong with anybody anymore, Bob," Jantzen said.

Later in the afternoon when the diner was empty, Jantzen sent the Hurkins home for the day. As he walked them to the door and said good-bye, he spotted Buddy Simpson's Chevy pickup parked beside the lumberyard. Simpson, at the wheel, was chatting with Hurley and Gibbons, the two yard-men obviously having as much idle time on their hands as anybody else that day. But Simpson's attention was focused down the street as he talked to the two men. Then Simpson handed them a bot-tle, glanced at them as they passed the bottle between them, then handed it back. Finally Hurley and Gibbons left, but Simpson sat in his truck, staring down the street. Fixed, mesmerized by something.

Jantzen almost called out to Simpson, consid-ered going over and asking his friend if he wanted to go for a drink. But even at distance, Jantzen was disturbed about something on Simpson's face he couldn't quite pin down. Simpson should have noticed him standing in the doorway; there was no one else around, after all. Why was Buddy just sit-ting there, a piece of stone, with a weird expression on his face? It struck Jantzen that he was seeing the same mean, lustful expression he had seen the other day when Simpson had railed about Jackie Rawlins and Toni Jacklin. Only now Jantzen sensed something predatory in the man's vigilant watch.

Something was wrong with Simpson. Jantzen watched him lift his bottle, take a deep swig.

With a bad feeling, Jantzen slowly walked inside to a position at the edge of the plate glass window where he could monitor the street.

It was then his suspicions were confirmed.

Jackie Rawlins was sliding into her own pickup

truck with a sack full of groceries. She had her young daughter with her. Sunlight glistened off the golden blond manes of both mother and daughter.

Disgust balled up inside Jantzen. What the hell was wrong with Simpson? He could only imagine the dark thoughts going through the man's mind. After all, Jantzen had heard some of it with his own ears.

When Jackie Rawlins reversed away from the grocery store, Jantzen felt his fear growing. He was afraid of what he would find next.

At the door, he heard Simpson fire up the engine. Slowly the truck rolled away. He was following them.

Jantzen quickly locked up and bounded down the stoop. He spotted Simpson's truck cutting left at the edge of town. Jantzen turned on the engine.

He knew Simpson had a rifle rack in the cab, pretty much standard traveling gear in the town.

But this was not a normal situation. Whatever he thought he had seen on Simpson's face, whatever the man's motives, Jantzen was glad he had the .45 with him.

Chapter Fifteen

She lived at least fifteen miles due north of town. The Rawlins were Jantzen's closest neighbors. Since he drove it every day, Jantzen knew the road well. Eventually she would turn off on Red Oak Run, hit a five-mile stretch down dirt road that paralleled his own property. From town to his home there were long and lonely stretches of isolated highway. Perfect, Jantzen thought, if Simpson was up to something sinister; not even a farmhouse or a few head of cattle, just brown fields and tumbleweed.

But what was Simpson's plan? Cut Jackie off as she turned onto Red Oak and brandish a gun? What was Simpson thinking? What was driving the man?

Jantzen had seen the malevolent expression on Simpson's face, and he wasn't about to take any chances. He knew Simpson had been drinking, knew the man could change after a few belts, and he remembered the animal desire in the man's eyes the other day.

What was happening to Newton?

The town was living in fear, yet there seemed to be a number of individuals—Reilly, Stallins, maybe Jock Peters and his barflies, and Simpson—who began to strike Jantzen as cold to the point of lifeless. Had he been living so locked in himself for so long that he had not noticed those subtle changes in the eyes, in their behavior? Go to work, another day, not look beyond himself. Had something been happening all along around him that he didn't know about?

He was clipping along at around fifty mph. Ahead, Simpson moved at roughly the same speed. Jantzen maintained about a hundred-meter distance behind. Beyond Simpson's truck, mother and daughter were five car lengths ahead of their pursuer.

Pursuer? Enough! He decided he had to confront Simpson, and now. Hitting the gas, he rocketed ahead, pushing it up to seventy. Closing the gap, he flicked on the headlights and hit the high beams.

Simpson's eyes appeared to flash with rage as Jantzen saw the man's face, sharp as the edge of an ax, filling the rearview. Jantzen waved for Simpson to pull over. Another quarter-mile, then Simpson slowed and pulled off onto the dirt shoulder of the road. Jantzen slid in behind the truck, a spool of dust blowing over him. For a moment, with the dust wall billowing over Simpson's vehicle, the man was merely a shadow in the cab.

Long moments passed, then the dust thinned.

As Jantzen sat there, he began to wonder if he really knew Buddy Simpson at all.

In the next moment he discovered he didn't.

He saw Simpson pluck a rifle off the rack hanging against the back window. It was a Winchester .30-30, and Simpson was jacking the lever action, chambering a live one. Utter terror ripped through Jantzen as the door to Simpson's truck opened. Then Simpson seemed to hesitate in the doorway.

Swiftly, his gaze on Simpson, Jantzen opened the glove box. He took out the .45 and tucked it in the waistband in the small of his back.

Slowly he opened his door and stepped out. He wasn't sure what he was going to do next, but he was braced for the worst.

Rage burned inside him, a living force that felt like fire. He was going to be denied.

Simpson heard the endless stream of vicious cursing in his mind, echoing back and forth in his skull. Unforeseen circumstance had thwarted his plan, trampled his desire. *Relax,* he told himself, *only for now*. There would always be another time. But it had to be soon.

Michael was right, though, about one thing. Desire fed on itself and it had to be fed continually in order to stay strong. For weeks he had been hungry for both the mother and the daughter. At night his mind screamed with lust as he watched his porno videos, drinking alone, thinking of all he could do to them.

Now this. Jantzen.

The man had followed him. He suspected something.

Now the women were getting away. His plan had been to cut them off when they turned onto Red Oak. Plenty of trees would have covered them from the highway. Use his rifle, force them to do what he wanted. When he was finished, kill them both, a gunshot to the head, then carve out their hearts, take them to Michael, both as proof he was worthy to be one of them and as an offering.

Damn it, he wished he had more meth on him that morning. Lately Michael seemed stingy with both the peyote and the meth. At least he had his bottle to help feed his desire. He'd been drinking whiskey all day as he staked out the road that led to the Rawlins ranch. Finally the two women had emerged. He knew the mother ventured into town every day, whether to drink, rent videos or grocery shop. It was double luck when he saw her young daughter with her.

Desire must feed itself. Those were Michael's words. They came from his own book, the history of his people, the chronicles of the entire clan.

Knowledge and a way to new power was why Simpson had sought out the man after their first contact. The man knew something. The man even sensed that Simpson was a soldier, asked if he had been in Vietnam.

"Did you do things over there that most humans would find an abomination?" Michael had asked him. Of course. He had seen entire Vietnamese villages slaughtered, the women raped, their homes put to the torch. He had even enjoyed it, a license to rape and to kill, knowing they could get away with it, that no one would miss a bunch of suspected VC.

"Then you have brought home the same desires, the cravings for power and domination, for release of your aggressions. Only now you are stuck in this small, nowhere, nothing place where good-looking women are few and far between. Your aggression builds, you probably indulge in pornography to satisfy yourself, you have anger inside you cannot understand, and you despise and hold in contempt this weak town at large. So you need something else, something more. You are a warrior and you need a renewed warrior's existence." How did the man know him so well? Those black eyes seemed to bore into the darkest corners of his heart. "We will help you, but you must be willing, and there will be a price."

He sat there in the doorway of his truck, the Winchester rifle in his hands. He wondered if he should kill Jantzen. They were alone at the moment, but someone could drive by. If it had been night....

In the rearview he saw Jantzen stepping out of his truck. That cop's natural suspicion and cynicism were all over Jantzen's face. He had come to despise Jantzen. The man was weak; he clung to a guilty past that paralyzed him with doubt and fear. Simpson chuckled. If the man only knew what he knew.

Slowly Simpson rolled out the doorway, the rifle low by his side.

* * *

At first Jantzen saw the ferocity in Simpson's eyes as the man unfolded from the doorway of his vehicle. Then the look faded into confusion. Then Simpson chuckled.

Jantzen felt the weight of the .45 low by his right leg. He was ready to pull the gun and swing it around if Simpson even brought his rifle up a few inches. How could this be happening? They were friends, or so he thought.

"Mark, what the hell are you doing?"

Jantzen licked dry lips, felt the sweat burn into the corner of his eye. "I was about to ask you the same thing, Buddy."

"You following me?"

"I was curious."

The rifle seemed to move, a half-inch or so, toward Simpson's free hand.

"Curious? About what?" Simpson's chuckle sounded forced.

"Why you seemed to be following Mrs. Rawlins and her daughter."

Another chuckle, Simpson shaking his head softly. The man's eyes looked lit with something that Jantzen couldn't pin down. The eyes were bloodshot, and Jantzen watching them as they darted from side to side for several moments. Simpson, he suspected, was hopped up on more than just booze.

"Come on, Mark. I wasn't following them. Why would you say such a thing? You think I'm a pervert?"

"Were you?"

"Was I what?"

Jantzen felt his jaw clench. Right then he realized he didn't know Simpson at all. The man was dangerous. If Simpson moved another muscle, Jantzen would have his .45 out in the blink of an eye.

"Following them."

Simpson's face turned serious. Slowly he let the rifle fall by his side. "Okay, yeah, I was following them. But before you say anything else, let me explain. This town's on edge. People are dying horrible deaths all around us. I see a mother and daughter out by themselves, well, I figured I'd make sure they got home safe. That's it, that's all it was."

Jantzen had seen enough liars in his day to know when someone was lying. "The Good Samaritan, that it, Buddy?"

"Mark, Mark. Come on, you and I been friends for a long time. You ever known me to be dishonest with you?"

"Can't say I have."

"So lose the suspicious tone, old buddy."

That vicious predatory glint flashed through Simpson's eyes, then was gone.

For the moment, it was a standoff. Jantzen figured there was nothing left to do but say good-bye, get in his truck and drive away. Alive. He wasn't about to take his eyes off Simpson.

"All right. Let's forget this ever happened." Jantzen could lie also. "Just a big misunderstanding."

Simpson chuckled. "No problem. I understand. Everyone's a little on edge these days."

"I'll see you around, Buddy."

"Hey, how about stopping by the Bluff later? I heard Mary's out of town, we can drink the night away. Kiss and make up. I don't have any hard feelings."

News about Mary being gone had spread fast. Jantzen didn't like that, but in a small town he didn't expect anything less.

"Some other time."

Keeping his gaze fixed on Simpson, Jantzen slid back into his truck. He watched as Simpson's expression hardened. A huge gap had just opened between them. He wouldn't trust Simpson ever again. Something was wrong with Simpson, and it went beyond booze.

Jantzen swung out onto the highway. Driving past the man, he watched as Simpson remained beside his truck, man and rifle soon growing smaller in his side mirror.

Jantzen didn't pry his stare off the mirror until Simpson vanished. He realized he was trembling.

Jantzen was still shaking when he got home.

He was surprised he didn't go for a drink right away. Instead, he sat down on the living room couch, concentrated on staring at nothing, tried to think of nothing. The silence, plus being utterly alone, suddenly washed over him with a great sense of relief. Strange, but right then he almost found a sense of peace in his isolation. People out there, both the seen and the unseen, were beginning to terrify him. It was getting to the point where he didn't know who was who, what was what. Just like that, life had shoved on a great big mask. Clown, gargoyle, demon face, pick one, he thought. A gigantic rubber face over life, at once laughing, sneering, ferocious. He was starting to wonder if he was going insane. All the guilt, paranoia, fear and anxiety were eating away at him like a cancer.

Breathing deep, he somehow emptied his mind, even put his thoughts of Simpson, the animal ferocity he'd seen in the man's eyes, behind him. There. Sit in silence, feel nothing.

It didn't last long.

Something was terribly wrong in, and with, Newton. Why was everything changing so quickly? All dignity, respect and trust had been ripped from the town and its people in the past few days. Was it all beyond hope? Would anything ever again be the same? If the killers were not caught soon, or at least identified, would neighbors and friends just continue to live in fear of one another?

Finally he lit a cigarette. It was then he became aware of the bulky object poking into his back. Damn! He was so distracted he hadn't been aware of the .45 Colt. Reaching behind him, he took the gun and gently laid it on the coffee table.

Next he gave serious consideration to calling Mary. And say what? "Hi, hon, how was your day, that's nice. Things here? It's all getting back to normal. I even thwarted what I suspected was going to be a rape attempt today by a good friend of mine. But I think I've gotten beyond my paranoia. How 'bout coming home, I'll make you dinner, we'll drink a few bottles of wine, make love, just like old times.'"

He didn't dare call her. She would know something was more wrong with him than when she left.

He couldn't stop his mind. Images and faces kept flashing in his head. Visions of nightmares boiled and meshed and screamed. He kept trembling, began sweating.

Before he knew it, he was in the kitchen building a stiff Wild Turkey. The drink somewhat calmed his nerves.

Another drink hardened his resolve. He knew the number was in their personal phone book. He pulled the book from the kitchen drawer. Mary kept the numbers listed alphabetically, but she was all about order and neatness anyway.

He found the number, picked up the phone and dialed. A man's voice he didn't recognize answered.

"Yes, hello," Jantzen said. He hesitated, thought about hanging up, but fear drove him on. If he didn't follow through now, he dreaded it might prove the worst mistake in a long time. "I would like to speak with Father McMartin. Is he there?"

The voice said the priest was there, who was calling?

"It's been a while, he might not remember. Tell him it's Mark Jantzen, the policeman from Atlanta. Tell him it's urgent. Maybe even a matter of life or death."

Chapter Sixteen

The receiving room of the rectory was exactly as he remembered it. Small, with only two couches facing each other, a nightstand with a lamp, and a crucifix on the wall. Jantzen supposed the room was meant to surround anyone who came here in spiritual unrest with a comfortable and unpretentious ambience.

Sitting on the couch, Jantzen took some time to reflect and gather himself while he waited for Father McMartin. It had been five years since he had last come to Saint Charles, he recalled, back then searching out the only Catholic parish he could locate near Newton. A man in dire trouble turning to the church, wanting answers. But the more he heard, the less he listened.

Now he was back, and worse than ever.

At the edge of Tulsa, the small church, rectory

and school were situated in a suburb east of Broken Arrow. He knew Father McMartin was originally from back East, Baltimore if memory served him right. He hadn't pried back then, wondering why the priest had decided to relocate in Oklahoma. Jantzen sensed, though, that something had haunted the elderly priest from wherever he came. Perhaps they shared something he wasn't aware of. Either way, Father McMartin knew far more about him than he did about the priest. It was unsettling to Jantzen that someone knew so much about him.

He waited some more, gradually growing agitated. Jantzen was tired, becoming more worried and afraid the longer he was without his wife, the longer the law did not find the killers. He began giving serious consideration to calling Mary after he left the rectory and ask her to meet him. He would decide later.

It had been a long morning already, making the hundred-plus-mile drive north. Last night had been another heavy and grim affair. Gun under his pillow, sleep restless, but he was grateful there were no nightmares.

Now Jantzen felt a puzzling sense of relief but also a stirring unease. Long ago, he had confided so much in the priest, revealed his entire past and reason for fleeing to Oklahoma. The failed police career, the adultery, subsequent failed marriage, the murders of his family, the descent into alcoholism. Father McMartin had told him pretty much the core of his spiritual problem, and he suspected he might hear the same thing again. The guilt he suffered from, his inability to forgive himself. So what was he looking for? Why was he even there if he already knew the answers? Or was there something more going on in his life?

Finally Father McMartin entered the room. Jantzen stood. They shook hands.

"Mark, it's been a long time."

"Good to see you, Father."

"Likewise. Sorry to keep you waiting."

"No problem."

The priest was in collar, dressed in black clerical shirt and trousers. He was slightly built, a little stoop-shouldered, perhaps the weight of the world and too many confessions on his back. Jantzen figured the man was well into his sixties, his face lean to the high cheekbones around the sunken eyes, but the jowls sagged. His blue eyes looked tired, world weary, as if they knew things no man should know. Certainly the priest looked more troubled than he remembered; the shock of white hair had thinned up top since the last time Jantzen had seen him. It hit him then that years can pass, a man grows older, sadder, hopefully wiser, and the outward self mirrors what is inside.

"Please, sit."

When they both settled onto their respective couches, Jantzen wishing he had a cigarette, a long moment of tight silence passed. Jantzen felt the priest's stare.

"You made it sound urgent when I spoke with you last night. Are you in trouble, Mark?"

"Not outwardly, Father, but you could say I'm most certainly in trouble. By the way, I didn't mean to sound so dramatic last night. I should've at least given you some idea."

Father McMartin nodded. "You're here now, that's all that matters."

"Yes. All that matters." He heard his voice trail off, felt that awful haunting feeling boil inside. He sat in silence, not even aware he was drifting from the moment until Father McMartin spoke.

"Mark, if you'll kindly allow me to be blunt?"

"I wouldn't have it any other way."

"I see the same man I did five years ago. You look like you're at death's door. I see a man whose soul is dying quickly. You're clearly disturbed, and I suspect not much has changed since the last time we spoke."

"Not much."

"Things are worse?"

"I suspect you've heard what's happened in Newton?"

The priest turned grim for a moment, and nodded. "Is that why you're here? Yes, I've seen the news. Five murders. It's taken you back to that time in your life?"

"It's one reason why I'm here, Father." Quickly he explained how he'd seen two of the three crime scenes.

"So you're thinking there's some connection with the present killings and your past?"

Jantzen sucked in a deep breath. "I do."

"And all your guilt and torment over that has you overwhelmed. All that fear and anxiety has seized you again."

"Nearly possessed me, you might say." He thought he saw the priest wince.

Jantzen quickly went on. "I remember what you told me about what I'd done to my last marriage, how I believed I had destroyed, inadvertently, my family. You told me to forgive myself, that I had to move on with my life. That even though I've sinned in the past, God hates the sin and not the sinner."

The priest studied him for a moment. "I can see you didn't heed my advice."

"Not by a long shot. The nightmares have come back, Father. I can't sleep, I can't think, I'm off running, from my wife, chasing after—I don't know what."

"How is Mary?"

Jantzen hesitated, the question catching him by surpise. "Can I smoke?"

Nodding, the priest left the room, then returned a moment later with an ashtray. When Jantzen got his smoke going and took a few drags, he said, "She's left me, at least for a few days." He told the priest her reasoning.

"Your wife is scared. And with good reason. She's afraid for herself, for you, your marriage. She doesn't know how to deal with all this, and your being overwhelmed is overwhelming her."

"I should be stronger, is that it?"

Father McMartin didn't answer right away. "You're strong in your own way, particularly in your defiance and stubbornness. But you're also much stronger in other ways you won't even see."

"How so?"

The priest shook his head, as if he'd thrown out a riddle Jantzen was supposed to answer for himself.

"Mark, I saw a man years ago who was clearly driving himself to insanity. If I may be frank, your faith is weak. And you're still angry with God."

"If that's true, then why?"

"It's simple, at least to me. Your thinking is that you didn't ask to be here, you don't want to be here to deal with this, so in your heart you silently curse God. In some ways, well, what I hear from you and what I see, if you can't be God you don't want to be anything. It's why the devil and his followers were cast from heaven and given their own kingdom in hell."

"Really?"

"Really. What's more, you stay mired in the past and things you cannot change. You drag the past into the present, and all you're doing is simply creating another past, more painful memories to feed your unrest. Five years later we're having the same conversation."

"My suffering keeps me going?"

"To some extent you enjoy your suffering, only because you won't accept suffering for the sake of suffering. But men suffer, Mark, we all suffer, but that's the cost of sin, and suffering is the way back to the Lord. You can't accept suffering. The fact is, you can't accept anything. Your unacceptance of life, of yourself, where you've been and what you've done, against whoever it is you blame for your own perceived plight, well, it's always driven you to commit acts that only reinforced your sense of hopelessness, and, of course, your anger toward life."

"Is there a way out? Is there any hope?"

"The way out is to have courage and face yourself, face whatever you've done. And, yes, beyond asking for forgiveness, receive it and forgive yourself. In that, there will be hope. And hope will give you courage. Right now you have no hope."

"I know. I don't know how to get it."

"Pray. Ask for help. Repent through actions and not words. That you've even come back here, well, that's something of a good sign. But it's only a start."

"Do you believe in the devil, Father?"

The priest seemed momentarily surprised. "Satan is real. That you even ask that question tells me your faith is weak."

"The reason I ask..."

He stopped, but Father McMartin forged on. "I know why you ask; we've discussed it before. The murders are the work of some group that worships the devil. Long ago you told me about that bookstore, your experience reading some of those writings. You told me you considered buying this Satanic bible because you wanted to understand your enemies. You were convinced the murders were committed by a group involved in Satan worship."

"Was I wrong on both counts?"

"No. First, what you read was evil, but it touched some part in you that you were both repulsed by and afraid of. It was best you never took possession of such an evil thing. In fact, you might have saved yourself from even greater torment. Satan is not called the Great Liar for no reason. He is the master at creating confusion and chaos and unrest. You've always lived in dangerous territory inside yourself. Your soul has always been pulled in opposite directions. One day the light, the next moment you're slipping toward the abyss. But the reality of it is that you actually have the same problem the rest of the human race does. The flesh. You live in the world, you want the world, your heart wants what it wants because you have no faith and no trust that God will aid you, that God could possibly love you, and that He will prevail. The fact that you can't let what you've done and known go, it shows me you even take pride in your own sin. In your mind, you may not even realize that because you were a policemen and since the law was behind you there was no way you could be like the criminals you were after or arrested. What was always the first thing someone you knew was guilty wanted to do?"

"Lie."

"Exactly. Lie. Why? Pride, essentially, and it does go before the fall." He paused. "Second matter: from what you've told me about the past and the present killings, it does read as if one of these cults is responsible. You believe that, I believe that. I'm sure this is one thing you came to me to hear. These people, they are sick and dangerous people, living in evil, and they are beyond hope in their present state. Now, what do you do? What I'm seeing in you is that you believe, or want to believe, since the guilty were never caught back then, that it is the same ones."

"And if it is?"

"Mark, you're heading into... well, you're staying stuck in very dangerous territory. Listen to me carefully. The people who took the lives of your wife and daughter will one day be punished."

Jantzen felt his gaze narrow. "Vengeance is mine, sayeth the Lord?"

"That's what's eating you up. You want it your

way, you want to shed their blood with your own hands."

"Let it go, just like that? Love thine enemy? Turn the other cheek?"

The priest leaned back, solemn in the face of Jantzen's sudden anger.

"Do you ever think, Father, that in some cases perhaps God uses us as instruments to exact His will, even if it is vengeance? I mean, if these... individuals have turned over, or offered, or sold their souls to the devil or whatever and are committing atrocities against the innocent, don't you think God wants them found and punished—even if it means taking their lives?"

Father McMartin seemed to ponder something long and hard. Jantzen thought he might quote Scripture, but the priest surprised him and said, "You make a convincing argument."

"How come you don't sound all that convinced?"

"I'd have to give it some thought."

Jantzen ground out his cigarette. He felt a sudden strain in the pause between them.

"Mark. Why did you come to see me?"

"I wanted... help. And answers."

"I smell the alcohol on you."

"I haven't had a drink since last night."

"Where's your mind now?"

"On a drink."

"I won't get into that with you. You're going to do what you want. But if you can clear your head, perhaps your soul will follow, at least somewhat. Give it some thought anyway. As for answers, you have the answers, you're just not asking the right questions. And perhaps you shouldn't even be asking questions of things no man has a clear knowledge of and insight into."

"Such as what?"

"Such as why your wife and daughter were taken from you."

He felt resentment. "Just accept it?"

"There is no answer, other than there is evil in the world."

"My whole point."

The priest appeared to grow heavy in deep thought. "What does your wife want from you?"

"For me to be happy, joyous and free." He detested the note of sarcasm in his voice, regretted sounding that way.

The priest chuckled, but it was a grim sound. "I will pray for you, my son."

For a moment Jantzen saw a profound sorrow burn into the priest's eyes. Then the priest's expression hardened.

"What do you want from your wife?"

"For her...to come home."

"So that you won't feel lonely? Isn't that selfish? You are incredible, and I have to believe I'm echoing Mary's thoughts. The world revolves around you. You primarily take and very rarely give, especially of yourself. Everything is a struggle for you."

"Does that make me a bad man, Father?"

The priest shook his head. "No. It just keeps you...alone. The fact is, Mark, and I'm sure you need to hear this, but you're a good man. The simple fact that you're tormented like this, well, it's a sign of hope in a way. You want to change, you need to change or you will die. But I'm here to tell you, you're no Paul. There won't be any blinding light. You'll have to look at yourself, very hard.

"I won't hurl Scripture at you, but your view is a lot like Solomon's. Wickedness is in the world. Nothing is worthwhile, everything is futility. Basically, why bother? Everything, every breath you take, is a struggle, but you struggle on. And, yes, you bother, more than most. Still, even worse, you have no peace because of that, but I hope you find some. You won't find it in a bottle, nor all the things you used to do as a policemen, the drugs, the gambling, the prostitutes. Believe me. I've tried it—the drinking, that is, though I've certainly had my moments of desire where I had to pray like I never had before. Oh, yes, it's a little-known fact, but I was a terrible alcoholic. Mostly did my drinking alone." He smiled. "You see, even a priest has need for confession."

"I never doubted that."

"But, of course, ever the policeman."

"Thank you, Father, for spending some time with me."

"Has it helped?"

"I'm not sure. I... may I feel free to call you?"

"I insist you do. When was the last time you went to Mass?"

"I don't know, I can't remember."

The priest seemed to choose his next words carefully. "I know Mary goes to church. You told me that when we first met. How you would like to, but couldn't. Why?"

"I felt... unworthy."

"Why don't you try sometime? Maybe, well, maybe it will help bridge the gap between you and your wife."

"A kinder, gentler me?"

"It would be a start."

"I'll think about it."

"But now you're going to go have a drink."

"I'm giving it some serious thought."

"And then?"

"Go home."

"And then?"

"Hope for a better tomorrow."

Father McMartin paused, looking even more weary and saddened. "Before you go, do you want to make your confession?"

"Yes."

Chapter Seventeen

After the fifth whiskey, Jantzen started nursing his drinks. When Mary showed up he didn't want to be all the way in the bag. She expected him to have a few at the end of the day, but not consume so much he couldn't function, or perhaps lapse into a Jekyll-and-Hyde mode, put up a surly and sarcastic wall which could prove equally unsettling. If nothing else, he wanted to show his wife some progress, that he was attempting to change. But why? Surely she would see the same anger and distress. And surely she would decide that a little more time to herself was in order.

For the sixth time in the past forty-five minutes he checked his watch. She was late, but then again she had to make the drive from northern Tulsa to the southern outskirts of the city.

He drummed his fingers on the table, worked on

his drink, fired up another cigarette. What was his life becoming? A circle of madness and mystery, tightening a little more every day around him.

He put his thoughts back on his wife. He had to restore their marriage somehow. He had to change something. He could understand how he was driving her away. But it wasn't his fault.

She had sounded surprised to hear that he was in Tulsa, but he explained his visit to Father McMartin. A lame excuse, perhaps, but they were married, and he wanted to see her. He couldn't read what was in her voice until he saw her. Would she be disappointed? Happy to see him? Would she think he wanted to pressure her to return home?

Waiting for her began to make him angry. He had given her the name of the place. In fact, they had dinner here long ago. They were no strangers to the city. Every few months they used to get away, just pack a few things and spend some time together, away from the diner and Newton.

He settled back into the booth. He was in the deepest corner of the restaurant, alone. It was an establishment that catered to the new urban cowboys—guys in suits with Stetsons, or just guys in suits, with a few scattered roughnecks, maybe oil workers. Everyone was chatting and laughing, suits and roughnecks talking to a lot of pretty women in skirts or pantsuits, the whole cast lining the long mahogany bar for happy hour. Here they played soft rock, not country and western. A few couples sat in booths or at tables near the bar. The walls were adorned with oil paintings of everything from rodeo riders to gunslingers and scenes of shootouts, to sunsets and tugboats in the Tulsa port of Catoosa. Beside him hung a painting of the sun going down over the prairie, a few forlorn-looking cattle, dark lumps in the shadows. Cheers.

In brooding silence, he took the felt pen and cocktail napkins he had asked the waitress for. Slowly, methodically, he drew a pentagram. He knew the five-pointed star was the traditional weapon of power in magic. Symbolically it represented the number five, which in the world of mystics and magicians stood for the living world of Nature with man as its lord and master. There were, he knew, two ways for the pentagram to be used, either worn or in ritual. The five points symbolized Christ on the cross, meant to frighten off evil spirits. One point going up was used for calling on good influences to wipe out evil influences. Invert the pentagram and the two upper points represented the horns of the devil, thus becoming a symbol of evil. There were centuries and centuries of lore and legend surrounding the pentagram. There was the Pentagram of Solomon, drawn on parchment, to be carried in a magical ceremony. There was the star of the magi, the symbol of the Word made flesh, or of a man with arms and legs extended, symbolizing man's divine spirit. There were many other meanings and legends he couldn't remember at the moment.

But he could clearly recall the meaning of the reversed pentagram.

Staring at the pentagram, he recalled how he read in the police report how the reversed symbol had been drawn around the bodies of his wife and daughter.

He felt his blood throbbing in his ears. He would never rest until he found the animals who had made their sick offering to Satan.

Shoving painful memories to the back of his mind, he thought of the crime scenes at the Delmarvins and the Donner place. No pentagram at either scene. But there had been the black circle, broken with the upside down crucifix, around the Fenner girls. Beyond the obvious sacrilege, what did the circle represent? Was it some new symbol for Satanic ritual? Surely if other such crime scenes had been found in the state or anywhere else in the country, Special Agent Thomkins would know about it. It was Jantzen's contention that this particular cult was sophisticated and mobile, perhaps with cells throughout the country. Murder at whim, move on, vanish like ghosts into the night. He could ask Thomkins all the questions he wanted, and he knew he'd get nothing but stony silence or an implied threat.

So what to do? Search out the killers himself? How? Patrol the county, looking for strangers? Interview Newton residents?

"Mark?"

He jumped. Mary was standing by the table. She looked tense, uncertain. She was staring at the pentagram.

"Drawing pentagrams now?"

Flat, no accusation. Same thing, different place. She sounded disappointed.

"Hi," he said as she slid into the booth next to him. He stared into her eyes, hoping to find a glimmer of something, anything, even if it was anger. Gently she kissed him.

"Does that mean you've missed me?" he asked, a smile dancing over his lips.

She returned the smile, but there was sadness in her expression. "Yes. I missed you."

"But what?"

She sighed. Jantzen caught the waitress's eye. Mary ordered a beer. She opened her purse, took out her cigarettes, and he lit one for her.

"I don't know. There is no 'but what,' I guess."

"How's your girlfriend?"

"Under her present circumstances, Judy's as good as she can be." A heavy expression fell over her face. "She divorced about a year ago. Husband's a pilot, apparently fell madly in love with some stewardess. It was a messy divorce, but she got custody of their two children."

"Can I ask you what made you think to call her?"

She smiled, wistful. "We grew up together, went to school together, we did all the small-town things together. The homecomings, going to the rodeos, you know. So... we got to talking, you know, going back. I guess we just missed each other. She moved away from Newton long before we met."

"Miss the old days?"

"Mark, please. It isn't as serious as you make it sound. What I miss is the quiet, simple, structured life we had."

"Had? I hope you're not kicking me around too much."

She thanked the waitress when her beer was set down. When they were alone, she said, "I'm not kicking you around at all."

"You just needed to get away."

"I'm scared, Mark, I've told you that."

"What good does it do us to be apart? Don't you think that whatever gap is growing between us won't be bridged by you staying here?"

"Actually, Judy called me a few weeks ago at the diner. She was depressed, what with the divorce, the breakup of a ten-year marriage. I hadn't talked to her in two years. She asked me if I would come and see her. At the time I told her I'd think about it, run it by you."

"So recent events helped your decision to come here."

She worked on her beer and cigarette. "How's things at the diner?" she asked.

"It's still there."

She cast him an admonishing eye, silently warning him to cut out the sarcasm, the cynical remarks.

"Everyone's been asking about you. They miss you."

"What about . . . anything on what's been happening?"

"Beyond what you heard on the news, nothing. It's as if whoever's killing our friends and neighbors has vanished into thin air. If the police or the FBI know something, they're keeping it to themselves."

"What was your reason for going to see Father McMartin?"

"You said I needed help."

"Do it for yourself, not me."

"I was, I am."

"You told me something of what you discussed with him on the phone. What else did he have to say?"

He gave her a quick review. "Just in case you

were wondering, I didn't use Father McMartin as an excuse to see you."

"Mark, we're not separated, okay? If you wanted to see me, all you had to do was ask."

"How come I feel like everything I say or do these days is a test?"

"It's in your mind. I don't need to test you or us."

"We've had five solid years of marriage. We've never been apart. Just like that, there's this strain between us."

"I just... I told you... I just want you to deal with what you have to deal with." She sighed. "The fact is, you were starting to alarm me. I've begged you to get help—"

"And I am. I can't just turn off the nightmares. They're real, Mary."

"It's because you have no peace."

"So how do I find that?"

"I don't know."

"I intend to see Father McMartin again."

"I bet he told you that five years later you and he were having the same conversation, didn't he?"

"You must be pyschic."

"Don't be smart. This whole thing... this awful thing that's happened in Newton has worn my nerves. You still have that same angry, haunted look, you're still hiding behind sarcasm and contempt."

"I was a cop, Mary. I have contempt for a lot of things, but us and our marriage is not one of them. I want our marriage more than anything."

"Well, now you're drawing pentagrams. What's next? You sink completely into the bottle and our lives become a daily living hell?"

"I don't know what's going to happen. I can't see into the future."

"Exactly my point."

"You want assurances, I can't give you any. Look, I don't want to argue."

"Neither do I."

"You know, you make it sound as if going to Father McMartin was a waste of time."

"Well, did what he say fall on deaf ears?"

He softened his voice. "He told me I should think about going to church with you. He seems to think I should pray for help and guidance. Just suggestions, mind you; he's not one to shove all that down your throat."

"'All that'?"

"What did I say?"

"It's what and how you said it."

"I'm supposed to change the way I speak?"

"The way you speak," she said, "is a reflection of the way you feel and think."

He decided to drop it. They were heading for a bad argument. He called the waitress over and ordered another drink. They sat in an awkward silence that had never existed between them. Mary was clearly disturbed, and he wanted to understand her point. Still, he felt some resentment. She was here in Tulsa, and he was going back to Newton and a cold, empty house. He tried harder to understand, thinking he was being selfish, believing it was good for her to get away for a while. After all, given his talk with Father McMartin, he concluded there was a lunatic asylum in his mind. He wondered if he would ever be free of what he felt and thought. He didn't care too much for the idea that he had been alarming his wife.

He told her, "I just don't like the fact that you're away, that you feel you need to get away from me."

"That's not what it's really about."

"Then what?"

After the waitress brought his drink, Mary cleared her throat. "Mark, there's another reason I had to see Judy."

Alarm bells sounded in his mind. Paranoia flared in him.

"How come I don't like the sound of that?"

"It's always you, isn't it? Well, this time it isn't about you." She drew angrily on her cigarette. "When I first spoke with Judy, she told me she has cancer. Breast cancer. She's scared and she told me she has no one now, no man, very few friends, she doesn't have a job. She's all alone. She was desperate for me to see her."

He felt his face muscles untense. He cursed his selfishness.

"I'm sorry to hear that. I'm... I'm sorry."

Another heavy pause.

"So you see," she said, "a lot of my reasoning was to just be there for a friend."

"You could've told me that."

"I don't know how it would have sounded to you. You've been so lost in yourself."

"What, did you think I was conjuring up the worst-case scenario in my mind?"

A moment of anger sparked in her eyes. "You know me better than that, Mark. I would never do anything to shame you or do something that crosses the point of no return."

"Likewise. I've learned my lesson." Impatient, annoyed with himself, he shook his head. "Listen, I want you to be with your girlfriend. I can ride this out. The more I think about it, the more I think you should be out of Newton."

"You have your gun, I'm not worried about you protecting me."

"But that I even have it bothers you."

"Okay, yes. I hate it, I hate violence, or anything that even has the potential for violence. You know my own past, that I was beaten by my...anyway. I also know you've seen a side of life beyond my comprehension. And, now...that I've seen...death... murder...I've seen what you've seen."

He put his arm around her, felt her shoulders trembling. "It's going to be okay, baby, I promise."

She nestled her head into his shoulder. "Is it? Will anything ever be normal again?"

"Yes, it will. Whatever I've been going through will pass."

He knew that was a lie as soon as he said the words. He was asking her to have faith when he had so very little in anything, much less himself. Indeed, there wouldn't be closure until he knew the truth about the murders, the identities of the killers. From both the past and present. And there was some connection, he was sure of it. There had to be. At this point in his life there were no options, no choices. He was on his own, and his wife knew it.

"Mark, don't say things you don't mean. I know you. I'm your wife. I know your worst secrets, I know everything about you." She sat up. She put her hand on his face. It felt good to have her touch him like that, gentle and warm. "Do me a favor when you go home."

"What?"

"Take my Bible. Now, before you say anything, you know I've never shoved religion at you. But you may take some comfort in it."

"Just what is it I should read?"

"Ecclesiastes. It was written—"

"By Solomon. Funny you should say that. Father McMartin mentioned Solomon. Funny you two see what I see, at least in some ways. Maybe I keep myself blind to certain things."

"I know. You feel that everything's hopeless, and useless and futile."

"That I've what? Lived a wasted life?"

"No. You've wasted a lot of life, but the fact that you can see it means you have the power to turn it around."

"I'll think about it."

He saw the flicker of disappointment in her eyes. He wasn't about to tell her what his real agenda was for the night.

"You hungry?" he asked her.

She hesitated, then nodded.

She would stay awhile, and right then that was enough.

"Can I call you later tonight?" he asked.

"I insist."

He kissed her. "I understand. Forgive me if I doubted you in any way. You need to be here with your friend. You're a good woman. I love you."

She smiled, the warmest, most genuine smile he had seen in weeks.

He shoved down his sadness, his feeling of loneliness without his wife. She was back with her ill friend, giving comfort. But that was his wife, he knew. She had a selflessness about her that he envied. She tried to find the good in life, whereas he struggled every day just to try and find some humanness around him.

When he forged on into the blackness of the prairie country and crossed the county line into Newton, he knew he was coming back to nothing but inhumanity.

The pentagram tortured him. Back in Tulsa he had mentally mapped out his course of action for the night. He decided to investigate the Donner house for himself. He wasn't sure why, but a nagging gut instinct seemed to be pulling him toward the house and its nearby crime scene. There would be something in the house, he believed, that would confirm his suspicions. If not...

Finally he was driving down the long dirt road that led to his destination. Ahead, the white farmhouse loomed, isolated and utterly abandoned in his headlights. So still, dark and silent that images of a graveyard flashed through his head. As he drew close, gravel crunching under his tires was the only sound he heard. A chill went down his spine as his gaze searched the house, the surrounding woods where the two murdered girls had been found.

He killed the engine, the headlights. From the glove box he took his gun, tucked it in the small of his back, covered it with his windbreaker. Then he took the flashlight.

Stepping out, he flicked on the light and advanced on the front porch. Yellow tape was still strung across the door. They would have already swept the place clean, the police, forensics, the FBI.

Crickets chirped, a maddening symphony of insect noises filling his ears. His heart started thumping, sweat beading on his brow even as the chilly night air shrouded his approach.

Wood creaked under his shoes. He crossed the porch and stood at the threshold. Strangely enough, he found the front door unlocked. He ripped through the tape. He didn't care what the police or the FBI thought. Chalk it up to some kids breaking into the house.

He aimed the light down the narrow foyer that led to the living room. He was struck by how cold the air felt. There was an odor in the house, a mixture of roses and incense.

With the roving light, he checked the kitchen. He went through all the drawers, the refrigerator. Everything was empty. Cobwebs hung from the ceiling. A spider crawled down the refrigerator door.

Next he found the living room empty. There was no sign that anyone had ever lived here. He assumed that if there had been any furniture it was possible the FBI had taken it away for analysis of fibers, or anything else that would give them clues—but they would have to find a suspect or suspects first. Without a suspect to match anything, there was no evidence to connect them to the crime scenes.

Still, there was something in the eerily cold air. A presence, something lingering in the emptiness. Or was it his imagination?

Then he saw the edges in the floor at the end of the living room. The trapdoor would lead to the storm cellar.

He went to the trapdoor. He suspected that if the Fenner girls had been in the house, they would have been kept in the cellar. Yes. Down in the darkness, in the cold, alone, isolated in the blackness and the silence. Everything meant to feed their fear. It was only logical; that was how the sick minds of the killers would work. But still he found it strange that there had been sightings of individuals residing at the Donner house and not much had been made of it by the locals. Were people in Newton just minding their own business? Strangers didn't go unnoticed in a small town.

He took the metal ring and pulled up the heavy oak door. He almost gagged at the vile odor that assaulted his senses.

Hot rage in his belly, he sucked in a deep breath. It smelled like all manner of bodily fluids down there, a stench straight from the bowels of hell.

Wood groaned under his feet as he descended the steps.

And he saw it.

In fact, the light seemed drawn right away to the pentagram.

The girls had been there. He had seen enough crime scenes to feel the presence of violence and horror. Even long after the act itself, some malevolent force seemed to cling to the air, even after the body was removed.

His head swam with nausea. He believed he could almost hear the tortured cries of pain and terror and pleading from the Fenner girls. Among other odors, he could smell the sweat and the lingering fear in the cellar.

He swept the light around the room. There was a large wooden bench against the wall. It was big enough to accommodate two full-grown adults. Shining the light on the bench, he saw the dark splotches, stains of God knew what. He could only imagine what those two girls endured.

He'd seen enough.

Sickened, he moved up the steps. His heart ached. He was lost in his own world, going back to a terrible time, wondering how much his wife and daughter had suffered before they died.

He heaved a deep breath when he cleared the opening. Hanging his head, he shut the door. He was sucking in more long, deep breaths to clear his head when the scratching sound of a match flaring to life jolted him. He was reaching around for his gun, searching the living room, when he spotted the flickering match.

Then his light fell on the angry face behind the match and the cigarette.

"Get that out of my face, Jantzen," Sheriff Stephens rasped.

Chapter Eighteen

It was a dangerous moment, and Jantzen knew it could fall either way.

Standoff or shootout.

It was one of those captured instances in life where a man made a decision—or hesitated—and everything changed forever. He had a fleeting vision of a patrolman he once rode with who walked up to a motorist he had pulled over for speeding. Officer Gary Hankins, moving right up to the window. The driver looked like a respectable, middle-aged banker or lawyer. Hankins asked for driver's license and ID. While Jantzen called it in, he saw Hankins take a bullet in the face, dead on the scene. Later it turned out the driver was a courier for a major drug operation. He was captured less than an hour later with thirty kilos hidden in the doors of his vehicle.

Staring at the sheriff, Jantzen was reminded of that driver. All was not what it appeared on the surface; men wear masks. For one thing, Stephens wore a badge, and he had a gun. Second, Jantzen knew how much the man hated his guts, but he suspected there was much more going on with the sheriff than he knew. Last, the two of them were alone.

Something dark and threatening lit the sheriff's eyes.

So Jantzen remained frozen, his hand just inches from the .45 Colt. For another stretched second he kept the light on the sheriff's face. Dark anger kept boiling in the lawman's eyes, but he kept his gaze narrowed, away from the light. In the light and the smoke, Stephens didn't even appear human to Jantzen, but rather an animal poised to tear apart its prey.

That Stephens was there was no mere coincidence. Briefly Jantzen imagined the report the sheriff would make. Man with gun, caught breaking into a crime scene. Suspect pulls gun, self-defense.

Stephens puffed on his cigarette for several more eternal heartbeats. Large clouds of white smoke wreathed his face, his eyes glowing like two coals. His hand lowered for his revolver.

"I told you to get that light out of my face."

Jantzen hesitated. Clearly there was something wrong with the sheriff. Jantzen was certain Stephens wanted to kill him. There was a coldness in the man's eyes that Jantzen wouldn't trust even long enough to take his eyes off Stephens for an instant. Primal fear gripped Jantzen. He was a civilian, ready to shoot a lawman, but in self-defense. It wouldn't play in the courts.

Finally Jantzen let the light drop, but he held the beam on the bare wooden floor near the sheriff's boots. Tension and fear kept his hand near his gun. From where the sheriff stood, Jantzen didn't think Stephens could see the bulge of the weapon, but he wasn't certain.

He could feel the sheriff boring holes into him with the same menacing stare he'd felt the other day outside the diner.

"Did you see what you needed to see?" Stephens asked.

"I saw enough. You people know I was right."

"That we have a Satanic cult in Newton? Why? Because there's a pentagram drawn on the floor of the cellar?"

"That, among other things."

"Some kids could have broken in here and drawn that."

"What's with you, Stephens? First you want to tell everyone Tom Delmarvin killed his wife and himself, now you don't even want to believe what's right in front of your face."

The sheriff draped his hand over the butt of his .357 Magnum. Jantzen tensed.

Smoke curling out his nose, Stephens said, "What I see is a problem. What I see is a man making something his business which isn't. What I see is a man I'm liking less and less all the time. Kinda like a sick animal, needs to be put to sleep."

"Threatening me, sheriff?"

"Not necessarily."

"So, I suppose you're going to run to Wiley and Thomkins and tell them I broke in here."

Stephens chuckled, a cold sound that filled the living room like a death knell. "Don't want to, don't need to. This is just between you and me. I leave, I'll forget you were even here, Jantzen."

Puzzled, Jantzen stared at the smoke-sheathed face. Stephens was acting completely out of character.

"You know something about what's going on, don't you?"

Again Stephens chuckled. "I know a lot, but not because of the State Police or the FBI."

"You were following me?" Jantzen asked.

"Not exactly. I had the place staked out. Something told me you might come here and find what you found. I just like to know when I'm right."

"Whatever else was here, the FBI took it, didn't they?"

"Always the cop, asking questions. You know, asking too many questions of folks around here might get you in a real jam. I'd be very careful if I were you. Have a nice night, Jantzen. Say hi to your wife, if and when she decides to come home."

Jantzen felt his blood boil. Beyond that, though, he was confused, and still very much afraid. Stephens was definitely acting very strangely, even ominous. His every expression, every cloaked word, every veiled threat was meant to suggest something, but Jantzen couldn't figure out what.

Stephens slowly walked down the hall. Smoke followed the sheriff out the front door as Jantzen kept the beam trained on the lawman's backside.

Jantzen didn't budge until he heard the growl of the cruiser's engine, followed by tire tread grabbing at gravel.

Even when he knew the sheriff's cruiser was rolling up the drive, he didn't move. He could only stand there and wonder what the hell was going on.

It was a little after midnight when the phone rang for the second time since Jantzen returned home. The first time it was Mary calling. Surprisingly enough, it had been a warm and pleasant talk. She was coming home in the next couple of days. She said she needed to be home again with her husband, and hoped he understood now about her girlfriend. It seemed Judy was seeing a doctor in the morning and was terrified about what the procedure would be to remove the cancer. He told his wife he understood, missed her, loved her. She said they'd both be in and out a lot, it would be difficult to reach her. Judy didn't like answering machines. When they said good night he had a strange and terrible feeling of being utterly cut off from his wife. Worse, something in the back of his mind kept pricking at him, all his instincts wanting to warn him that neither of them had yet seen the worst.

Now the second call. He let it ring until the answering machine kicked in. Gut instinct told him it wasn't Mary.

He let the Bible slide off his lap as he went for his drink. Swinging his legs off the bed, he listened to Mary's recorded voice on the machine. After the beeps, there was only an ominous silence.

Jantzen stared at the answering machine on the bedroom nightstand. It was his mystery caller.

He heard the connection severed on the other end.

Gun in hand, he went to the window, searching the drive, the road that led to the mailbox and highway, the black field. Nothing. Fear wanted him to tell Mary to remain in Tulsa. Then again, if she was there with him, he could watch over her, make certain she was safe.

It took at least fifteen minutes, but he checked the entire house, made a circuit outside of the house, then made sure the doors and windows were locked when he went inside.

Back in bed, he closed the Bible. He had done what his wife asked, but didn't see the point in reading about the futility and foolishness and even the valuelessness of wisdom in the world. Solomon. A king. Like Job, Solomon had known the pinnacle of life and the abyss of human suffering and despair. Jantzen knew he was no Solomon, no Job, no Paul. No blinding light for him. He had known the abyss, all right, and beyond that, he had merely skirted the edges of the pit for most of his adult life.

He couldn't help but know there was a message in what he'd read, and the message became clearer as he thought about it.

How *not* to live. Avoid the mistakes of others and one will not live a wasted life. Everything by man and from man turns to ashes, rendering him old, bitter, angry and with no passion for anything in life.

Made sense, Jantzen decided.

It was how he felt these days.

It was perhaps how he'd felt most of his life, at least since he'd been on the police force. He'd seen the folly of the world, and become dead inside.

But the good father said there was hope and hope came in courage and facing oneself. Still, Father...

Fools die just as the wise man does.

So what good is knowledge and experience?

Old Solomon was a piece of work, Jantzen decided.

Jantzen became depressed. Had he really lived a wasted life? Why had he gone to Father McMartin anyway? What had he been looking for? The good father had really done nothing more than tell him the answers were inside of him.

So, was what was in his heart unclean? Were his motives dark and twisted?

He didn't think so. In fact, he concluded right then he *knew* so.

His primary obsession was a clear and driving force.

Vengeance was what he truly sought, and he had tried to rationalize that to the priest. What was wrong with wanting justice done anyway? Something had been taken from him, and forever. He deserved retribution.

Then he wondered, if his wife and daughter had lived, would he have been able to make it right, make it work?

He would have never known Mary.

And he would have never lived through the horror he had seen in Newton.

Angry, he tossed the Bible aside. He had been

reared in Catholicism but chosen to walk away from it years ago. Many times, he had heard the argument that the Catholic church was one of the richest institutions in the world, but did that make it wrong? Would the church turn away the poor and the starving if they showed up one Sunday morning, hands out?

All he knew was that he was his own man, had always done it his way and always would. Indeed, pride goes before the fall. Or does it? And if he was his own man, why had he left himself vulnerable to the priest? In short, he had heard what he already suspected about himself. Maybe that's what he needed—to hear certain truths he wanted to bury. He couldn't deny he liked Father McMartin. He felt some kinship with the old priest, a man who had seen something of the worst in others, jaded in his own right. Surely the priest had his own problems in the world, but Jantzen would not judge him for that. If anything, the priest's allusions to his own troubles made him more human to Jantzen.

Some pieces wanted to fit, some didn't. But pieces to what exactly?

Was everything that had been happening coming full cycle? Even Solomon said history repeats itself. But the wise learn from their mistakes and do not repeat them.

It occurred to him then that in all the time he had lived in Newton he really had no friends. Scratch Buddy Simpson. The man was not the man he thought he had known, beyond a drinking crony. It was disturbing, this sudden bizarre behavior in Simpson, the animal aggression he had seen on the man's face. Then there was

Stephens. Cold, quiet, a menacing aura about him, not the blustering small-town sheriff waddling around, groping through another oblivious day.

It hit him deep. He had not even known these people, had not really ever bothered to get involved with them, or in their lives. They had always been just faces, bodies to deal with. Suddenly they had life. For years, it was all just a passing, day-to-day existence which he had allowed to sink into drudgery and anger.

Now there were certain individuals changing right before his eyes.

He started to wonder if that was even true about himself when he heard a sudden loud noise. He was jolted by the crash, the jarring, thudding sound from beyond the bedroom. It sounded ominously loud in the utter silence of the house.

Jantzen was out of the bedroom, gun in one hand, flashlight in the other in an instant. The thud sounded as if it had come from the front. Quickly he went to the front hallway. Crouching at the door, he lifted the drape an inch.

There. He saw shadows darting into the thinly wood area beside the drive.

With grim determination he barged out the door. Something seemed to rise up from the front porch, clipping his feet. In the next instant he was tumbling head over heels down the porch steps. Outstretched on his back, snapping on the flashlight, he aimed the beam up the steps.

And felt his heart skip a beat.

The beam of light seemed absorbed by the lifeless black eyes of a cow. Rising, Jantzen gave the obscene warning—and he was sure it was a warning—a quick and angry look. The cow's head had been severed clean at the neck. There was very little blood, indicating it had been some time since the killing.

The ritualistic slaughter.

He started running after the shadows. He wasn't sure how many dark figures he'd glimpsed, but he was prepared to shoot first and ask questions later.

He swept the flashlight's beam around the brush and trees. He forged cautiously into the wooded area. Visions of Gruber and all the other victims flashed into his mind. He was being stalked, maybe even hunted.

Ahead, he spotted a shadow dashing for the highway. In the distance his beam wandered over the black hulk of a van. The same van he'd seen on the road the night his wife had left, he was certain.

"You!" he shouted, hastening his strides. "Stop! I have a gun! Stop now or I'll shoot!"

Suddenly the figure stopped, held its arms up in the air. Then a strange fit of cold laughter erupted from the shadow. Puzzled, sensing danger, Janzten checked his flank. Ahead the tall figure turned—slowly, ever so slowly. In Jantzen's mind it was like some pantomime of a ballet move.

Jantzen took several steps toward the figure, his light lifting. He froze, a wave of terror washing through him, as the light shone on the grinning face of the man with the shaved head and black eyes.

For an eternal second he couldn't believe that what he was seeing was real. He was taking another step toward the ghastly white figure who was now sidling out of the light when Jantzen felt a crushing blow to the back of his head. He heard his own grunt ringing in his ears, fading quick. Then he saw the earth rush up to his face before the world went black.

Chapter Nineteen

Darkness.

Light.

Voices.

Shadows.

Flickering, fading black orbs staring down.

From the bottom of some dark and suffocating ocean the world returned with a crashing roar. His head pounded mercilessly, a jackhammer inside his skull. All sight and sound warped, the distant, grumbling noises, growling voices falling down from above. So far away, yet so close. The throbbing in his brain made him feel as if his head would explode from the pressure.

Drifting voices in the night swept over him. A prairie wind with fire in the air scorched his face, driving into his skull, a hot branding iron sizzling from the core of his brain.

"Breathe the putrid air."

"Smelling of death. Fear."

"Taint of blood."

His words? His own voice in his skull? Or their sick prayers? Chanting? Taunting him?

A coppery smell bit like serpent fangs into his nose. Jantzen tasted his own blood on his lips. His eyes were open but he couldn't focus on anything. The world spun. Nausea bubbled in his stomach. Light pierced his eyes, blinding him. He closed his eyes, saw the shine against his lids. Then his flashlight died, leaving a white sheen, penetrating his lids, inflaming the pulsing in his head. Long moments later, he opened his eyes again. Panic seized him. His gun? Where was it? It was his only hope.

He looked up into the black, black night, a swirling ocean of velvet and eternal emptiness that eventually broke through the lingering sheen of white. There. Above. Beyond. Dark figures, at least three, loomed over him. He was a dead man. His soul turned into a pure fire of outrage. He wasn't going out meek as a lamb.

It was them, he was sure of it. The Satanist animals. The one with the shaved head and black eyes spoke in a cold, aggressive voice. Their leader. Someone was asking a question, something about killing him.

"Not yet."

"Why?"

"He's dangerous. He believes he has some knowledge of us."

Jantzen recognized the cold, deep voice of the bald-headed leader. He struggled to hold onto consciousness, and listened. With the pain and the nausea and the darkness, he felt as if everything was not quite real, even though he knew it was all too terribly real.

"Precisely my point, brother. The forces are not yet aligned. Let him grope and stumble and suspect all he wants. His words are but the ramblings of a madman, they fall on deaf and soon to be dead ears. Besides, his other is gone and we must wait for their union again."

Mary. They were waiting for his wife to come back. And then...

Rage started to clear his head some more. He struggled to sit up but collapsed as the pain seared through every limb.

"I don't understand."

"I do. I sense...I know this one from someplace."

"Look at him now. He is the blood for our lamb of an offering to the Master."

"No. I see in his future the offered blood of the lion. A far greater and more noble offering is one that is performed when the sacrifice is from the blood of a fighter, one who has been broken into submission." There was a pause that felt like an hour to Jantzen before the deep voice said, "Where do I sense I know him from?"

"Look at him now, this cop."

"Former. He's a tortured animal now. Full of anger. No peace, nothing but an eternal and futile struggle, this one. I look into his eyes. Look. Do you not see, brothers? When you know what to look for, you can see a man's soul, his every secret, his every desire. From the bottomless well of want, you can even determine where a man came from, his past, and since nothing much changes in human nature, the one constant, you can read his future. It is how all the great sorcerers and seers perform their task for our Lord."

"What is it you see, Great One?"

The voice came to Jantzen, sounding disembodied.

"This one has suffered, or so he believes. A great loss, perhaps a family member. See the rage in his eyes, even as they try to focus on us? He hungers for blood over some perceived injustice. He sees but does not see. He hears but does not hear. All the torment inside has locked him up at this moment, then, now and forever. He is incapable of change. He believes his will is his and his alone. Oh, he, this bastard seed of a whore, I strongly suspect, will keep."

"Why do you call him a bastard? Seed of a whore?"

Jantzen couldn't move from the pain. He felt as if he couldn't stop them—or at least the bald one—from penetrating into his soul.

"He has known woman. He has hungered, I feel, for woman all of his life. Seed was taken, seed was planted, the whore, his whore of a mother, was the seed for this tortured animal. I believe..."

The thing touched him. Jantzen wanted to rise up, strike back. Revulsion and fury mingled, driving him down into a spiraling inky pit inside himself. He nearly slipped into blackness. The bald-headed ghoul's fingers were on his neck, then the clammy palm rested on his forehead. Jantzen felt something cold, vile, like icy worms, run down his face.

"I think...this one...had a mother, of course. A whore, he sees her as. Has not...seen her...since her flight to total whoredom and her own service to our Master. He walks the line, brothers. It is a precarious toehold he maintains between the left and the right."

Cold laughter. How could this animal, this monster, this creature dare to even suspect he knew something about him? Yet, he did.

It seemed like forever, but finally the moist and icy touch was removed from his face. Jantzen felt as if his entire being had just been raped.

"Yes, death is too easy for him. I want to know more of this one. He could prove useful to us. Besides, there is much to do, much for him to know and to see and to fear. I believe even his lust for his perverted justice will serve us. Tomorrow our forces will begin to be unleashed around him. They will all wonder and continue to live in fear of the unknown."

"The Others are ready."

"Indeed they are. Perhaps they are merely unworthy fools, we shall see. Even so, there are others among the Others. Their want is our way and our will. Listen to me! Tomorrow—you, down there—if you can hear me, and I know you can."

Some of the nausea subsided in Jantzen. Still, the voices hovered in his ears like eerie music. Even more terrifying was the way they talked about him, around him, as if he were some subhuman species, an insect studied and about to be dissected. They were the monsters, inhuman things in human skin.

"You will come to see that those who were are not, those who are not were and are. There will be nowhere for you to run, or to hide, no one to turn to for comfort. Even the bosom of your wife will turn cold as ice and the milk from her tit will be bitter poison in your mouth. She is merely another Great Whore in his service, one who has existed from the time of Babylon, from women whose lusts knew how to live and to truly love and who bore today's fruits so long ago from those two Great Cities by the Sea which perished in fire, but will arise once more." Laughter, then, "The power of the Great One will be unleashed, then vanish in the blink of an eye before you. Tomorrow a great twister of his will will rip through your town. Here, then gone. We will meet again, and you will come to understand. I spare your life and you will give me homage. For there is a choice and a way out for you. I know something about you and you cannot hide ever again."

Jantzen felt strength return to his limbs. Groaning, he was about to sit up, digging for the final reserves of strength and determination to explode into his captors.

Then something heavy plunked on his stomach, knocked the wind out of him. It was his gun.

"Take it back. Not even that will save you. You are powerless, and you are without the only real weapons which can defeat us. For one, you are of the world and all its impurities. You cling to them, enslaved. You do not even see yet that you are one of us. But you will. In time, I will offer you freedom."

Slowly, vision returned to Jantzen, but he only saw the black maw of night. Quiet rustling. They were leaving. He looked, squeezed his eyes shut, opened them. Vision. Shadows in the distance were swallowed up by darkness. He took the gun, aimed at the back of one of the shadows, curled his finger around the trigger.

Squeezed.

Click.

He checked his gun. No clip.

The shadows faded.

"Who...who are you?"

He wasn't sure if he said it or thought it. Unnerved, as if the one with the shaved head could either read his thoughts or had heard his voice, Jantzen heard the answer swirling over him, laughter and coldness, from a great distance.

"My name is Legion. For we are many."

Laughter roared as doors slammed.

Like some slug, he wriggled on the ground, sweeping the dirt. His hand found and grabbed up the clip. He slapped it in, cocked the gun, but the van was already racing down the highway.

The sun rose. Shafts of light knifed through the curtained window.

Red-eyed, exhausted but awake from the hot and constant flow of adrenaline, Jantzen sat on the living room couch. For what seemed hours he had not taken his eyes off the front door. He had left it open, could see the cow's head. With sunrise came the flies. A horde of buzzing flies now covered the head, a black and writhing mat. Soon he would dispose of the head, bury it, clean up whatever blood was on the stoop.

He had not let go of the .45 Colt since somehow, hours earlier, he had found the strength to make it back to his house. He had cleaned the wound on his head. Using his wife's handheld mirror, taking a needle and thread, he had closed the deep gash on his scalp. His skull still throbbed; he was still queasy.

But at that point he enjoyed the pain, intent on dishing it back tenfold.

Several things had cemented his determination during the hours he had sat alone in the silence and the darkness, on the couch.

Mentally he reviewed the list.

He would not tell Mary what had happened. He wanted her home by his side, but he would let her determine the time of return. No more alarming his wife. He'd take care of her or die trying. He was no hero, but never in his life had he felt more determined and driven to see this nightmare through.

Second, he would not go to Wiley, the FBI. And certainly not Stephens.

He would unlock his shotgun from the diner. And never leave home without it.

Last, he was on his own. Sheer knowledge of that fact iced the entire list and gave it meaning.

It was personal.

The encounter with them stormed through his mind.

He was fighting against some force that was in

and of the world, but somehow beyond it, he believed. Human but demonic, perhaps so entrenched in evil that they were gripped by some form of demonic possession.

Father McMartin came to mind. He would decide later if he needed another visit to the priest. Perhaps the good father knew something about possession, or how to destroy such an evil. It could be as simple as a crucifix dipped in holy water. Then again...

Words from the bald-headed leader tumbled back through his mind.

He was powerless.

His soul was impure.

He was of the world.

He was one of them and he would come to see that.

"Fat chance," he said aloud.

He recalled the final words from the one with the shaved head.

"Legion. We are many."

Jantzen had opened the Bible, had searched for a good hour for that passage from which he had heard those words so many years ago. Even beyond the Bible, he had heard accounts of demonic possession. Was that what he was faced with?

Surely possession was believed to be very real in biblical times, and even in certain circles of the Catholic church in history. But was it today merely regarded as mental illness? Perhaps Father McMartin had some insight.

Still...he was faced with something, a presence of pure evil he had never known.

Mark 5. He glanced over it again. A possessed man, living among gravestones. With such strength he could snap handcuffs and whatever passed for manacles back then, fighting off entire mobs who came to subdue him. Screaming and shrieking all day and all night. Jesus in a boat seeing the possessed man, running to the shore of the lake. Jesus: "Come out, you evil spirit."

The demon shook in terror of what God would do to him. Jesus: "Your name?"

"Legion, for there are many of us here within this man."

The possessed one demanded to be cast into a herd of swine. So it was written that Jesus did just that, and the herd rushed down the hillside into the lake, drowning themselves.

Mark Jantzen stood.

He walked toward the cow's head, the swarm of angrily feeding flies.

He had a wife to consider. Two lives, one soul, and a marriage to save.

The worst, he knew now more than ever, had yet to arrive. He would be ready for the worst.

For some reason, the words spilled out of his mouth, quiet but grim with determination.

Staring at the cow's black eyes, he said, "God in heaven, help me."

He had yet to see the darkest hour, he believed. And as much as he told himself he could do it alone, he knew he needed help.

Or he would perish.

They were ready for the promise. Everything told to them would come to great glory and reward.

The drugs had helped fuse their souls to the Master. After listening to the man for so long, meeting with him, they were believers in another way.

First, Reilly and Stallins needed money.

Together they would get it, then return to Michael, who needed proof of their worthiness to be one of them. It was their mission, their offering to create terror and mayhem.

They had been out of work for too long. But why work? Michael had said. He even quoted the Bible to them after an incantation to the Master. Something about turning in despair from hard work, search for satisfaction through pleasure. Why should they work so hard all day long on a ranch or an oil field for chicken feed and struggle so much? They were young, virile, the whole world before them.

It made sense to them.

Silently Reilly drove into Newton from the north. It was early morning, not too many of the locals out and about.

"You despise this place as much as I do?" Stallins asked.

"More. I was born here. Couldn't wait for my parents to die so I could inherit the farm. Fixed the brakes for them one night. My brother got the house, in name, but he couldn't stay away from the big cities."

They wore dark sunglasses; the light hurt their eyes. As the drugs wore off, leaving them agitated, paranoid, they sweated, fidgeted, talked in rapid-fire voices.

"Told me. Liked his drugs."

"Too much, no sense in him. And spending our

parents' money like no tomorrow. I helped him out one night. I bought him a nice little batch of smack."

"Laced?"

"Strychnine."

"Use that to kill vermin."

"Vermin was what he was."

"Autopsy?"

"Drug overdose was what it appeared. Sonofabitch waste of life died alone in a motel room near Oklahoma City. Watched him die, face turning all kinds of colors, gasping for air."

Stallins checked the load on the .44 Magnum, spun the cylinder, snapped it shut. "Sweet. I never knew that about you."

Reilly knew it was the drug making his tongue loose. But he didn't care. The man was his only friend in the world. They shared everything together, a home, food and drink, each other's love.

Reilly took the .38 from the seat, tucked it in the waistband of his pants. Behind them, two pump shotguns rested on the backseat of their Camaro.

They were primed for the promise.

Michael said the world was theirs, and everything in it. They just had to want it bad enough, go to any lengths. They wanted money? Simple enough. Take it. That's how it was done these days in America. What, you think a CEO of a major corporation was any different than a mid-level drug dealer? What, you think criminal defense lawyers cared if their client was guilty? Money, son, it was all about money. The Great American Dream. Go take your slice of the pie before someone else eats it first.

"Old fucks should be easy," Reilly said.

"Mr. and Mrs. Sterns. Bank of Newton. How much you think we can take?"

Reilly wheeled around, pointed the Camaro toward the north end of town. Their escape route lay in that direction, with their allies waiting.

"Who gives a shit? Few thousand. It'll be more than we have. My parents weren't exactly wealthy people," Reilly said.

"Who needs to work for a living? We've been down on our luck for too long."

"Exactly what Michael told us. He's a good friend."

"He promised to be waiting outside town."

"Everything will run like clockwork," Reilly said.

The bank had just opened. Having lived in Newton so long, they knew these sleepy, dull people didn't exactly go rushing to the bank every day, first thing in the morning.

Hatred for his life, the emptiness and bitterness the two of them had known in a town they so despised for so long, was about to change forever.

"Shall we?" Stallins rasped, reaching over the backseat and hauling up both shotguns.

"We shall. Today is the first day of the rest of our lives. Just like we were promised."

Chapter Twenty

It was a new day, but he feared today was going to be the worst in Newton's history. It was a combination of instinct and knowledge that led Jantzen to conclude that a day unlike anything they had yet seen would descend on the town. Indeed, the list of problems was growing, the ominous danger was intensifying, and solutions were nowhere in sight.

And all day Mark Jantzen knew he would feel the specter of the bald ghoul on his back, hear his cold laughter in his mind.

He told himself he wouldn't make himself crazy with paranoia and fear.

So he did what he would have normally done, which was open the diner. Anyway, all he could do was wait and see what would happen. Then again, what if he didn't report what had happened last night to Wiley or Thomkins? Would any knowledge he kept to himself prevent the law from finding the suspects? Prevent an arrest? Find him guilty of obstructing justice?

Okay, when he saw Colonel Wiley again, he decided he would tell the man everything that had happened last night. Including his bizarre encounter with Sheriff Stephens. Only he couldn't accurately draw any firm conclusion about the strange behavior of the sheriff. And what was he thinking anyway? That there was some Satanic conspiracy in Newton?

He shoved that thought out of his mind. He needed solid proof.

A new day dawning. Right.

From six to nine all of six customers had wandered in. These days it was the usual talk in the diner, done in grim and fearful tones, about the killings. Moods were somber all around. Grumbling about police inefficiency or the law keeping knowledge to themselves. Clearly resentment about police silence was mounting. Jantzen knew why. Police kept leads to themselves for fear of not wanting a suspect to know they were onto the scent, thus allowing the suspect to elude them, destroy evidence, sweep up the tracks of their crimes, or establish alibis. He knew that the longer a crime went unsolved, the more likely that it would never be solved. Still, Jantzen figured he had a right to know something, civilian or not.

During the morning Jantzen had kept to himself and gone through the motions of tending to routine. He was exhausted, nerves frayed. There was a knot on his scalp, but he hoped combing his hair over the lump would hide it.

At eight sharp he had called his wife. No answer. He would try again later until he reached her. He didn't want her going back to their home without him.

"You look like hell, Mark," Tim Hurkins commented as Jantzen walked into the kitchen to get an order of scrambled eggs and bacon. "Look like you haven't slept in days."

"Who could get a good night's sleep these days?"

"Miss Mary, do you?"

He glanced at Tim, felt a stab of anger at the intrusive observation. "Yeah, I do."

"When she coming home?"

"Soon."

For some reason he felt a strange compulsion to check his watch. It was exactly nine. Either time was dragging or it was racing ahead, he couldn't be sure.

Move. One foot in front of the other. Keep going.

But something was out there. He could feel it beyond the walls of the diner. Look straight ahead. Stay centered. Pull it back, deal with the fear and the paranoia.

How much worse could things get?

Back at the counter, he shoved a plate of food at Burt Martin, the only customer at the counter. He was returning to his coffee when he spotted both of the sheriff's deputies sitting in a booth. Puzzled, he stared at them. Neither deputy looked his way as they focused on their menus with stony faces.

He hadn't seen much of Deputy Jenkins or Dooley lately. But he knew they both were part-time, owned ranches, had wives and children. Stephens liked to run the show, keeping them either in the office answering phone calls or staked out for speeders around the county. Jantzen couldn't recall seeing either one of them at the crime scenes, or even with the sheriff lately. He noted the handhelds on their gunbelts, meant to keep them in around-the-clock alert with their boss.

That they were there today struck Jantzen as odd. He wasn't in the mood for games, much less being spied on.

Slowly, jaw clenching, Jantzen approached them. He studied their clean-shaven, sun-burnished faces. Solemn as pallbearers, neither deputy looked up. They were both lean, raw-boned men, dressed in brown khakis, with Stetsons on their heads, each carrying a Glock 17 in a hip holster.

"Morning, gentlemen," Janzten said with his usual what-can-I-get-you impersonal touch. "Haven't seen you in a while."

"Well, there hasn't been anything to do up 'til now," Jenkins said, tight-lipped.

"Now we've got a full plate, so to speak," Dooley said.

Jantzen's gaze narrowed. He smelled something, all right.

Finally they looked up. Two pairs of dark eyes stared back at, him.

"Fact, I rarely see either of you in here, much less in town these days. Mind me asking what's up?"

"What do you mean?" Dooley asked.

"We just came in for coffee and a bite," Jenkins added.

"Your boss have the day off?"

Both deputies peered at each other. Jenkins said, "You're asking a lot of questions for a man making a lot of noise around here."

"Oh, I get it, how stupid of me. You're here to keep an eye on me."

"Sheriff wasn't feeling well today, if you must know," Jenkins said, an edge to his voice. "He wants us at the office just in case there's a breaking lead."

"If you're done asking questions, we'd like to order," Dooley said.

Both deputies studied the menus.

"Fact is, I've got a lot to say." They looked up, and Jantzen read a flash of surprise and anger in their eyes. He stared down at them, held his ground, unmoving, unflinching. "I find it damn strange that the two of you suddenly show up in my diner." Dooley bared his teeth, set to interrupt, but Jantzen held up his hand. "You're in my place and you're on my time. Like anybody else around here, I pay taxes in this county, so I'd like to think I have a little say in what's been going on.

"First, I've been under suspicion of murder by your sheriff, who I'm sure has burned your ears off about me, and I'm here to tell you, just in case you were wondering, your boss is dead damn wrong. Second, this whole town is locked up tighter than a drum with terror. Every day now I find Tyler Street, even the roads around the county, practically deserted. No one of any kind of authority is telling anyone around here who has a right to know a thing about the murders, meaning fear is feeding more fear. No one knows if there's a suspect or suspects, should we stay in our homes, should we lock the doors and arm ourselves to the teeth and shoot anyone who sets foot on our property. In short, what the hell is going on? Third, I haven't seen either you in here in two, three months. I'm led to conclude your boss sent you here to keep an eye on me."

Dooley scowled and Jenkins fidgeted in his seat.

"You look like you've been on a weeklong bender, Jantzen," Dooley said. "You're not thinking straight since your wife's been gone."

"My wife's not gone, and that has nothing to do with anything."

"Okay," Jenkins said. "You want to know something. All right, Stephens wants us in or close to town until there's some answers. We've got a list of folks he wants us to interview. Since we're duly elected and sworn-in deputies, we've got a job to do and we'll do it."

"But you don't like it?"

"Like what, Jantzen?" Dooley said. "Nobody could like any of this. We have families, we own a few head of cattle, we've got lives of our own beyond this badge. Tell you the truth, neither one of us exactly likes being a deputy—but it pays a little extra." He shook his head, exasperated. "What I'm saying, we're as concerned as anybody else."

"We both have children," Jenkins added. "My wife and kids aren't allowed out of the house unless I'm with them. We even keep the doors and windows locked during the day. I gave her a gun and told her to shoot the first sonofabitch shows up and looks funny at her."

"Why don't you get out there and find who's

killing off people around here then?" Burt Martin growled from the counter.

"Why don't you mind your own business, Burt?" Dooley rasped.

"What's happening around here is my business and anybody else's," Martin shot back. "Folks are being carved up and you two are sittin' here twiddlin' your thumbs!"

An angry pause hung in the diner. Jantzen looked over his shoulder at Martin, who sat on his stool glaring at the deputies. When Jantzen returned his attention to the deputies, he saw the anger had drained from their faces. Now they looked uncomfortable, embarrassed.

"Listen, Jantzen," Dooley said, "we know the sheriff doesn't like you, for whatever reason. But you've never caused any problems around here. Run a business, have a good wife, your own home. You're a former policeman."

"If it makes you feel better, we don't buy a word of what Stephens might or might not say about you," Jenkins added.

"Thing is," Dooley went on, "we've been given our orders by the sheriff. That you haven't seen us doesn't mean we haven't been combing the county, looking for anything out of the ordinary, strangers, drifters. We've been conducting our own interviews, scouring isolated areas, wooded areas, talking to sheriffs in neighboring counties. So far, nothing. What can we tell you?"

"I never meant to imply you weren't doing your job," Jantzen said, believing they were sincere. "If it sounded that way, I apologize. I know you're under the gun with this thing."

"These murders will be solved," Dooley said.

Jantzen nodded, but he wasn't so sure the deputies or even the State Police or FBI would be the ones to solve them.

He asked the deputies, "What are you having?"

The world exploded in a white-hot light of rage in Reilly's eyes.

"Four hundred and sixty-six dollars!"

Fury mixed with despair crashed over Reilly. He leveled the shotgun on the elderly couple behind the wooden counter. Their arms trembled, and the old woman looked about to faint. Through the shimmering light he saw Stallins standing guard by the door. Reilly felt his legs threaten to turn to jelly. He had been up so many nights lately, using the drugs, pulling all-nighters of prayers and incantations, that suddenly the world did not look real. Everything was a bright, painful light despite the shades. It was a piercing sensation that cored through his brain, cleaving him in half. Was everything meant to come to nothing?

"It's all there is!" he heard old man Sterns wail.

"You're lying!"

"What's wrong?" Stallins rasped.

"He says there's only less than five hundred in the bank!"

"He's fucking lying! What about a vault, a safe?"

"There is no vault! I cleaned out the safe!"

Rage kept churning in his belly like a chained animal rattling to break free. For a full half-minute, Reilly waved the shotgun in their faces as he unleashed a stream of vile curses.

"Where you two been livin' all these years?" he

heard old man Sterns cry through the roar in his ears. "Everyone uses the same checks around here. You get IOUs, credit. People mostly keep their own cash. Bury it in a jar in the backyard. Hide it in the floor. Town businesses pay with checks that get cashed in the next county. You ever even seen an armored car on this street, boy?"

Now the old man was getting surly, tough.

It was incredible. It wasn't supposed to happen like this. Michael had promised them success, glory.

Reilly heard the old woman say, "He's telling you the truth!"

"You boys gone crazy. I always thought you were a little strange, but not this stupid kinda crazy!"

"Shut up!" Stallins roared. "Shut your stupid old mouth! You got money here and you're fucking lying to us!"

"I'm not!"

Why hadn't he known this? Reilly wondered. He assumed these yokels kept money in the bank like everyone else. But he always operated in cash himself, kept it squirreled away in his home, just like the old fuck said everybody else did. What was wrong with these people? No IRAs, no bearer bonds, no nothing, not even a few grand in the safe. They weren't normal, these people, they were ugly, they were thieves from the Master. Well, if this was reality, then he had just crawled out of his hole. A raw and burning hatred for this old couple seized him. It was their fault. They had cheated him.

Reilly bellowed, reached over and snatched up

the money, shoved it in his pants pocket. A part of his mind wanted to tell himself it was better than nothing but not by much. Another darker, stronger part of him overwhelmed him with a flood of twisted emotions. Life had cheated them. Everyone was out to get them. It would be the last time. Utter coldness dropped over him. They must have seen the change in his expression, and he savored their terror.

He heard the old man holler, "Noooo! Don't!"

He heard Stallins scream his name.

He caught the old woman pleading for him not to kill them.

The shotgun seemed to take on a life of its own as he drew a bead on the old man's face and squeezed the trigger.

Chapter Twenty-one

When he heard the distant and muffled but unmistakable thunder of a shotgun blast, Jantzen nearly dropped the coffee in the laps of the deputies. A heartbeat later he clearly caught the horrified shriek of a woman, followed by another muted thunderclap.

The screaming died abruptly.

Silence, thick and total, settled in the diner and out on the street.

Eerie and awful in its finality.

"What the hell was that?" Burt Martin called seemingly from a great distance.

"Sounded like it came from the bank!" Dooley said.

From outside, Jantzen heard feet pounding the boardwalk, a pair of familiar voices shouting, cursing. Jantzen slung the cups on the table. Behind him he saw Martin lurch off his stool while the Hurkins burst out the kitchen door.

The deputies were out of the booth drawing their weapons, racing for the doorway.

"Everyone stay where you are!" Dooley barked.

Jantzen echoed the order, but then followed them outside, several steps behind the deputies.

"Freeze!"

"Halt! Drop your weapons!"

Before he knew it, Jantzen was hugging the doorway as thunder from shotguns sounded and his window was blasted into a thousand pieces.

Dooley and Jenkins bounded off the stoop, triggering their Glocks on the run. They were dashing for their vehicles, Chevy Blazers with Newton County insignias and crossbar lights on the roof.

Peering around the corner, Jantzen caught sight of Stallins and Reilly angling away from the Bank of Newton. A shotgun was blazing in Reilly's hands, while Stallins triggered a large-caliber revolver in one hand, holding a shotgun in the other.

Jantzen heard a sharp cry of pain. Whirling, he saw Deputy Jenkins topple, blood spurting from his chest. The deputy collapsed near his Chevy Blazer. He lay outstretched, arms and legs twitching, his eyes rolling around in their sockets, thick crimson bubbles forming in his mouth. Then the man lay utterly still.

Jantzen didn't need to check the deputy to know he was dead.

Dooley cried. "Call an ambulance, Jantzen!"

Jantzen made his own decision, both out of instinct and years of training, and out of the need to do something and to redeem himself.

He wasn't about to see Reilly and Stallins rob the Bank of Newton and get away. It could have just as easily been his place. And he could be certain both Mr. and Mrs. Bradley Sterns were lying in pools of blood inside the bank they owned, dead or dying. It could have been him and Mary.

He caught enough of a look of the robbers standing in front of their car, triggering their weapons like there was no tomorrow, to know they were hell-bent on either making good their escape or dying where they stood.

He bolted away from the door across the front porch and down the steps, braving a shotgun blast that sheared up planks behind him while he felt the hot slipstream of a bullet scorching the air behind his skull. He crouched beside Jenkins and touched the man's throat. No pulse.

"Jantzen! Call an ambulance!"

"He's dead, Dooley!" Jantzen shouted back, then scooped up the Glock.

Then a din of weapons fire shattered the air.

At the back end of the Blazer, Janzten was stunned at the sight of a dozen townspeople firing an array of weapons at the bank robbers.

The match fell from his fingers. Flames fluttered like an orange bat, winging its way downward to the golden chalice. He stared at the reflection of his black eyes, the white sheen of his skull, reflected in the gasoline, the blood and the semen which filled the object stolen from a Catholic church. The flames whooshed to brilliance, his image seeming to come alive in the fire.

It was happening. His will was once more being done.

He could almost feel the death and the terror, even though they were in a motel room two counties north. Funny how it worked that way. Souls were energy, and energy couldn't die. No matter where energy traveled, it could be felt by one who knew the precise nature of a soul's energy. In some, the energy was distorted, going in all directions, chaotic because there was no direction. In others, the energy was precise with lust, or greed, or anger.

Chaotic energy in two, precision energy in one. He knew them better than they knew themselves. Three men he had spent weeks with, after all, using drugs, drinking, using the women and the men to attain power, the connection of the flesh to the spirit. The Others, doing the Master's work. If they were true believers, then he would soon know.

At the moment, he was alone with three girls of the clan. He called them Sadie, Macie and Lacy. Not quite eighteen, still young enough to satisfy him, fairly unsoiled, creamy and ivory, breasty and leggy, still eager to please and to learn. They were kneeling before the flaming chalice. Before he was through he would know their every orifice. Beneath his robe he could already feel himself stiffening.

Naked before him, they held the crucifix by the feet upside down, kept the thorn-wrapped head near the fire. At one time they had merely been whores. Now they would be cleansed, used in his service. If they didn't whore for the Master, they could never be truly worthy. If nothing else, they yearned to serve.

Women of the clan who were not immediate blood sisters or cousins were recruited off the city streets across the country. These three with him now he had bought from a pimp in Pittsburgh. Of course, the pimp had come back, demanding his merchandise be returned. It seemed he had changed his mind, unless there was more money involved. And, of course, the pimp had been killed, shot four times in the head. Michael smiled at the memory of pulling the gun so lightning-fast the giant black pimp—so tough, so in control, such the big cock when he had been on the streets slapping around scared and defenseless girls—had looked set to shit himself.

These days the girls were easy, and it was getting easier all the time. It seemed the Great One was hard at work across the land, and his army of souls was multiplying daily. They came to him from broken homes, divorced families, claimed abuse, physical, emotional and sexual. What they really wanted, he believed, was a life of sex and drugs. After all, wasn't money and pleasure the meaning of life in this land? So he provided that, took care of their every need, put food in them, drugs in them, allowed them to realize all of their fantasies. Whatever money they had he convinced them it was in their best interest to turn it over to the Family. After all, a family was what they had always wanted.

His needs were being met, and that was what

really, only, always mattered. Today, both in Newton and in Tulsa.

It had been no fluke that they had located the woman. It had been part of his plan since first hearing of, and seeing, that one for himself. That tortured animal-cop had no idea he had been followed to the restaurant where he'd met his wife. Of course, he might have been suspicious of a black van, but they owned many vehicles. They were always moving, changing places, dispersing the clan to different neighboring counties, maybe the next state. But they were always in contact, always arranging the next site for an offering.

Texas was close. Texas was next.

First the woman and her tortured-animal cop.

It would be interesting, and amusing.

"Children," he told the girls. "Let us pray for our three brothers who are now, at this moment, doing his will."

Together: "Our father who art in hell..."

At first Jantzen couldn't believe his eyes.

Had Newton gone insane? Or was this simply frontier justice on the Oklahoma prairie, unleashed by pure primal fear?

They came from the barbershop, the grocery store, they barreled out of the lumberyard and the furniture repair shop. They walked out of Mom's Trinkets and Things, they rushed from the post office and reached into old model vehicles or trucks, all men, and all with grim intent. He even saw Jock Peters drop a sack of groceries and haul a rifle out of his truck.

Fear had obviously pushed the townspeople over the edge. They weren't taking any more, and they weren't taking any chances. It hit Jantzen that perhaps the townsmen had been thinking along the same lines he had. Every man was on his own. Each man for himself, to save his life, his property, his loved ones. Any threat that showed would be dealt with in short and brutally swift order.

If he had judged them as short on intellectual or reasoning powers or lack of experience and knowledge beyond the confines of their own small, dusty world of cattle and twisters and small-town talk at the edge of the prairie, he couldn't judge them short on guts.

Reilly and Stallins turned in every direction, firing their weapons at the storefronts.

"Fuck you people! Fuck you all!"

They screamed and cursed, obscenities and blasphemies Jantzen couldn't even fathom, their shouted words of rage and hate clearly heard above the din of weapons fire unleashed on them.

Bullets and buckshot tore into the bank robbers. Chunks of ragged meat were sheared from their bodies but they didn't go down.

If anything, the horrible agony of their wounds seemed to stimulate the townsmen, light their faces with some weird light of defiance, harden their resolve.

Jantzen joined the madness, if only now to put two wounded animals out of their misery. Still, he found it incredible how the two wannabe bank robbers held their ground even as bloody holes were punched into their bodies, front and center, up and down. He triggered the Glock in unison with the cracking sound of 9mm bullets chugging from Dooley's gun.

Stallins squeezed off the last round from his revolver, his chest soaked with blood. He twitched, convulsed in the hurricane of bullets and buckshot, twirling one way, then the other. His sunglasses flew off his face, revealing to Jantzen eyes that bulged with a ferocity and a hatred he had never seen in his life.

Cursing, Stallins started to topple; then the shotgun boomed in his other hand, the barrel aimed at Reilly's legs. The ensuing scream from Reilly was one long horrific wail as cloth, blood and flesh erupted from his thigh and groin. A pink-brownish mist showered the air around Reilly, raining the muck of blood and flesh and other bodily fluids on the car. Through the gore, tattered strips of dollar bills blew in the whirlwind of blood and gunfire.

Still the man wouldn't go down. Jantzen had heard stories about suspects so jacked up on drugs that it took as many as eight to ten officers to subdue one man. Or how it took a dozen bullets to an armed suspect's vitals to bring him down.

Whether or not that was the case here—and he had never seen one personally—Jantzen couldn't be sure. But he was sure a toxicology report would turn up drugs later.

It was clear Reilly and Stallins were going to die where they stood, no matter how long it took, no matter how many bullets. Under other circumstances, it would have seemed sadistic overkill. But something else was going on here, Jantzen knew. With Reilly and Stallins. With the people of Newton.

Critical mass had erupted.

Reilly was almost amputated at the hip by the accidental shotgun blast from his buddy. There was no meat around at least three-quarters of his thigh—just gristle, and gleaming femur bone. Raging, cursing, Reilly slumped against the side of his Camaro, still jacking the shotgun's action. His eyes nearly popped from their sockets in a disturbing mix of agony and—what? Pleasure?

A burst of laughter ripped from Reilly's mouth, mingled with vile curses.

"You will all burn in hell forever!" Reilly shrieked. "I will see you in hell sucking the devil's cock! It's his will! You fucks!"

Like a drunken sailor, Stallins staggered out into the middle of the street. Blood pumped from his shattered skull but he fired his shotgun one more time. It appeared that a smile creased his crimson lips before he collapsed in a boneless sprawl.

"You are all going to hell!"

It was the last thing Reilly shouted. Jock Peters had a Winchester .30–30, was drilling one round after another into Reilly, jacking the action lever, shooting, jacking, shooting. Gore and brain burst from the man's skull. Reilly jerked under the impact, then pitched to the ground.

Silence hovered over the street. Slowly Jantzen stepped away from the Blazer. He heard Dooley cry, "Dear God in heaven!"

He felt the deputy's eyes on him. All around him, Jantzen saw their faces. Beside him, he saw Jason Collins peering from a crouch through the window of his newspaper office. The townsmen with weapons moved out into the street, through the acrid clouds of gunsmoke.

Adrenaline raced through Janzten, the world looking white-hot bright. Cold sweat soaked through his shirt. He saw Dooley angling for the bank, the deputy frantically trying to reach his boss on the handheld. Jantzen followed the deputy.

"I want every man on this street," Dooley ordered, "to stay put, stay right where you are until the sheriff gets here!"

Bob Tamlin called out from the stoop of his barbershop, "So the sheriff can do what, Dooley? Slap us on the wrist for saving our bank from that scum, or pin a medal on us?"

"Spare me the lip, Bob. That's an order, you understand me?"

For a full half-minute, Jantzen watched as Dooley unsuccessfully tried to reach the sheriff. "Where the hell is he?" Dooley growled to himself.

"You have Colonel Wiley's frequency on that?" Jantzen asked.

"Yes. Why?"

"Why? Radio him and get him here."

Dooley cast Jantzen a resentful eye, but nodded. "In a minute. You people, stay out here!"

Dooley moved toward the bank. Gun poised to fire, he went into the small lobby. Jantzen followed him inside the bank.

"I thought I told you to stay outside, Jantzen."

"Dooley, whether you're aware of it or not, I may be the only thing standing between you and total insanity."

Dooley cast him an odd look, then crept toward the counter.

Jantzen saw the great washes of blood and the grayish gob stuck to the wall. He didn't need to look over the counter to know what he would find. But he looked.

Either Reilly or Stallins or both had cleanly blown the heads off the elderly couple who owned and ran the Bank of Newton.

Dooley took one look, dropped to his knees and vomited.

Chapter Twenty-two

The head count of all the men who had pulled a trigger was taken by a badly shaken Dooley. Relentless firing from the weapons of thirteen men had finally brought down Reilly and Stallins. Jantzen had a nagging, twisted feeling that the bizarre, terrifying, extended time it had taken to kill the two men was only the beginning of a bad day about to get worse.

Smoking, he waited on the stoop of the diner for either Sheriff Stephens or the State Police to arrive. The Hurkins were mingling near the post office with Tamlin, Martin and a few other townspeople. He had tried to call Mary twice, but no luck.

Nearly an hour dragged by. No sign of any law.

So the sun rose, the temperature climbed and Newton baked. Grim faces lined the boardwalks on both sides of the town, and men and women gathered in pockets near parked vehicles. Occasional distant murmurs hit Jantzen's ears, and there was some grumbling about having to turn over arms. But it was Standard Operating Procedure, Jantzen knew, for each man to turn over the weapon he had had used in the gun battle. Forensics and ballistics were going to be damn busy the next twenty-four hours. Two more murders, then two brutal killings, done, of course, in self-defense. It would be a stretch to charge any man there with even disorderly conduct, much less a weapons charge, much less manslaughter. No matter what, the State Police were in for a long, tough day in Newton.

But where were they?

Blankets had been draped over the dead until the ambulance crews could arrive. Still, flies swarmed over the bloodstains around Jenkins, Reilly and Stallins. There were doctors in the countryside, Jantzen knew, one who resided near the county line, a retired M.D. from Oklahoma. But there was only one hospital in the area, which served Newton and its two neighbor counties. It also doubled as the morgue.

While he waited, Jantzen had time to reflect on what had happened. Just what had driven Reilly and Stallins over the edge? He had seen something of a subtle change in the two men over the past few days. The quiet seething, the growing coldness, the strange, distant looks in their eyes. But this? Had it been drugs that had given them the strength to stand, nearly unflinching and still blasting away, against a hurricane of bullets and buckshot? What exactly had he seen in their eyes?

It was more than ninety minutes after the killings before Colonel Wiley arrived in town. Within minutes a dozen cruisers had kicked up a cloud of dust from both ends of town while grim-faced troopers emerged from their vehicles. To sort through this latest mess, the interviews, the endless streams of questions, were going to be a grueling, time-consuming affair.

Jantzen went into the diner, shuffled his way to the back office. He was more disturbed than ever. The possession question nagged him. Was there even such a thing as demonic possession?

He called Mary again. After the tenth ring he hung up. For long moments he stared at the phone, debating whether to call Father McMartin.

Finally he dialed the rectory, asked to speak to Father McMartin, told the woman on the other end who he was, and waited.

"Hello, this is Father McMartin."

"Mark Jantzen here, Father."

"Mark. How are you doing?"

"Just fine, thank you. Father, there's something I need to ask you."

"Yes?"

"Point-blank—do you believe in demonic possession?"

The pause on the other end was long and heavy. Jantzen almost believed he could feel the priest tense up.

"Why do you ask?"

"Well, Father, let's just say...I've seen some things. Strange behavior. Behavior I can't explain."

The priest sighed into the phone.

"Father, please, I wouldn't ask if I didn't think it was important."

"All right. Yes. Demonic possession is real. Understand, it's rare, and there are only a few isolated documented cases in this century."

"By that, you mean today we call it schizophrenia, paranoid delusions, psychosis?"

"It's...much more involved than that."

"Explain. What are some of the signs, say, in an individual who may be possessed?"

"Mark, I think it best if we meet again. You don't sound well."

"Father, I haven't had a drink in...it's been maybe a day. I'm as sober, as lucid as I've been in weeks, maybe months. You have some idea what's happening here in Newton, but there are things that have happened...well, at the moment I don't want to get into the details."

Another long pause. Jantzen sensed the priest was uncomfortable discussing the subject of demonic possession.

"The signs, Father."

"The signs are dramatic, no question about it. A change in behavior is slow at first in coming. But once a soul is possessed...it's a terrifying sight."

"You sound like a man who has had some experience."

The priest lapsed into a long silence, clearly wrestling with his decision to continue the discussion.

"Father, are you there?"

"Mark, I urge you to come and see me."

There was something in the priest's past that was making him this uncomfortable, Jantzen suspected. Perhaps Father McMartin had even performed an exorcism, or had aided in one. Either way, Jantzen didn't want to pry.

"I may just do that, Father. But I'm faced with something here and I need to know what it is I may be dealing with."

Another sigh.

"Father McMartin, please continue."

"Very well. In one who is possessed you see a ferocious rage. There are convulsions, erratic mood swings. Then the individual will collapse, fall exhausted into what I can only refer to as a catatonic state. This state may last for hours, even days. Then the convulsions and the unleashing of this... inhuman rage will begin again. There is also superhuman strength displayed; it may take as many as four to six grown men to hold down a possessed person. There will be shrieking, and all manner of vile blasphemies and obscenities will pour from the mouth of a possessed individual. The face may even change before your eyes. Say, a grimace that can stretch the skin to the point where bone protrudes. Eyes rolling clear into the back of the sockets. Foam at the mouth."

"Like a rabid animal?"

"Yes. I've heard you will hear strange fits of laughter. One may even speak in a foreign language that the individual has never studied, has never even heard of. The language may even be spoken backwards. Whole sentences, that is. Their voice may even change."

"What more?"

"Well..." He paused, cleared his throat. "The possessed may know things about your life. They may know dark secrets that will be used against...an exorcist, or one performing the rite of exorcism."

"Is that something that can be discounted as, say, psychic phenomenon?"

"No."

Just like that, Jantzen had no doubt that demonic possession was real. He was unnerved by what the priest had told him. If he was paranoid and afraid before...

Then Father McMartin said, "Mark, you're asking an awful lot of questions. You sound very mysterious, very troubled."

"Father, I need to know something. How could I defend myself against...say a small army of such...individuals who may be possessed or who may believe they are possessed?"

"Mark, I don't know what it is you're planning, but before you do something you may regret, I urge you to see me."

"Father, please answer the question."

"Do you believe in the power of Our Lord Jesus Christ? That He is the Light and the Way, and our Salvation?"

"I must confess that recently I haven't given that much thought. But, yes, I am a believer."

"A crucifix then, blessed with holy water. But that's only one thing. Remember that Satan and his legions are consumed in the fires of eternal damnation. God is an eternal and all-consuming fire."

Fire. There it was. His weapon. But could he actually do what he was thinking? Burn a possessed individual alive? And how? Only if his life was threatened, or the life of Mary, would he burn such a creature alive. If there was no alternative.

Certainly he had seen how difficult it had been to kill Reilly and Stallins. But he couldn't even be sure they were, in fact, possessed. Still, according to what Father McMartin had just told him, he had seen some of the signs on the two men.

"Father, I may have to ask you a favor in the near future."

"Which would be?"

"I'll stay in touch. Thank you for your time and your help."

"Mark, before you hang up, promise me that you'll come and see me before you make any decisions that may change your life forever."

"I will."

Jantzen said good-bye and hung up. He took a key from the desk, unlocked the cabinet, took out the pump shotgun and two boxes of .12 gauge shells.

The biopsy had shown the tumor was benign. It was the best possible news for her girlfriend. For the first time in days it seemed to Mary Jantzen that life made some sense. After all the madness swirling around her, a ray of hope had shone through. Perhaps it was a sign that her prayers were being heard and answered. All she wanted was for life to return to normal.

So she had felt confident enough to leave Judy at her home and pack up her things. It was a bittersweet good-bye between long-time friends who had not seen each other in years.

Mary reflected over the past few days. They had talked about many things. Past memories, the men they had married. Unfortunately, Judy viewed herself as a failure in marriage, as a wife and mother. She had been depressed, wondering if there weren't things she could or couldn't have done to have saved her marriage.

Somehow Mary had turned the solemn talk and mood around. She talked of hope and courage to Judy, and of belief that everything would work out for the best. She still had her children to consider. They needed her. Judy held strong until the fearful morning. Then came the good news.

Now it was time to go home to Mark.

An hour south of Tulsa Mary was stepping out of her truck. The diner and gas station were part of a rest area just off the Interstate. She needed to call Mark. He didn't like surprises, and she figured he might be worried if he had tried to call her during the day.

All along, she intended to follow through on her own message to her girlfriend. Indeed, she had faith in her husband. Their marriage had always been strong, and he was a good man. Nothing could ruin their lives together, unless there was infidelity. This was not the case. If nothing else, Mark had gone to see Father McMartin. He wanted answers, he was seeking help. She didn't believe it was a smokescreen, a snow job. The marriage was important to him, their lives together meant everything. Mark was good at faking certain things, but she knew he was the kind of man who wouldn't fake it just to be with somebody. He would rather be miserable alone. The real problem was Mark's inability to forgive himself. Lately her husband had been nothing but self-involved. It was long since time for him to snap out of it. Perhaps this brief respite from each other had awakened him some. Perhaps Father McMartin could shed some light on his disturbance. But she wanted him to continue to see the priest.

She called the house. No answer. She called the diner. No answer. She called the pay phone in the dining room. No answer. Strange. She started to worry but hoped there was some logical reason why no one—not even the Hurkins—answered the phone. She checked her watch. It was dinner time. Somebody should be in the diner. What was going on? In a way, though, she was glad there was no answer. If one of the Hurkins had picked up the phone and told her Mark was not there...

She tried both the office and dining room phones again. Still no answer. Now she became worried.

Head bent, she was heading back for her truck. Lost in a sudden sense of urgency to return to Newton, she didn't see two men step from a dark blue Charger, approaching her. At first they were shadows in the corner of her eye. Then some vague sense of danger sounded a distant alarm bell in her mind. She hastened her strides, was about to open the door to her truck when she felt something hard jab into her ribs.

She heard the man's gruff voice in her ear as he

whispered, "I have a gun. I will not hesitate to use it. Get in and do not make a scene. I will kill you and anyone who tries to stop us."

She felt her knees shake. Her mind screamed with terror. This wasn't happening, she told herself.

The door was opened for her and she was shoved behind the wheel. Then a big, bearded man with wild, bulging eyes jumped into the passenger side. She saw the ugly little gun in his lap, pointed her way.

"What is this about?" she demanded. "Do you want money?"

"We want your husband, Mrs. Jantzen. And, of course, we want you."

"You want what? My husband? Who are you?"

Frantic, she looked around the parking lot. Hadn't anyone seen she was in trouble? But no one was nearby except her abductors.

"Drive and don't do anything stupid!"

Jantzen had waited long enough. For the past four hours, no one from the State Police had seen fit to interview him. The Hurkins had returned to the diner after being questioned by troopers, then informed they were free to go. Jantzen gave them the rest of the day off. As far as business went, the day was shot.

For the past hour, Jantzen had wandered around town. Troopers had taken statements from everyone but him. There was angry discussion about the brutal nature in which Reilly and Stallins had blown the heads off the elderly Sterns. There was more angry talk about weapons being confiscated, how everyone had to protect themselves, since the police sure as hell couldn't do it.

Now with the entire town paralyzed by formal police moves, Jantzen made his move.

Blanket wrapped around the shotgun, he cautiously moved for his vehicle. There was no sign of Wiley, just a gaggle of troopers with cameras. Deputy Jenkins had been one of the first to be loaded into an ambulance. Even when the troopers had done their field exam of the deputy's body and forensics had gathered what evidence they could from around the diner, no one had spoken to Jantzen. He didn't like it. He suspected Wiley was saving the worst for the last.

Quickly Jantzen put the shotgun under the backseat, then tucked the shells next to it.

Fire. He kept thinking of fire.

Suddenly he heard the phone ringing in the diner. Bounding up the stoop, he rushed into the dining room. It was the pay phone. He was sure it was Mary. If it was his wife, he dreaded laying this latest news on her. But it was too soon for word to get out about the bank robbery and killings unless she'd been trying to reach him unsuccessfully and decided to call a neighbor.

He reached the phone, mentally counting the rings. At least eight, maybe nine. He picked it up.

And a chill went down his spine as he heard the low breathing on the other end.

"Who the hell is this? I know someone's there! Speak up, God damn you! Is it you, baldy?"

Click.

Jantzen slammed the receiver back, rattling himself to the bone with the force.

"Jantzen!"

Whirling, he found Colonel Wiley. The colonel stood just inside the door, unmoving as stone.

"I'd like to talk to you for a minute."

Chapter Twenty-three

Jantzen was braced for a severe butt-chewing. Instead, Colonel Wiley, calm but looking shaken by what he'd seen, said, "I have a few questions for you, if you don't mind."

The colonel looked twenty years older than the first time Jantzen had laid eyes on him. As the colonel took off his hat, rubbed his face and heaved a sigh, Jantzen hoped the lawman hadn't heard or seen his strange behavior at the pay phone. Either way, Jantzen was about to be grilled, and his mind was already searching for evasive maneuvers. At this point, he didn't know whom to trust, whom to believe. Seconds passed as the colonel seemed to choose his words carefully.

Jantzen figured he'd prod the colonel along. "If this is about what's just happened, Colonel, I'm sure you've asked enough questions already—"

"It isn't. And what am I going to do anyway? Arrest the whole town? I'm sure every weapon used is registered and licensed. It'll go down in my report as self-defense, but I'm not sure yet exactly how this will all play. I still have superiors to answer to, and I'm sure the media will be back. Don't get me wrong, Jantzen, I don't much care for vigilantes. Whatever your role, I'm not here about that. Fact is, I even understand."

"Cutting slack?"

"This time. Given what's happened around here, I can understand people being pushed to the edge. Now, I've already given every man who fired a weapon strong and fair warning that this will not be tolerated again. Anyway..." The colonel paused, sucked in a deep breath, cleared his throat. "Were you at home last night?"

Jantzen felt the hackles on the back of his neck stand up. "Yes. Why?"

"If you don't mind, I'd like to ask the questions. You were home from when to when?"

"All night. After dark. Had a drink, watched some television and turned in early."

This was going somewhere ugly, Jantzen knew. Something was wrong.

"Didn't see or hear anything unusual?"

Jantzen lit a cigarette, moved to the counter. He purposely faced the colonel, hoping the man didn't observe the knot on the back of his head. Gut instinct warned Jantzen it was best to lie to the man.

"Such as?"

"Damn it, Jantzen, answer the question."

"I told you. I went to bed early. Nothing out of the ordinary happened."

The colonel peered suspiciously at Jantzen. "You're positive."

"I'm positive. Colonel, you're acting very mysterious. You've seen what fear has done to this town. I get the feeling something else is going on. If anybody deserves some answers, I feel I'm entitled to them. You don't want my help, that's fine. But I have a wife to consider. Like the others, I'll protect myself and my wife and my home. Tell me—why are you here asking questions about where I was last night?" No answer. "If you want, I can find answers on my own. I was a cop."

"Don't keep reminding me of that. I'm certain you've been watching out for anything unusual. I'm sure any stranger in these parts has come under your scrutiny. It's why I'm asking you if you've seen any strangers lately, anything at all you can tell me that might help in my investigation."

"Sounds like you and the FBI don't have the first clue."

"We've got zip, zero. Now. When you drove home last night, did you notice any vehicles in the vicinity of your closest neighbors?"

Alarm bells rang in Jantzen's head. "What's happened to the Rawlins, Colonel?"

Wiley squeezed his eyes shut and scowled. When he opened his eyes and stared with cold anger at Jantzen, he said, "I hope nothing, but I fear the worst. You'll find out soon enough, but this you must keep strictly to yourself. And this is a strong warning. You're going to see my men and the FBI around the Rawlins place. They may even comb your property...with your permission, of course."

"For what? Wiley, what the hell is going on?"

"The Rawlins girl is missing."

Jantzen felt his heart skip a beat. An image of an ugly lean face with wild eyes full of lust suddenly flashed through his mind. Simpson.

"I'm ordering the parents to stay home," Wiley said, "not take calls, not receive visitors. My men are staying with them. I don't need a fresh wave of panic and terror hitting this town. Or before I know it, you people will start shooting each other."

"When? How was she taken?"

Wiley grunted. "You read this as a kidnapping?"

"Or worse, Colonel. What happened?"

"Well, apparently, she was—God, I hate to say it."

"Snatched?"

"Right out of her bedroom. The...whoever came through the window. The girl's room is on the bottom floor, her room faces east toward a wooded area. Parents say they always lock all the doors and windows. But for some reason, I don't know, maybe she wanted some fresh air, she might've opened it."

"Or heard a noise and looked out the window."

"I don't think so. Girl that age, all that's going on, parents would have warned her. She wouldn't just open the window and start looking around herself. She'd go to her parents."

"Any sign of forced entry?"

"No. Way I read it, the girl just opened the window herself. Why, I don't know. Someone just came through the window and took her, that's the way it looks."

"Her parents didn't hear anything?"

"No. They didn't even know she was gone until this morning."

Jantzen felt sick to his stomach. "She's dead, Colonel, you know that, don't you?"

"I don't know that, Jantzen. Only reason I told you is because you're going to wonder why half of the state's law officialdom will be all over the Rawlins' place, and scouring around your property. Now—do I have your permission to look around?"

"Looking for some evidence, I assume?"

"You're not a suspect, Jantzen, all right?"

"I never said I was."

Jantzen fell silent. He debated coming clean with the colonel about last night. The cow's head was buried well off his property, but if they used dogs there was a chance the scent of blood would be picked up. He'd buried the head three, four feet deep. Still, if they found it, if Wiley suspected something, Jantzen worried he could be run in for obstruction.

"It's SOP, I understand, Colonel. Of course, you can look over my property."

The colonel heaved another sigh. "Good enough. If you'll excuse me then. Anything you can think of that might help me..."

"I'll stay in touch."

The colonel paused near the doorway. He looked back, and Jantzen felt the man's probing stare.

"Anything you need to tell me before I go?"

"No."

"How come I get the feeling there's something you want to say?"

"How come I get the same feeling the other way around?"

"Don't mess with me, Jantzen."

"I'm not. I want answers as badly as you do."

Grunting, the colonel stared at Jantzen for another moment, then left.

A great, terrible and terrifying weight settled on Jantzen's shoulders.

He knew what he had to do. He knew where he had to go.

The night, he feared, would bring a revelation of a horror he could not even begin to imagine.

At home, he took the lockbox from a desk drawer in the basement, keyed it open. After retiring from Atlanta P.D. he had kept a few items, momentos from his days as a detective. His service revolver and handcuffs were in the box. He took the cuffs. If what he suspected turned out to be true, he was prepared to take the law into his own hands, no matter what.

True to Colonel Wiley's word, Jantzen had found troopers scouring his property. Two hours ago, they had left. If they'd found anything—footprints, blood—they hadn't informed him.

Night had now fallen, full, total, black.

Venturing outside, Jantzen hopped into his vehicle, fired up the engine and set off into the darkness.

He had reached an agonizing decision.

During the drive to the remote, small farmhouse at the southeast edge of the county, Jantzen came to the grim conclusion that the Rawlins girl had been kidnapped by Buddy Simpson. He hoped the girl was still alive, but he had serious doubts.

Insanity had seized Newton.

And madness was what he was now sure he had viewed in the eyes of Buddy Simpson. It was the same raging, animal hunger he had observed in Reilly and Stallins.

The look was terrifying. He didn't understand it, at least not yet.

But he would. And he was going to take action.

He hoped he was wrong, would find nothing out of the ordinary with Simpson. Jantzen didn't think that would be the case.

Jantzen rolled slowly down the dirt drive. Ahead, his lights washed over the one-story white farmhouse. Simpson didn't have a dog, no warning, no alert.

It didn't matter. This far out in the country, Simpson would hear the smallest noise around his home. Jantzen saw lights flickering against the curtain of the living room window. Surely Simpson would know he had visitors.

Simpson's truck was parked out front. Other than that, the look and feel of the night was eerily still and silent.

Jantzen killed the lights and stepped out of the truck.

A moment later, he saw the tall shadow move against the curtain, stand there, then disappear. The way the light wavered, Jantzen knew the man was burning candles.

Jantzen tensed, sensing something ominously out of the ordinary inside the man's home.

Suddenly the front door creaked open on rusty hinges.

Jantzen drew his Colt, stopped, watched the dancing light in the doorway.

"Buddy? Buddy? It's Mark! I'd like to come in."

A long moment of awful silence.

Then a voice, cold and distant, called, "So come in."

Heart pounding, Jantzen moved up the steps. Cautiously he walked through the doorway. He was scared to death of what he would find inside.

He turned and looked down the short, narrow hall.

He froze, his heart throbbing in his ears.

Black candles in black holders were burning in the living room. There was a coppery smell in the air. Blood. And something else. A rancid odor, like sweat, but different.

Wood creaked under Jantzen's weight as he moved down the hallway.

Then he heard a noise, vague, distant, coming from the living room. It was the television. He heard grunting, groaning, a woman crying in a weird mix of pain and pleasure. The volume was turned up and the sounds of people engaged in the throes of passion registered in the misty shroud of fear that gripped Jantzen.

It seemed to take forever, but Jantzen reached the living room.

The first thing he saw was the back of Simpson's head.

The man was sitting in a leather recliner, obviously fixated on the naked woman with two men on the giant-screen TV.

"How you been, Mark?"

The voice sounded ominously cold, deep, like the throaty growl of an animal.

But it was the living room that sent a cold shiver down Jantzen's spine. Sight and sound whirled around him. Nothing clicked in his mind as he tried to grasp everything in one instant. Nothing sank in. Time froze.

He had never been to Simpson's home, but what he saw shocked him.

The man's home was a shrine to pornography.

And other darker, uglier things.

The world blurred for what seemed like an eternity in Jantzen's eyes. Because of the flickering candlelight it took several long moments for everything in the living room to register.

And even longer to comprehend the horror of it all.

"What kept you so long anyway, Mark?"

With wooden legs, Jantzen slid off to the side of the man in the chair, training his gun on him. Simpson didn't look his way. Instead, as the woman appeared to reach climax on the video and the two men ejaculated on her in great white spurts, Simpson froze the frame, then kept reversing and replaying the image.

Jantzen took in the ring of candles around Simpson. He followed what appeared to be a black circle from the television. His eyes knew what they would see—just before he saw it.

A human heart and two eyeballs were at Simpson's feet.

Chapter Twenty-four

Eyes wide in utter disbelief, heart pounding with fear, Jantzen kept the gun pointed at the back of Simpson's head. The man had removed the heart and the eyeballs with what appeared to be surgical precision. In Jantzen's observation, there was very little blood, no ragged edges of gristle, just a clean severing of muscle and sinew. Beyond that, he only hoped the girl had been dead before Simpson had set upon her with his demonic work. He could only imagine what else this monster had done to the girl.

Everything leapt, spun and swirled around Jantzen. It was all he could do to not vomit.

Visions. Smells. A living picture of hell on earth.

While keeping one eye on Simpson, Jantzen tried to take the room in, all the sights, stenches, get his bearings, try to fathom something that would give any shred of a clue as to the madness he viewed. His eyes flickered around the room. He already knew there was no making any sense of what he saw, nothing but unreason and pure evil.

The world had turned upside down.

A large bucket reeking of gasoline but looking dark with a scarlet liquid on top—blood, he guessed—sat in front of the television.

He saw bookcase after bookcase stuffed with videos, all labels indicating hardcore porn. Then there were magazines depicting every natural and unnatural act known to men and women.

The walls were plastered with naked women, some alone, but many together in lesbian positions. Using devices. Even animals. Wild, leering faces, eyes laughing with lust and pleasure stared back at him.

And pictures of children, mostly young girls. Pictures so grotesque Jantzen told himself they weren't even there, that it was too horrible to imagine what someone had done to children to have taken pictures like that.

Circle of candles surrounded the recliner, broken only at the top by a crucifix, the head of Jesus pointed at Simpson.

Another upside-down crucifix hung above the television.

A plate of some brownish substance, probably some kind of hallucinogenic mushrooms, and another small plate with white powder, cocaine or crystal meth, were on a nightstand beside Simpson.

Simpson kept clicking the image on the screen, back and forth. Freeze it, reverse, forward, freeze again, back and forth, flashing images, sound forward, reversed, the woman's cry of unleashed orgasm filling the silence with an unearthly sound.

"Watch what the whore does to him, Mark. I like this part."

Jantzen stepped in front of Simpson. It was only then he noticed the incredible, shocking change as he came face to face with a vision from hell.

Simpson wore only white underwear. There was a jar of Vaseline in his lap, his shorts soiled. A large puddle of his semen had spattered the floor. There was a weird grin on the man's lips, giving his face a distorted, jack-o'-lantern appearance. The eyes were red, bulging with some strange light of warped desire. His face looked gaunt, stretched paper-thin over razor-sharp bones in the cheeks and forehead.

Jantzen's head swam from the combined noxious smells of sweat, semen, blood and gasoline.

In a language Jantzen had never heard, the man muttered something. A shiver went down Jantzen's spine as Simpson burst into a strange fit of laughter. Was Simpson merely fried on drugs? Or was it something else?

"Do you know what I just said, Mark? But of course you don't. That was ancient Hebrew. I offered my prayer to the dark lords of the netherworld. Galgall and Bethaleh. I quoted Scripture in honor of the town's destruction. Hosea, chapter five, verse three—'I have seen your evil deeds, Israel, you have left me as a prostitute leaves her husband; you are utterly defiled.'" Another fit of laughter, only this time Simpson convulsed, jerked. Then he fell strangely still and silent.

Stunned, Jantzen could only stare in utter fear. Simpson appeared catatonic. The man's chest didn't even rise and fall.

Reaching out with a trembling hand, Jantzen took the remote.

Sudden life, laughter erupted from Simpson. "See? Even we, the damned, can quote Scripture. The fact of the matter is, we know your Lord far better than the holiest of holy saints. We suffer our eternal damnation with pride, and we are growing stronger every day. Sins of the flesh, Mark, they are the easiest to bring down upon the human heart." He giggled. "Heart, the little girl had a lot of heart. I enjoyed her. Heart, the home of the soul. Eyes, the seekers and holders of knowledge and wisdom, the windows opening the heart to all it wants and desires. Just in case you were wondering about the significance.

"'There your daughters turn to prostitution and your brides commit adultery. But why should I punish them? For you men are doing the same thing, sinning with harlots and temple prostitutes.'" Another short fit of laughter. "See. See! It's everywhere! Here in my temple! Give praise, give honor to the harlot, for she is the mother of your sorry existence!"

Jantzen snapped off the television.

Silence.

"Why did you do that, Mark? I need my temple prostitutes."

Jantzen took the cuffs, dropped them in Simpson's lap.

"Put those on, Simpson."

The man didn't budge. Jantzen grew angry, gritted his teeth. He was about to repeat his order when Simpson, moving in slow motion, took the cuffs, slipped them on, snapped them shut.

Simpson stared ahead. Something shadowy, dark and cold hardened his face.

"Where's the girl's body?"

Simpson laughed for a moment. He cocked his head as if he wasn't sure he'd heard the question. "She's around, Mark. Spread around, that is."

"What the... what are you, Simpson? What have you become?"

"I have become God, my friend. I am in the power of Assinikan, the Lord of Perversion."

"You're a monster. Why did you..." He glanced at the heart and eyeballs. "How could you?"

The voice changed again, deeper, colder. "Because it was the will of the Master. You wonder how this has happened, how I could be this. Accept it. It was, it is what I was always meant to be. You cannot even begin to understand. You choose not to choose. You are neither here nor there. You are a chameleon. But there's hope for you."

Simpson giggled, shuddered.

"You're insane."

"No, I have never been more sane in all of my life. The way was merely shown, and opened. Just as the Lord you think you want to believe in has a book of life written in heaven with all the names of those saved in His light, so, too, the true Master has his own book. And his book is far more full."

"Where is the body?"

Again the voice changed, this time level, matter-of-fact. "About two miles north in the woods. I buried what was left of her. She was tasty, that one. Sweet, too, and tight. She screamed nice."

Jantzen had the urge to club the man half to death. In fact, he took a step forward, lifting the gun.

"What, Mark? You going to beat me to death? For merely acting on the same impulse others felt toward the little girl?"

"Impulse? What you did...was beyond sick."

"Judging me, are you? Why not judge your mother, Mark? You always hated her for leaving you as a child." Simpson rolled his head, and Jantzen felt the full force of the penetrating stare. The voice seemed to reach Jantzen from a new and great distance.

Simpson bared his teeth, then smiled; then his expression melted into a stony mask. "You were eight years old, it was raining that day and you were in your room crying, oh, crying so terrible, shrieking inside yourself for your parents to stop fighting. To kiss and make up. What fool are you? You were writing a poem to your mother that day, the tears streaming down your cheeks. Would you like me to recite it for you?"

Jantzen felt his jaw go slack. "I...I never..."

"Of course you never told me. There are many things you kept from your good friend here. For instance, your father would always beat you with a belt, Mommy, too, once in a while. Make you drop your pants, show your little ass to them. You grew to enjoy the pain because in your twisted mind you believed you deserved it, that you were the problem, the wedge between your parents. You even overheard Mom one tell day your father, 'I wish he had never been born. I should have had an abortion.'"

Jantzen felt acid bile squirm into his throat. He didn't want to hear this, it was all too terribly true. How? How could Simpson know this?

"Mark, remember all those temple prostitutes you yourself tasted when you were a policeman? Remember all the things they did to you to indulge your dark side—"

"That's enough!"

"You liked the belt, you enjoyed two whores at one time, one suckling on you, the other suckling on the other. The smell of sweet and wanton vagina in your nose. Guilt and shame, a mere detective's salary, used for whores, taking food and comfort out of the mouths of your wife and daughter. What kind of man are you? What was the name of the woman you cheated on your wife for? Maggie, that's it, it was Maggie."

He couldn't stand to hear any more. Whether it was terror or outrage, Jantzen didn't know, but he cracked Simpson over the head with the barrel of the Colt. The blow hardly fazed Simpson. The man didn't even flinch. Instead, as blood trickled down the side of his face, Simpson flicked out his tongue and lapped at his own blood.

"Not as good as the little girl's but I have her flesh in my stomach. Perhaps she has been digested into my system."

"Where are the others?"

"Others? Funny you should mention them in that way. They call the new ones, us, the Others. But now I am one of them. The Master is pleased with me tonight."

"Where?"

"Oh, they're around. They move, like ghosts. The man, he knows, he can feel things, see things, sense things. He can feel souls near him, knows where to go to do what is necessary and avoid capture, even mere detection or suspicion. Don't you see? Man wants knowledge, man wants wisdom and insight and power. The God you think you want to believe in wants to keep man ignorant. If man attains wisdom and truth, he is branded a sorcerer, a magi of the black arts. The truth is, man can have knowledge and wisdom and your God becomes a jealous God because man is that much closer to the secrets of the universe."

"You lie...you blas—"

"I do not blaspheme. I merely know and speak the truth."

Jantzen was becoming furious, more impatient, more terrified. "The bald one. Where can I find him?"

"Michael?"

"That's his name?"

"I just told you, you asshole cocksucker faggot piece of shit!"

The sudden explosion of rage made Jantzen flinch.

"You dripping sperm of a mule's dick! You're fucking weak and spineless and gutless, Jantzen. You drink the piss and eat the shit of life because piss and shit are all you're filled with! You bow before a woman's vagina! You are a whore and a coward!"

The eyes bulged, nearly seemed to pop from their sockets. Simpson held up his cuffed hands, stretching, straining to break them apart. Foam spilled from his mouth.

Jantzen staggered back, a fresh wave of terror washing over him. He lifted the Colt.

"Don't do that, Simpson!"

"Fuck you and your whore of a wife! She's been gone only a few days and do you know how many cocks she's sucked? She sucks balls, too, big fucking balls!"

"Shut up! *Shut Up*! Stop moving! I'll shoot you!"

"No! You won't! You are a woman in a man's body! You're too weak! You're nothing, you are nobody and you know you are and you know I'm right!"

Before he knew it, Jantzen saw Simpson snap the cuffs apart. In an eyeblink, Simpson was a blur of movement. Jantzen squeezed the trigger, aiming at the man's leg. The gun boomed, sheared off a hunk of the man's thigh, but Simpson charged into him like an enraged bull. Jantzen felt himself swept up in Simpson's arms, lifted like he weighed no more than an infant, and hurled into the bookcase. The force of the impact made stars explode in Jantzen's eyes. Videos bounced off his head, torn pictures fluttering in the white haze of his eyes.

He looked up, saw Simpson looming over him. He tried to raise the gun, managed to swing it around, draw a bead on the man's chest, but the foot shot out of nowhere. The gun went flying from his numb hand. Jantzen drove a punch into Simpson's gut. It was like hitting stone. Still the man grunted, then Jantzen felt hands like steel digging into his shoulders. Again he was lifted into the air.

Jantzen stared into the burning pools of Simpson's eyes. Wild laughter and a vile stench erupted from Simpson's mouth. Jantzen drove his fist into the man's nose, repeatedly, coming down over his shoulder, driving, smashing. Simpson laughed off the punishing blows, even as blood spurted from his mashed nose.

Jantzen was airborne in the next moment. As he slammed against the wall, wind was driven from his lungs. Then the face of demonic rage and hate swept over him. Out of nowhere a fist battered his jaw, and he felt his head bounce off the wall.

Legs turning to rubber, Jantzen melted to the floor.

Jantzen drifted in and out of a white, sick haze. Somehow he struggled to his knees, then slumped against the wall. He felt cold fear as his vision cleared and he found Simpson crouched on his haunches. The monster was just inside the circle of candles, toying with the Colt, pulling out, then slapping the clip into the gun, over and over, the same frenzied motion Jantzen had seen him use with the porn video. Simpson grinned his awful grin.

Then, like some giant insect, Simpson skittered on his haunches across the floor. Chuckling, Simpson held up a porn picture and thrust it in Jantzen's face.

Laughing, Simpson said, "Take a look."

Jantzen glimpsed the picture. It showed two naked women, one squatting over the other and having a huge phallus shoved up her, a red ball jammed in her mouth. Jantzen swatted the picture away.

"Kind of reminds you of good times gone by?"

"That—"

"What? Wasn't you with whores? Don't lie to me, Mark, it's very unbecoming. He knows your soul just as well as the Other."

"I—"

"Oh, listen to this. You've what? Changed? Seen the light? You're no Paul. But you're lucky, Mark. Michael doesn't want you killed. Not yet. Seems the man has plans for you and your bitch-whore wife. Michael seems to think he knows you from somewhere. I'm sure when you finally meet the man, you can ask him about Atlanta. Hey, cheer up, it's not your time." Cold, Simpson added, "I'll be back in a minute, soon as I can find something to tie you up with. Try something stupid, well, I'm not opposed to shooting you in the balls." Laughter. "You had your chance to kill me, Mark. But I know you, you don't have the guts. That's always been one of your problems. Can't face reality. The truth about yourself you cannot face."

Simpson stood and walked out of the room.

Rage and fear cleared Jantzen's head. He had to do something fast, escape, fight back or he was dead. But he just toppled onto his side, against his will. He thought he would lapse into unconsciousness when something dug into his hip. Pain revived him. He reached into his pocket and pulled out his Zippo.

He heard Simpson in the other room.

"Be a good coward, Mark, and cooperate. If you do, you will know pleasures like you've never known. Michael is merely a conduit to the all-wise and all-powerful Master. But you must pray our prayers, drink the blood of our victims, seek hidden knowledge. In your Bible they called it sorcery, but with us it's far more. What I am saying is, you may have a chance to become one of us. Michael claims he sees something in you. What, I don't know. I never even liked you all that much. You're too soft, you're too ready to cut the other guy a break, even when it gets broken off in your ass. See yourself as generous, but you're a weak-willed fool. No balls. Never made a real stand in all your life. You're a slave to your past."

The whole time Simpson railed on, Jantzen made his way to the bucket of gore. He heard feet scraping wood in the next room. He picked up the bucket. It was far heavier than he had imagined. At least a ten-gallon bucket. Whatever else was mixed in with the fuel, he couldn't imagine. But the smell of gasoline nearly made him pass out. Jantzen willed himself to stay on his feet.

He should have killed Simpson, a monster in human skin, or was Simpson something else? Incredibly, the man had just bled and walked on after being shot in the leg, not even a limp.

A shadow appeared in the nearby door. Jantzen stepped forward.

"Now, Mark, old friend..."

Simpson reached for the Colt as angry realization bulged his eyes and his face contorted with fury.

Too late.

Jantzen hurled the gore in the man's face, had the Zippo opened and flaring to life. The fuel ran down Simpson's chest and stomach, momentarily blinding him. Simpson bellowed in rage. He was swinging the Colt around when Jantzen raced up to him and dropped the Zippo into the man's gas-soaked shorts.

Jantzen dove to the side, away from the gun.

Instantly Simpson burst into flames. The Colt fired once, a blind shot, the bullet burrowing into the ceiling. Shrieking, Simpson dropped the gun, bounced off the doorway, then flailed around the living room, a living ball of flame.

"You bastard son of a whore!" Simpson screamed. "*Not fire*! Oh, God of the damned! *Noooooo*!"

Terrified, Jantzen staggered away from the flaming demon. Simpson slapped at his face and head as he slammed into the television. The video machine toppled, was crushed under Simpson's frenzied flaming feet. The giant-screen TV fell over beneath Simpson's crashing weight as he pitched to the floor in a frantic attempt to extinguish the fire eating him alive. The banshee-like wailing seemed to go on forever in Jantzen's ears, echoing in his mind.

Jantzen scooped up the Colt and began firing at near point-blank range into Simpson.

The man merely jerked and twitched under the impact of the thundering rounds. Flesh exploded and blood burst through the flames, but Simpson shrieked on.

"You can't kill me!"

A warning or a plea?

Even as Simpson's eyes seemed to melt from their sockets, Jantzen watched in cold disbelief as Simpson seemed to find him. The flaming thing struggled to its feet and staggered toward Jantzen, arms outstretched as if Simpson meant to sweep him up and have them both eaten alive in the fire.

Jantzen fired three more rounds, coring the .45 ACP slugs into the man's brain. Bone cracked like eggshell and blood and muck rained around the living room.

Simpson took one long step toward Jantzen.

The thing was nearly on top of Jantzen. Time, sound, sight—froze.

Desperately Jantzen squeezed the trigger—to a dry click. He was searching his pocket for another clip when suddenly Simpson folded and thudded to the floor.

Jantzen watched as the skin bubbled, melted off Simpson's skull. A sickly-sweet stench pierced his senses.

Jantzen had to get out of there.

Numb, he staggered from the house. Whether or not the place would burn to the ground, he didn't know. He didn't even care.

He hopped into his truck. He wasn't sure how far the closest neighbor was, if anyone had heard anything. His mind was racing, his blood rushing hot.

He fired up the engine, reversed it and sped up the drive.

Within two hours, Jantzen had what he needed to fight them. Or almost everything. Father McMartin leapt in and out of his head.

His first stop was an all-night truck stop near the Interstate north of Newton. He kept a ten-gallon gasoline can in the back of his vehicle in case of an emergency. Everything about tonight was classified as an emergency in the extreme. He topped the can.

Visions of Simpson burning alive, screaming about fire, kept flashing through his head. He shoved them aside as he drove to the diner.

Still...

"God is an all-consuming fire."

He reached destination two. In the kitchen he found several empty crates. He took large plastic jugs and emptied their contents, whether cooking oil, dressing, whatever. Then he cleaned them thoroughly and filled the crates with the empties.

As he was driving back home, reality sank in. He was now confronted with a new series of problems, and an ever-growing list of dire trouble. Even if he survived, he could be a hunted fugitive.

First, Mary. Call her. Tell her to stay where she was. Don't ask questions. She would know he was in serious trouble, but he would deal with it, make something up. Still, wives could tell. Just a tone of voice. A look. There was no hiding from her. Perhaps he should come clean. He would decide later.

Forget the law, Wiley, the FBI. The Rawlins girl was dead, butchered, hacked up and buried on or near Simpson's property. Later, when he had picked up the trail of this Michael, he would phone Wiley. But tell him what? That the man responsible for murdering the girl had been torched by his hand?

Stephens. The sheriff boiled in his mind, lingering on. There was a taint of corruption in that man. No doubt, there was something odd about the sheriff. Eerie. Or was he stretching it? Still, the encounter in the Donner home the other night had unnerved him, made him suspect that Stephens knew something—or was covering for someone. More stretching? Jantzen didn't think so. And why had the sheriff been so hard to reach by his deputies the morning of the bank robbery? Jantzen couldn't even recall the sheriff even being on the scene after the fact. Why? Or had Jantzen simply not seen him? No. He couldn't even recall finding the sheriff's cruiser in town that morning.

Eventually, through the dark and eternal night, when he reached the driveway to his property Jantzen was relieved to find no cruisers, no unmarked vehicles waiting for him. After parking in the dirt drive, giving the immediate vicinity around the house a thorough scouring, finding nothing but silent darkness, he rushed into the house but with his gun in hand, a fresh clip in the magazine. He turned on the living room light. As he moved for the phone, he listened to the house. His senses were electrified from both fear and adrenaline.

The silence was so deafening he heard the angry beating of his heart.

He was trembling as he picked up the phone and dialed the number that was branded into his memory. He waited a long time. Ten, twelve rings. It was only when he checked his watch that he realized how late it was. Eleven. Maybe everyone was in bed. Sleeping. While he had been killing a man.

Finally a sleepy, slightly irritated voice of a woman answered. "Hello?"

"Uh, yes, this is Mark Jantzen. I'm sorry to bother you at this hour...Is this Judy?"

"Oh, yes, Mark. Hi, yes, this is Judy."

He struggled for words, any words. "Yes, hi. I need to talk to Mary."

A pause, then the girlfriend, sounding tentative, said, "Well, Mark, she left here a long time ago."

His heart skipped a beat. "What? When?"

"Well, it was, I don't know, maybe three this afternoon. We had lunch after she took me to the doctor's. She was already packed. She told me she was going straight home. She wanted to surprise you."

His throat constricted, went dry. "She hasn't called here. Did she call you at some time...this afternoon?"

"No. I thought she would have been home long ago."

Suddenly headlights were striking the curtains of the living room window. He thought it was Mary, but a moment later he knew it wasn't. He knew the low, throaty grumble of her truck's engine, and this was a small engine sound.

Frozen on the couch, he lifted the gun, heard the woman on the other end call his name.

A door opened and closed out front.

"I have to go. Sorry to have bothered you," he said, and hung up.

Swiftly he moved for the front door. Soft footsteps sounded out front. Then there was a rap on the door.

Tense, Jantzen called out, "Who's there?"

"Mark, it's Father McMartin."

"Father McMartin?" he heard his voice whisper. "Father, what are you doing here?"

"Please, Mark, open the door. We need to talk."

Stunned, Jantzen swung the door open. He

stared at the shadowy face of the priest, framed in the glow of the outer limits of the living room light.

The priest was clearly disturbed. Jantzen thought the man looked haunted.

Chapter Twenty-five

Judging by the priest's hard stare of concern and confusion, Jantzen could be sure he was something of a frightening sight to Father McMartin. Jantzen stood stone still before the priest, sweating, burning with adrenaline. The ghosts of that night haunted Jantzen, living, flaming memories of what he'd seen and done branded in his mind.

Perhaps for the rest of his life. Provided, of course, there was even life left to live.

Right now, he knew it was down to survival. And to hunt or become the hunted. He had no options. Not after what he had done to Simpson, what he now knew.

"Mark, it's plain to see you're not well."

"Understatement of the century, Father."

"What's wrong, Mark?"

"What isn't wrong is a better question."

Jantzen brushed past the priest, searched the drive, the woods, the field for any sign of an invader. Total darkness. Silence. Not even the wind moved tonight. Somewhere in the distance the plaintive cry of a coyote. Jantzen flinched at the haunting animal noise. Turning back, Jantzen found the priest staring at the gun in his hand.

"Mark, may I come in so we can talk?"

"Why are you here, Father?"

He didn't mean to sound suspicious or skeptical, but Jantzen found it impossible to take anything at face value any longer.

"The more I thought about our last conversation, the more worried I became. I needed to see you. I fear where you may be headed."

"I'm not in the mood for confession, Father."

"I'm in the business of saving souls; you needn't be suspicious of me."

"I'm a little on edge, Father. You'll have to forgive my abrupt manner."

"I can see that there's been a definite and frightening change in you. Whatever you may think, I'm glad I'm here. I couldn't very well just let you leave the rectory the other day and embark on some course of self-destruction. What kind of priest would I be if I allowed that?"

"Yeah, well, at this point somebody needs to get in the business of saving lives."

"I'm not sure I understand."

"I do. Right now that's enough."

"Has your wife returned home yet?"

Jantzen looked at the priest, shook his head, then moved into the doorway.

"Come on in, Father."

Jantzen closed the door behind the priest. It was then Jantzen saw the dried blood on his shirt and pants. Looking up, he noted the priest looking at his soiled clothing.

"Mark, what happened tonight?"

"Father, I'm in serious trouble. I don't even know where to begin."

"You've done something . . . terrible, haven't you?"

"That depends on how you look at it. First of all, I'm scared to death for my wife. I need to find her, then I need to get the hell out of this town—with Mary."

The priest gave Jantzen a puzzled look. "What do you mean? Is something wrong with Mary? Has something happened to her? Mark, slow down. You're acting very strange."

"Strange, huh? I'll tell you what's strange. My wife left her girlfriend's place in Tulsa in mid afternoon, her girlfriend said. It's at best a two-and-a-half hour drive. Here we are approaching midnight and I haven't seen nor heard from her."

"Have you called the police?"

They moved side by side to the couch. "Do you want something to drink, Father?"

"No, thank you."

Jantzen plopped down on the couch and Father McMartin took a seat on the other end. Jantzen fired up a cigarette.

"So you're here out of concern for my well-being. Well, it may be a little late for that."

"I'm here because, as I said, I'm concerned for your soul, Mark. And perhaps even my own."

Jantzen peered at the priest. Exactly what did he mean?

"First, tell me what it is you've done."

Jantzen nodded. "You're not going to like it."

"I already don't like it."

"Whatever I decide to do, understand it's my decision and you will not try to talk me out of it."

The priest thought long and hard before he answered. "Allow me that choice. For someone who's right now seeking his own way, allow another to do likewise. I'm here as a confidant, a priest and a friend. Fair enough?"

"Good enough. All right..."

Jantzen told the priest the whole truth about his night. He also told Father McMartin about his encounter with the bald one he now knew as Michael. Beyond that, Jantzen didn't need to give the priest any further proof that a Satanic cult was at large and responsible for the murder and mayhem that had descended on Newton.

A half-pack cigarettes later, Jantzen and Father McMartin sat in tight silence. He couldn't read any reaction in the priest, who sat there with a flat expression on his wizened features. But the priest's eyes seemed to fill with a haunted sorrow.

"It's just like you told me, Father. The man...he was...possessed."

"So you're inclined to believe."

"What would you call it?"

"You say there was drugs involved?"

"Yes."

"This man had built some temple to pornography?"

"There was the upside-down crucifix. The black circle I saw at the crime scene where the Fenner girls were found. The man had incredible, no, superhuman strength and a rage unlike anything I've ever seen. A bucket of some mix of gas and bodily fluids, I imagine. The girl's heart and eyes, cut out of her body. He talked in a foreign tongue, his voice, his whole face would change, just like you said. Foam at the mouth. He even knew things about me and my past no one ever should have known. Father, forgive me for saying this, but you're sounding skeptical."

"Hardly. What I understand is that certain areas of human behavior can be seen as forms of possession, which in this modern age we term obsession or mental illness. For example, drug addiction, alcoholism, even runaway appetites for sex, or all manner of perverted acts, the love and the chasing of money and power, these can so consume a person's soul, their entire energy, their life force, that they live for nothing else. It becomes, in essence, the desire for self but to the most extreme degree. It only leads to destruction. You only have to turn on the evening news to know what I mean. But of course, you were a policeman, you know what I'm talking about."

"You don't believe that what I saw was some form of pure evil?"

"You said you were once drinking companions with this man?"

"Yes. Long ago. And, yes, I know where you're headed with this. I never even alluded to things he told me about my past."

"You're certain?"

"Absolutely positive. I've never been a blackout drinker. Is it possible I'm dealing with individuals who . . . are either possessed or under the influence of some form of demonic possession?"

"It's possible."

"Father, I saw it with my own eyes. The man was like some wild animal. What do you think?"

"Perhaps possession, I can't say for sure. Or it could be a combination of the drugs, maybe even some self-induced state of hypnosis which gives the appearance of demonic possession."

"After I've told you, you still don't believe me?"

"I believe you. As I said, evil can so consume a person, though, that it may also come across as a form of possession. If certain individuals involved in the occult, the ritual of a Black Mass, well, their souls stray into very dark and dangerous territory. Just as a Christian can pray and ask for and even receive help in their lives from the Almighty, then the opposite is true of one who believes and seeks the power of the devil."

"So what is it I'm faced with exactly?"

"All I know is that something evil has happened tonight in this town. That this Simpson person murdered a girl, that you killed him—"

"In self-defense."

"Still. The police may have a different view of it."

"I won't turn myself in, Father. I have to find my wife. I can't do that sitting in jail."

The priest sat back on the couch, heaved a breath. Suddenly he looked ten years older.

"Father, I get the strong impression there's something you desperately want to say to me."

"Indeed. There's a reason I came to Oklahoma many years ago and began my own parish. I, like you, am running from a nightmare. I know about demonic possession, I've seen it with my own eyes. When I was a priest in Baltimore, there was a boy in my parish. Came from an upper-middle-class family. He was eight years old, no history of medical problems other than the flu or the common cold. The boy had been having convulsions for weeks. Naturally, the parents believed he was having seizures, believed the boy might even be epileptic. The doctors could find nothing medically wrong with the boy. All manner of tests were done, every specialist the parents could find attempting to uncover an answer about their son.

"I began to visit the boy at the parents' request. The same symptoms I described to you over the phone, this boy was afflicted by. But to an extreme degree. The speaking in foreign tongues, the contorted faces, the endless streams of some of the vilest language and blasphemy one can imagine. Suffice to say...well, performing an exorcism involves...certain steps, procedures, not to mention approval from the church. It was all kept very quiet, but the parents were desperate for help and willing to try anything. I procrastinated, I was somewhat skeptical about demonic possession. After all, this is not the Dark Ages. I kept hoping the doctors would find an answer. Finally the parents insisted I do something. They were, of course, terrified.

"What happened...well, I put it off and put it off until...one night I was going to their home, fully prepared to perform the rite of exorcism. When I got to their door, I could almost feel the presence of something terrible inside the house. I knocked. The door was ajar. I stepped inside and found...

the boy's mother at the foot of the door. She had been hacked up almost beyond recognition. I ventured upstairs in search of the father, and they also had a daughter. I know I should have called the police right away. Understand, I was much younger, more foolish actually than brave back then."

He paused, his gaze falling away from Jantzen. Finally the priest sucked in a deep breath and continued. "Upstairs, I found both the father and the daughter... murdered in the same horrible manner as the mother. I was in shock, mortal fear for my own life at that point.

"I heard this unearthly... bellow of pure rage, it's the only way I can describe it. I remember I was moving back down the hall, dazed but aware the boy was still somewhere in the house. I knew he had committed these murders, but I was asking myself at the moment, was it the boy or was it something that had taken control of him?

"From out of nowhere the boy charged me. He was wielding a large kitchen knife. He was covered in blood. I reacted. I reached for his knife hand, but was hurled into the wall with such an incredible force—mind you, this boy weighed no more than eighty pounds. What happened next, it's as if I see it as something hazy, dreamlike, it was so terrifying. He charged me again. I believe in my terror I tried to charge the boy to defend myself, only I didn't stand all the way. I recall the knife sweeping for my face, I ducked. Then... I can't accurately recall how, but the boy's furious momentum must have carried him over me. Only..." The priest swallowed hard, his eyes brimming with fear over the memory. "Only he...well, he went down the stairs...only it didn't appear that he was falling. It looked as if he was actually flying, or propelled down the stairs by some outside force. When he hit the bottom of the stairs...

"The police report said he died of a broken neck. It's entirely possible that was the cause of death. However, before the police arrived, I saw the boy. His neck had been broken in such a manner that his entire head was twisted backwards and his face was crushed inside his head. It was a sight I knew I would never forget. To this day, I still have nightmares over it."

Jantzen saw the priest's hand were shaking.

"A fall like that," Father McMartin said, "should not have produced that...manner of fatal injury."

Jantzen was silent for long moments. "You left Baltimore? You felt responsible somehow?"

"Had I not procrastinated, had I gone ahead with the exorcism sooner..."

"Who can say, Father? You may or may not have been able to save that family. Who can say?"

"Precisely my entire point with you about your past. Be that as it may, both of us are haunted by this specter of...whether it is pure evil in human form or demonic possession, I can't say. Let me ask you—what are you planning to do?"

"Hunt them down. And—I don't know this for a fact—if they have taken my wife, then God help them. If she's harmed, I'll show them no mercy."

The priest nodded. "I can only pray for the salvation of your soul, Mark. Here, I brought you something."

Jantzen watched as the priest took a crucifix the size of his hand from his pants pocket.

"I have blessed it in holy water."

"They're not vampires, Father."

"Indeed, but the principle works just the same. That's the eternal symbol of God's triumph over evil. Another thing about the boy which finally made me decide to go ahead with the exorcism—when I laid the crucifix on his forehead when he was deep in the throes of a convulsion, he began to shriek in a voice not his own that he was burning, that the cross was burning him, and he demanded that I stop. Feverishly I prayed over him, commanding the demons to leave this boy in the name of Jesus Christ. The boy's eyes rolled back in his head until only the whites of his eyes were showing. Then he collapsed into a state of total exhaustion, that catatonic state I mentioned."

Jantzen looked at the crucifix. "So you think this may prove a weapon against an individual who may be possessed?"

A grim smile crossed the priest's lips. "What would it hurt? If nothing else, if you are a believer, then you would at least have God on your side. It may prove, if you have faith, that faith alone may save you."

"Thank you, Father. I know it's tough for you to understand that I have to do this thing, that I need to take care of it. I'm also probably going to be considered a fugitive—until I can prove beyond a shadow of a doubt what has happened tonight and earlier."

"Believe me, I do understand. It's why I'm going to insist I go with you."

Jantzen shook his head. "Father—"

"If I can't talk you out of doing what it is you're thinking about doing—"

"Father, be smart. I'm intent on committing cold-blooded murder if I have to."

"I understand. Perhaps in this case...well, maybe the Lord does work in mysterious ways."

"It's too dangerous, Father. I don't want your blood on my hands."

"My decision is made. I have my own car. Would you prefer I follow you? Not even you know how you're going to proceed, do you?"

Jantzen was set to further protest when the phone rang. Flinching, he stared at the phone on the coffee table for a long moment. Then tentatively, he reached for the phone.

"Yes," Jantzen said.

Right away he recognized the cold and deep voice that sounded as if it came from the bottom of a tomb.

On the other end the bald one said, "We need to meet and discuss your future. And also the future of your lovely wife."

Enraged, Jantzen wished he could reach through the phone and rip the ghoul's throat out.

"You sick bastard," Jantzen growled. "If you harm my wife—"

"Please, spare me the threats. Get a pen and paper."

It seemed to take a full minute before Jantzen could find the strength to stand. His whole world, he feared, was about to be torn apart.

Again.

Chapter Twenty-six

"Don't you worry, asshole, I'll find it."

"Oh, and by the way. I would bring a fair amount of water with you."

Puzzled, Jantzen growled, "Why?"

"The desert is hot this time of year. As hot as hell."

Click.

Jantzen slammed the phone down on the coffee table. If nothing else, at least he now knew what had happened to his wife. Small consolation. He knew just what these sick monsters were capable of.

"They have Mary," he told Father McMartin. "They told me to come alone."

"Meaning no police."

"Right. Or meaning I simply come alone."

"I am clearly not the police."

"Father, this could get real ugly."

"It's already ugly."

"You sure you still want to go, Father?"

"Now more than ever. You need help. You can't do this alone. What do they want?"

"He wouldn't say. Father, I implore you to change your mind."

"Mark, you need to understand something. Like you, I have a past to confront."

"This isn't about redemption. Or penance. Or a guilty conscience."

"Then what is it about? You said something earlier about saving lives. Perhaps this is my chance to do just that."

He could tell the priest was determined to go along. But why? Would he interfere at some critical point? Or if these individuals of this Satanic cult in fact were possessed, did the priest believe he could exorcise them on the spot?

"Have it your way, Father. You want in, right now you can give me some help loading my vehicle."

A half-hour later they were ready. The Jeep Cherokee was loaded with six additional plastic jugs, all filled with gasoline.

Jantzen had some idea where they were headed. The ominous meet was set to take place at a motel near the Oklahoma-Texas border; he had marked off the way on the state map. He figured they would get there at around three in the morning. Beyond that, if they were going south and if they went deep into Texas, then they would be heading into rugged desert country. In that event, Jantzen was prepared. Three large canteens; two jackets for the cold of the night; other essentials were vitamin supplements and salt tablets, wide-brimmed hats and an extra pair of sunglasses for Father McMartin, in case this lasted into tomorrow.

Jantzen and the priest had already shredded bedsheets and pillows and tucked them into the tops of the jugs. Jantzen had noticed the way the priest had handled the task of making crude homemade Molotov cocktails. Anxious, uncertain, the priest had seemed to go through the motions, becoming more grim, more subdued as he went.

Finally, just before they boarded the Cherokee, Jantzen pulled out the shotgun. In the dim light shining from the open doorway of the Jeep, Jantzen caught the disturbed look on the priest's face. Jantzen took eight .12 gauge shells. He held the Mossberg 500, racked the slide until he had loaded the maneater to capacity.

Laying the shotgun on the floorboard behind the driver's seat, Jantzen asked, "Having second thoughts, Father?"

The priest shook his head, but Jantzen was dubious.

"We need to get you a change of clothes," he told the priest.

"Why?"

"In case they lead us into the desert. Black will draw the sun. You'll fry."

"My collar is my armor."

Jantzen nodded. There was no point in arguing small details.

Hopping in, Jantzen took one last long, hard look at the map of Oklahoma. He couldn't help but wonder with a deep sense of dread, as he fired up the engine, what was waiting for them at the state line.

Thirty minutes later, Jantzen picked up the tail. He had one eye on the road ahead, one eye on the sideview mirror. The tail—and he was sure they were being followed—boiled out of the night, lingered perhaps a half-mile back.

"What's wrong?" the priest asked.

"I'm not sure."

They were near the county line, with the Interstate now just a few miles west.

Jantzen slowed. The headlights came closer, then the car fell back. Jantzen pulled over, but the vehicle stopped. In the darkness, the headlights still gave shape to the vehicle. It looked like a Ford four-door. Or a Chevy Caprice.

Sheriff Stephens, he believed.

Jantzen waited as the vehicle sat on the shoulder of the road. If it was the sheriff, then the man had staked out the road leading from his home. But why? So far, their progress out of the county had been unimpeded. Jantzen suddenly feared a small army of state policemen barreling around him, guns drawn. For a full minute, they waited. The car behind didn't move either. The road ahead was dark, empty.

"You think we're being followed?"

"I know so," Jantzen said.

"Who?"

"The county sheriff."

"Why?"

"I couldn't say."

If the sheriff knew about Simpson and suspected Jantzen of killing him, then he should have roared up on him, demanding a search of the vehicle. And finding the weapons, the jugs of gas. In that event, Jantzen's hunt was finished before it even started.

Then suddenly the cruiser swung across the highway and roared off in the opposite direction. Jantzen watched until it vanished, far down the highway, into the black of night.

Jantzen didn't like it.

"Keep your eyes open, Father."

In tight silence, Jantzen drove on.

MOTEL.

The sign was lit, swaying on hinges against a low prairie wind, a beacon signaling them in the night, drawing them.

The place was one-story with a shabby office at the far end. Several miles west of I-35, it was perched in a remote area at the edge of far-reaching flatland.

Jantzen found the black van parked at the west end of the building. A few other vehicles were strung out in the small lot in front of the motel rooms. Tumbleweed rolled in front of the headlights.

Jantzen slid in beside the familiar black van, shut down the engine, killed the lights. He watched the curtain to Room 15. No movement, not even a faint glow of light against the curtain.

Jantzen hefted the .45 Colt. "Father, maybe you should stay here."

"And do what? I told you, I'm with you in this."

"And if I have to shoot one of them? If I'm forced to use violence to find out where my wife is?"

"I hope it doesn't come to that."

"My whole problem with you being here. You're still clutching to Thou Shalt Not Kill."

"If you must defend a life...please do not resort to violence as the only answer."

"I don't like being handcuffed, Father."

"Uncuff yourself, then. Let's go. Besides, I must see these individuals to determine what exactly they are."

Jantzen slid out of the truck. "Stay behind me, Father."

Gun low by his side, Jantzen moved up to the door. He hesitated, not hearing any movement, any sound from inside the room. He was about to knock when he heard, "It's open."

Jantzen didn't know what to expect, whether Mary was inside, or what they wanted. He hated unsolved mysteries, suspense, unanswered questions. It had always been the part of police work he had hated. He had no patience. He wanted answers right away. Despite the priest's warning, he would get answers. Beginning now.

He opened the door and watched the soft glow of light from the distant sign wash over the black eyes and shining white dome in the far corner of the room.

Chapter Twenty-seven

From the deep shadows, the stark white man laughed. "You bring guns? A man of your God? You bring violence and hatred to me?" More cold laughter. "That's good, that's very, very good. We need that. You give us both hope and strength. But this is not cop stuff."

Slowly Jantzen ventured into the room. He jumped, gun swinging around the room when he heard a match scratching, then flaring to life. The fire seemed to ignite malevolence in the eyes of the one who called himself Michael.

Jantzen's gun hand moved instinctively. He drew a bead on a large, bearded man with black hair who was in the deepest part of the room but moving into the outer limits of wavering light.

"Freeze!" Jantzen warned.

The big man stopped near the edge of the bed.

Jantzen quickly took in his surroundings as he closed the door. Twin beds, dresser, a television. An open door behind the big bearded one, leading to the bathroom. It was hot, stale and musty in the room.

Michael lit a candle on the dresser, remained seated in a wooden chair.

"Where is she?" Jantzen asked.

"Do you know, I could feel you arrive, even from a distance. I could feel the exquisite beauty of your fear and anger and thirst for vengeance."

"I asked you a question." Jantzen checked on Father McMartin out of the corner of his eye. The priest stood next to him, unmoving. He could feel the priest staring at these two men, a look of utter fear in his eyes. They were both in the presence of a pure and unnerving evil. They looked human enough, but something in their eyes, their voices, told Jantzen they were more than, or perhaps less than, human.

Again Jantzen was chilled by the weird light he found in the eyes of these Satanists.

"At the moment, she is safe."

"At the moment? Where is she?"

"Far to the south. My legion is already there. Preparing."

Jantzen felt his heart skip a beat. "Preparing? To offer my wife as a human sacrifice?"

Jantzen stepped forward, cursing, lifting the gun. Then he felt Father McMartin drop a restraining hand on his wrist.

"No, Mark. Stay calm in the face of their evil."

Michael laughed, a mocking sound. Then his voice took a deep snarling tone. "Yes, Mark, listen to the holy man. I see this one, I can smell the same guilt and fear on him as you. What brings you here, Father? Have you performed your absurd rite of exorcism in the past? Indeed, as I look into you, there is something you are trying to hide. Tell me, Father. Do you believe in the power of your Lord to defeat the eternal glory of my lord?"

"What kind of monsters are you? To murder children, to kidnap, to turn others into whatever it is you are?" Jantzen growled.

"Jonas," Michael said, tilting his head to the big man. "Tell them."

"We are the Children of Satan. Michael is the seed of Our Father. We are Family who have dwelled and wandered the earth, passing on his great work, down from generation to generation."

"You're insane. Where's my wife? What do you want?"

"Your fear, your hatred, your thirst for our blood, you rotten cocksucker! You hater of your own miserable existence!" Michael raged. "You feed us! But you need us even more than we need you!"

"Is that what this cat-and-mouse game is all about?" Jantzen asked. "You want me to feel fear?"

"It feeds them, Mark," he heard the priest say. "I see it now. It is how evil grows stronger. No matter what, I implore you to stay calm, keep yourself under control."

"Oh, you wise man," Michael scoffed. "Come closer, Father, let me know your own sin. What is in your past you are so desperately hiding?"

"My wife!" Jantzen demanded.

"I told you," the deep growling voice replied. "She is where she belongs. She is in a place far to the south where we, the Legion of the Damned, have tasted blood before."

"I'll kill you before I let you butcher my wife."

"Indeed. I know who you are. Cop. Atlanta."

Jantzen watched, his heart pounding with fear and anger, as the white ghoul dropped a large black book on the bed.

"As it was written, I had to go back to uncover the truth. It is marked in there. Almost six years ago it was. The girl, she had strawberry blond hair. The mother, I recall she was a fine specimen for an older whore."

"You bastard!"

"We're all bastards. The God you worship abandoned the human race from the beginning of time."

"Don't listen to his lies, Mark!"

"No, listen to me and you shall hear the truth. You ask many questions for which there are no answers. The whore! She had a mole right below her right breast, did she not?"

Jantzen felt his head swim. It was true. It was them. He was faced with the monsters from the past who had taken his first wife and daughter. How could it have all come to this? Coincidence? Destiny? Some divine, supernatural force bringing it all together?

"You..." He was speechless, the gun was lifting, drawing a bead on the ghoul, his finger tightening around the trigger.

"Shoot me and you have no hope for Mary, your Virgin Mary."

Laughter.

"We are who always was." Michael laughed; then a strange haunted look filled his black eyes. "I cannot expect you, who don't even understand your own life and your own sin, to understand us. We are the Damned. We are the Clan of Morton. The names have changed over the ages. We were once the Clan of Domishkin. The Clan of Yuraa. The Clan of Mabdul. The Clan of Rothschild and O'Malley. Even as far to the east as the Clan of Yoshimo. It is written in the Great Book."

Jantzen followed the long, bony, white finger to the cover of the book. It was then he saw the circle, broken with the upside-down crucifix.

"We are the undying. Of course, we all die. In body, that is. But my heritage goes back thousands of years. We have traveled the four corners of the earth. We have bred and interbred in almost every nation you can name. We are ageless and we are timeless. We, the Children of the Devil, carry on his work."

"I'll ask you once more or I'll shoot you dead, you sick asshole. What do you want from me?"

"And I'll tell you again, foolish man, we need your fear. We need your blood."

"Do you intend to kill my wife?"

No answer. Michael just sat there, staring back from the flickering shadows.

"You wonder about the circle, foolish man. The circle means life, broken by the symbol we abhor. It means that life ends in death. Everything comes full circle."

"Did you know I was living in Newton? Is that what this is really about? You followed me?"

"You might say I was guided to you. You are a fire, one that was unquenched from so long ago. You are drawn to me, whether you realize it or not, like a moth to the flame. You want reason, but there is no reason. You want truth, but there is no truth. There is only what is in front of you. Your town was the same way, calling us, beckoning us. The place where you hid from your sin and your past was ripe and ready for us. I can read others, even their minds and their thoughts. You wonder if someone in Newton is covering our tracks. You wonder how we could have moved about so freely. You don't understand our power. You don't understand that I can see what someone is going to do even before they do it. The police were never a threat. I could feel their energy, even when it was closing in, and thus, foolish man, I knew when to move on, to evade them."

"Reilly and Stallins are dead," Jantzen told him. "Did you know that?"

And he saw the man balk, the raging light fade slightly in his black eyes.

"And? They were mere fodder. There will be more, and more."

"Simpson's dead, too. I burned him alive."

Now fear was visible on the bald man's face, his jaw going slack for a moment.

"He screamed about the eternal fire as he died. You who know so much didn't know that, did you?"

"I know now. I can see their deaths in your eyes, in the memory of your own burning fire in your tortured soul. So? They are merely with the Master now. That they were weak and couldn't survive is not my problem."

"How do you do it, Michael, or whatever your name is? How do you make souls cave to your will?"

A chuckle. "Are you so naive? I merely offer weak men what they want. Those three were easy. They wanted pleasures of the flesh, they craved money, they so wanted the world it wasn't difficult at all."

"Are there others in Newton that you've offered the world to?"

"Perhaps. And perhaps not."

"I believe you followed me," Jantzen said. "I believe I've been your target all along. I believe you knew I would be onto you eventually and you made your move against me. You've watched me, you found out who I was."

"What you believe is unimportant."

"Is it?"

Michael looked at the priest, gestured with his hand at Jantzen and laughed. "Do you see that, Father? I bet he's confessed to you many times. All his weaknesses, it makes me ill. The world revolves around him. He's selfish to the extreme, is he not? He has committed adultery, I see it in his eyes. He, too, craves the world. One who is like us cannot hide from us."

Jantzen bared his teeth. "You're wrong. I am not a thing like you."

"But you can be, if you're not already. Come, join us. Shoot the priest."

Jantzen flinched at the sudden command, the

strange new tone of utter contempt in the figure's voice. "The only one I'll shoot is you if you don't give me back my wife—unharmed."

"Listen to me carefully. No longer must you be a fool and live in torture of a sin which is really not a sin. I offer you now a way out. Shoot the priest, and I will give you back your wife. Go on! Do it. Just put the gun to his head and squeeze the trigger."

"No."

"No?" the thing bellowed. "Very well. I leave then."

"No. You forget I have the gun."

"I give you Jonas. Take him. He will lead you to your destiny."

Jantzen was uncertain what to do, who or what to believe. It seemed he had no choice but to play their sick game.

"Mark, stay calm," Father McMartin warned.

Holding his arms out, taking a step toward Jantzen, the one called Jonas said, "Go on, take me as your hostage. You will find us sincere."

Suddenly Father McMartin pulled out the crucifix. No one moved. Even more strange, Jonas didn't even look at the priest as McMartin laid the cross on the man's forehead.

Michael roared with laughter.

"In the name—"

"Of Jesus Christ," Michael said, completing the priest's words as if reading his mind. "I command you, Satan, to leave this man. In the name of Christ, I compel you!"

McMartin froze, staggered back, horrified. But there was no visible reaction on the face of Jonas.

"What, good father?" Michael said. "Did you

think your cross, dipped in your so-called holy water, would prevail against our power? What you do not understand, of course, in your ignorance, is that you cannot expel one of our legion when we are part of Legion in the flesh."

"But I can burn you alive," Jantzen said.

And Jantzen could almost smell their fear in the long moments of hard silence.

"I leave you now with Jonas." Michael stood. "Do not attempt to follow me. Jonas will show you the way."

"You're not going anywhere," Jantzen said.

"Oh, but I am. If my followers do not see me by the middle of tomorrow morning, alone, they will kill your wife."

Angry and frustrated, Jantzen stood, frozen, staring at the Satanist. "How do I know you haven't already killed my wife?"

"An honest question, which deserves an honest reply. We have not."

"Yet."

"It's all up to you."

"In what way? You haven't told me what you want."

The priest said, "They have, Mark. I fear...I begin to understand it now."

"What? What do you understand?"

"Later. Not now."

"The good father understands we need your fear, your hatred to keep us strong. It is what I sought out, it is what brought us together. It is why I was guided to you. Not even I completely understand why I ended up in Newton and why we are now facing each other in this moment of truth."

"Get out of here!" Jantzen growled.

"You will find us, do not fear."

"Oh, I'll find you, all right."

"Hear me, foolish one. Your weakness, your folly will destroy and cast you into the eternal fires of hell. There is no hope; you have already entered there and the gates are slamming shut on your soul even as we speak. I am here only to show you the way and the truth and the darkness of eternity." Slowly the white demon, grinning, walked past the priest. Jantzen kept his guard up, suspicious of some trap being sprung, some sudden violent move on the bald demon's part.

In silence, though, the demon left, shutting the door behind him.

"Give him a few minutes, then we can leave," Jonas said.

Jantzen's rage grew. The demons were the ones giving the orders, dictating his course of action. But what could he do? Nothing. At least not at the moment.

It was total insanity, he thought. His wife's life was dangled over his head. But why? So that his fear and anger and hunger for vengeance could feed their dark souls?

Outside an engine rumbled to life. Headlights hit the curtain, then slowly faded, leaving only the three of them in the shadows and the flickering candlelight.

Chapter Twenty-eight

Mid-morning they passed Waco.

The new day was only a few hours old, and already Jantzen was exhausted, frayed, stretched to snapping. He felt old as time, angrier than any army of demons in hell.

Father McMartin drove, their hostage sat in the passenger seat, and Jantzen maintained vigilance from the back.

Two things kept Jantzen going.

A thermos of coffee. And fear.

They had given the bald demon a forty-five-minute head start last night, at the insistence of Jonas. Jantzen relented only because Jonas said if Michael was tailed outright, Jantzen's wife would be killed right away, no question. So be it.

Hope was something else that kept Jantzen running. Not to mention a burning hunger for total vengeance. How it all played out, he was grimly aware, was anybody's guess.

They continued to ride in silence, brown prairie sweeping past in both directions as the priest drove south at a steady sixty mph on I-35.

The sun, a flaming orange eye, baked the far-reaching prairie. The air-conditioning was up high, but still Jantzen felt beads of moisture break out on his forehead. With little or no sleep, no sustenance other than days of poisoning himself with alcohol and anger, Jantzen knew he was just about at the limits of physical endurance. Anger can take a man only so far, he knew.

Jantzen wasn't interested in comfort, though, or scenery; it all looked and felt the same. Brown on brown outside, black on black inside. More prairie, but he knew that soon, perhaps close to midday, the closer they drove to the border, the more lunar and harsh the landscape would become. Desert and hill country. Abandoned forts, maybe an old ghost town from the frontier days. Soon there would be nothing but the vast and cruel desert. It seemed that was where they were headed. It also appeared that the Satanists had been to some specific spot before where they had performed some atrocity.

And were preparing a new one.

Jantzen lit a cigarette, staring at the back of the Satanist's head. "Father, next rest area where there's a gas station, pull in. I need you to fill up the can. Purchase some rope, cord, anything you find."

The priest looked more troubled than ever. Silence lingered on.

"There's one just ahead."

"Good enough."

"When we get there," McMartin said, "if you and I could have a moment alone to talk."

"Don't worry," the one called Jonas said. "I have no intention of escaping."

"You have no fear of us, that it?" Jantzen said.

"You have enough fear for all of us."

"You understand that if anything happens to my wife, terror is the last thing you'll know in this world. Terror and pain."

"I fear no man."

"Right. You've got your great, bald leader with his connections to hell."

"You mock us. But we are real enough. And we are stronger than you know."

"You really believe all that crap, don't you?" No answer, so Jantzen pushed it. "All I see is a bunch of sick people who can only get any kind of thrill or any kind of feeling out of living by brutally murdering others."

"It's the way of the world. In many ways we are only the world's mirror."

"It's the way of sick people. Evil walks—"

"Judge not lest you be judged," Jonas said, and laughed.

"Didn't let me finish. I've been sick long enough. What you don't understand is that you've shown me the light."

They fell silent. A strange, defiant look hardened the face of the Satanist.

Jantzen waited, trying to keep himself calm and under control while the priest pulled into the rest area. It was one of those combo service station-diner deals that marked America from coast to coast. At that time of the morning the lot was packed. It was the middle of summer, after all, a lot of travelers, tourists, Jantzen figured, raking over Texas with their fast food, kids and cameras. One big holiday vacation. Welcome to the party. If he found himself cynical right then, Jantzen felt he'd earned it.

Nothing about the world made much sense any longer. Except saving his wife. Getting himself and Father McMartin back to Oklahoma in one piece. Hopefully, too, with some toehold on sanity.

"Mark, I'll get what you want, then will you meet me outside?"

The priest had parked near the diner. Jantzen gave him forty dollars. McMartin took the ten-gallon can from the back and moved toward the row of gas pumps.

Jantzen took a long swallow from the canteen, then offered it to Jonas, who accepted, drank.

"You share with me?"

There was mockery in the man's voice.

Jantzen smoked. "You don't have anything I could catch."

Jonas turned, pinned Jantzen with a laughing eye as he handed back the canteen.

"You're welcome," Jantzen said.

"It will be over soon enough."

Jantzen blew smoke in the man's face. "You're right about that one. One way or another. If you think you targeted a sheep being led to the slaughter, you're going to find out just how wrong you are."

"No sheep, Jantzen. A lion, that's what Michael wants."

"I forgot. You need my fear to stay strong. Tell me, is that what this is really all about? A game? Some sick game?"

"It's no game. It's real, and everything Michael told you is true. We used up what we could from your town and whoever we could use. It was time to move on. That's our way. We need something new. New life, new death, renewed fear. New blood."

In a large way, Jantzen had to accept that. He had seen Simpson, he had seen too much in the past few days that couldn't be explained. And maybe the bald ghoul was right. There was no getting reason from unreason. Maybe the only way to fight them, to fight "it," was to accept, stay strong, remain calm in the face of their pure and monstrous evil.

When Father McMartin returned, Jantzen opened the door. He looked up front, saw the keys in the ignition and reached over the seat and took them.

"You haven't even tied my hands up to this point," Jonas said. "Surely you must believe I'm not going to run."

"I have the gun. I'm itching for a reason to shoot you dead. I won't be far."

The shotgun was tucked firmly under the backseat. If Jonas made some grandstand move, the mood Jantzen was in—a killing mood—he would scratch his itch.

The priest had brought some rope, and Jantzen

decided not to take any chances. After looking around the lot, finding no one watching them, Jantzen pulled a pocket knife from the glove box, cut off a strip of rope, then quickly tied the Satanist's hands.

Then, taking a few steps away from the Jeep, one eye on Jonas, Jantzen faced the priest.

"What is it, Father?"

"Last night in the motel, I must tell you. What I heard, what I saw...I now know we are faced with something that is total and hopelessly unredeemable evil."

"Sounds like I've got your blessing."

"I'm afraid this is going to end badly. I must tell you now..." The priest hesitated. "The other night—I know this may sound bizarre, even crazy to you—but while I was asleep I had a dream. A dream so real it was as if I was living it. I saw you. It wasn't even a dream, I think, but a vision, I don't know. I saw you...in a dark place with a gun, the exact same shotgun you now have. There was screaming and these horrible creatures who looked human enough but came at you resembling wild animals in some way. Then a voice, unlike any voice I've ever heard, a soothing, warm voice, neither male nor female, I can't say—entered my dream, but I wasn't even sure I was dreaming.

"Suddenly you were no longer there. Nothing but light, a pure and blinding light, so warm, so peaceful, this—sudden rush of peace and tranquillity, a euphoria I have never known, it filled my...head, or my soul, I can't be sure. The voice told me to go to you, to help you. It was clear, it was determined, and I heard that the choice was mine but it was not mine, but that I knew what must be done. The voice told me that you could be saved and to do whatever was necessary. It said there will be darkness, but that light will follow, that only light can prevail. Time stood still, or rushed forward, I don't know, but it was a sensation I can't define. It was beyond anything of a human experience. It was only a full hour later...when I realized I was wide awake, that my eyes were open, that perhaps I had never even fallen asleep. I can't explain. But I'm here."

Jantzen didn't know what to say. He just stared at the priest, who looked at once utterly bewildered but somehow peaceful. His eyes even seemed to glow, whether from memory of the experience or from the lingering effects of the experience itself.

"I don't even know what it is I'm trying to tell you right now. All I know...what I believe, is that I've been guided here to you. That whatever is going to happen it's God's will."

"Even if it means killing?"

"They are evil beyond redemption, these...people. Evil, like good, is infectious. Now, are these individuals possessed? I can't say, but I believe they may even be beyond possession."

"Chosen by the devil?"

The priest shrugged. "Who can say? If they believe it, then they are. What I know is that the both of us are going to be faced with an evil that could well destroy us. And your wife. In the coming hours we must have faith, in ourselves and in God. If you are ready, then we must do whatever is necessary to defeat this evil."

* * *

It was well into the afternoon when Jonas gave the order for them to turn off the Interstate, some thirty miles south of San Antonio. The countryside turned barren, rocky, dotted with jagged hills.

Jantzen noticed the Satanist was checking the countryside, obviously looking for landmarks.

Eventually, maybe an hour later, he told the priest to turn off onto a narrow dirt trail that cut through some ominous-looking hills with saw-tooth peaks. For another good hour, the priest drove west, slowly, the Jeep bouncing over ruts and rocks.

"Where are we?" Jantzen asked. Not a soul, not even an isolated trailer home, marred the empty landscape.

"We're almost there."

On a trail overlooking a ghost town Jonas told them to stop. Shanties and blown-over falsefronts littered a narrow valley below.

Jantzen and the priest got out of the Jeep. They had parked on a hilltop, overlooking a stretch of desert that rolled in a series of crags and gulleys to the west where an outcropping of low-lying hills jutted.

Jantzen hauled out his prisoner. "All right, you said we're there. Now, where are they?"

"Not yet. They will come to you, right here."

"When?"

"Tonight."

"Not soon enough."

"It will have to be. I can't force Micheal's hand."

"Well, I can." Jantzen thrust the barrel of the

Colt under the Satanist's chin. "You're going to take me to them."

Jonas said nothing. Instead he smiled. "Kill me and you'll never find them. And your precious wife will surely die."

"Mark," Jantzen heard McMartin call out. "Perhaps we should do as he says."

"Wait?"

"Yes."

Jantzen scowled, pulled the gun away.

"May I have some water?"

Jantzen whirled on Jonas. "What?"

"Water. I need to piss, also."

"So piss."

"Would you mind? The water first. Please? I would like some privacy."

"You, of all people, worried about privacy?"

"Indulge me. Consider it a last request, if you want."

Jantzen stared into the Satanist's eyes. There was no life in the eyes, just something cold. It seemed a small favor. And what could this—thing—do anyway? From inside the Jeep, he grabbed a canteen, shoved it in the man's belly.

"Just go on the other side. I'll turn my back, okay?" Jantzen said, sarcastic. "Since you're the shy type."

Jonas looked back over his shoulder. The ex-cop was watching him at first, then turned away. Jantzen had bought it.

But he knew he'd have to move quickly. At least the lower half of his body was concealed by the Jeep. At least the fool, in his earlier quick frisking of his body for a weapon, had not found the small vial.

His hands were tied in front, which would make the task even more difficult. There was no choice but to try. He uncapped the canteen, unzipped himself, wanting it to look just as he said it would. He swallowed several deep gulps of water.

"Hey, easy on the water."

Jonas flinched. He looked back, saw Jantzen scowling, but turned away. He was moving to stand by the priest at the edge of the hill. Quickly Jonas took the small vial from his pants pocket, uncapped it, and dumped the brownish-white mixture into the canteen. If Jantzen saw him now...

He was just finishing dumping the combination sedative-hallucinogen into the canteen when he saw Jantzen look his way. Jonas held up the canteen and said, "Thank you."

"Hurry up."

He started pissing. It was awkward. He would look suspicious if he was closely watched. One hand holding the canteen, the other slipping the empty vial back into his pants while relieving himself. But he was tied up, so it was reasonable to conclude he was having difficulties.

He zipped up, walked around the front of the Jeep, and was met by Jantzen. He handed Jantzen the canteen.

Jantzen uncapped the canteen, his eyes suspicious. "You didn't piss in it, did you?"

"Why would I do that? I have to drink it myself."

Jantzen smelled it just the same. He was sweating. Dehydrated. He drank, deep and long. Jonas hoped Jantzen would offer the priest some. But the priest seemed to be far off in his own little world.

"Father, you want some water?"

"What? Oh, water."

Jonas saw Jantzen pin him with a hard look.

"What's so funny?"

Jonas shrugged. "Nothing. Nothing at all."

Two, maybe three minutes at worst, he figured. It was the beginning of the end for Jantzen and the priest.

"Mark, perhaps I will have some water."

Out of nowhere, Jantzen's world started to wobble, then waver. One second he was walking toward Father McMartin, who was standing on the edge of the hill locked in some distant world of his own, and then everything exploded, rolled, lit up in a flickering, darting flash of bright colors.

He knew what had happened. Even before Jantzen turned so slowly, he never thought his head would make it, a head attached to a body that felt like rubber. He saw the Satanist grinning.

He saw Father McMartin lift the canteen to his lips.

Janteen's own voice sounded a thousand miles away in his ears as he shouted—or thought he shouted, "No, Father! Don't drink it!"

The priest's face seemed to melt, dripping like wax. Garbled words seemed to float on the desert.

"What?"

"Poison . . . Fa-Father . . . don't . . ."

He felt his knees turn to jelly. He pulled his gun, which felt hot as a coal in his hand, but he knew it was the drug, some hallucinogen the bastard had slipped into the water. Jantzen waded through a bright but slogging muddy mist. The bastard stood there, grinning. His face seemed to change before his eyes into something hairy, with fangs. It wasn't real, Jantzen told himself.

"It *is* real, you cocksucker!"

No. Not his voice. Not the Satanist.

Jantzen lifted the gun, or thought he lifted the gun. Close, so close. Then the thing with the wolf's face charged him.

In and out of reality. First the mist, then the bright sunshine.

Focus on the face. Shoot the animal! Blow that smug grin off.

But he couldn't find his reflexes. No will.

The foot shot up, buried itself so deep in his gut he felt the pain knife up and down his spine, driving the air from his lungs. The world was falling, swallowing him up. Vomit was burning up his chest.

He looked up instinctively. Somehow he knew he had hit the ground.

There. Through the shimmering myriad-colored fog. The wolf-thing, running, back turned.

Where was the gun?

Desperate, Jantzen scrambled through the dirt. Rocks became razors in his eyes, but he knew it was an illusion.

He saw Father McMartin, the face now normal, not melting away. The priest had the gun.

Jantzen tried to find his voice, urge the priest to do the unnatural. To defy, make it count, stand the fuck up and be counted.

"Shoot him...shoot him..."

A cannon roared. But no scream.

Echo of gunshots. Lingering, piercing his mind, the light and the colors, collapsing on his face. Light, sound, all living and breathing and laughing at him.

"Oh, God."

Was it over?

Jantzen collapsed on his back. The sky was right in his face, crushing him, smothering him.

Chapter Twenty-nine

Time stood so still that the world appeared dead to Jantzen. Rubbery, lightheaded, nauseous, he remained seated, slumped against the edge of his vehicle. How long had he been like that? Sitting, a human mummy? What drug was in his body? Certainly some hallucinogen, but what? Acid? Peyote? Some combination that the Satanists had concocted?

The sky had turned many colors during however long he had been drugged. Long ago—hours, maybe even days it seemed—he had checked his watch. Stared at the hands of time which didn't seem to move. Then they did, the longer he stared, as if he could will time to move forward.

Three-thirty.

Four. Then five.

Sun burning.

Six.

Sky wavering, blue, purple, orange and pink bands. Was that a laughing face in the sky?

Seven-ten.

Time check.

No. The face of Father McMartin.

Now he tasted bile on his lips, squeezed his eyes shut against the burning flow of sweat. For some time, he had vomited on his own, then stuck his hand down his throat, inducing as much vomiting as possible to empty the contents of his stomach, hoping to flush out the drugs.

"Drink some more, Mark."

He took the other canteen. Father McMartin was hunched beside him. The priest's face was still shrouded in the foggy pink of Jantzen's drug stupor.

"Did...Jonas...he looked like a wolf to me. Did he look that way to you?"

"No. He looked quite human. It's only the drug."

Jantzen drank. Shadows were stretching over the flat tabletop in front of him. Obviously the priest had gotten him out of the sun.

"How long, Father...time...nothing moves..."

"Five hours I have sat with you."

"It'll be dark soon."

"It's getting dark now."

"Did you...I heard a gunshot."

"I...I missed him."

Jantzen looked up at the priest and saw shame in his eyes. "You mean you—"

"Please. I am a man of God, Mark."

"I understand. Let me do the killing."

"If there must be killing."

"Did you see which way he went?"

"The hills beyond this ghost town. To the northwest. Are you feeling any better?"

"Not much, but I'm getting some strength back. It doesn't matter. Help me stand. We have to get going."

The priest helped him rise. Jantzen went to the back of the Jeep, checked on the two crates. The jugs were packed tight beside each other. It didn't appear that the rough ride in this rough back country had knocked any of the jugs out of the crate or sloshed out their contents. Still, Jantzen took the time to check each one.

"I'm almost afraid to ask what you're going to do."

"Father, you said we must do whatever it takes, whatever's necessary."

"Do you have a plan?"

"No. But any of those people who stand between me and getting my wife back will die. I'll handle the guns, if that makes you feel any better."

Standing and moving seemed to clear his head a little more. Now Jantzen saw something uncertain flicker through the priest's eyes.

"Mark, before we go, is there anything you'd like to tell me?"

"Like what?"

"Confession?"

"Last rites?" Angry determination fueled Jantzen and seemed to put even more strength back in his limbs. "Father, I've got nothing to say, nothing to ask for but a little bit of help from my friends. And, yeah, okay, a little bit of divine intervention. You drive. Let's finish this. If you have any doubts, speak now."

The priest nodded. "Let's finish it."

It was then that the howling swept over the hill. Both Jantzen and the priest jumped. Startled, they looked toward the distant hills. Then Jantzen heard what sounded like chanting, washing over them from a great distance. He listened. What were they saying?

"Chomdun... Chomdun..."

Jantzen took his shotgun from the back, then relieved Father McMartin of the Colt, tucked it in his waistband. Walking to the edge of the hill, scouring the deep shadows around the base, he saw shadows darting up the gulley. Three in all, skittering about, hiding quickly in nooks and crevices when they thought they were spotted. There could be more.

"Let's go, Father. It's started."

While he swiftly moved back toward his vehicle, what they were chanting became clear to Jantzen.

They were praying.

And his blood turned ice-cold.

"Come. Come."

So be it. He was going.

Mary Jantzen didn't want to believe it was happening, but it was. They had her staked out on the cold, rocky floor of a large cave. They had lit candles around her. They were kneeling, praying some awful prayer to the devil.

Whatever drug they had given her was beginning to wear off. Shivering, she slowly realized she was stark naked. She looked around, saw the torches hung from the dark walls of the cave. Where was Mark? Did he know? She implored God to help her, to save her.

"We offer you, Lord of Darkness, her body and her soul. Come. Come. Take her fear, take her flesh. Come. Come."

She turned her head and choked off a scream somehow.

All around her were people—or were they even people?—with masks of animals. There were horns of goats and rams. White masks with red eyes. Reptile faces. Whites of eyes. Fangs. Claws. No. It couldn't be. Some of the animals' heads looked real; then she realized they were actually wearing animal heads.

She felt sick.

Then she saw a huge figure in a black robe loom over her. Black eyes stared down at her from behind the mask of a ram. He held a gold chalice, tipped it over. She squirmed as the slick, hot gore spattered her stomach and chest.

"Oh, yes, Mary, my sweet Mary, soon to be our Master's new whore in the pleasures of hell and eternal damnation," the cold voice laughed, filling her with dread. "He comes. His fear brings him to us. We need his fear. He is on the way."

Who? She heard herself cry, "Why are you doing this?"

"There is no why, there just is. Be still, child. But I will tell you, what will happen here will fill the pits of hell with enormous joy."

"My husband...where is he?...What have you done to him?"

"We have done nothing, my child-whore. This is the completion of his circle and the closing of our own."

What did that mean? Where was Mark?

She saw the huge knife, lowering. She screamed.

"Silence!"

The cold edge of the blade was rested on her breast.

"Feel it. Feel it. Soon, not now. He needs to see this. He missed the first time. Not even your husband understands that his fear will be complete and that your true lord and master, Satan, is ready to accept him. The circle is nearly closed."

"Come, come..."

They were near the base of the hill when Jantzen pinpointed the direction from which the chanting came. It was the flickering of light in the mouth of a cave, perhaps a hundred feet up and at the far edge of a ledge, another two hundred feet beside him, that betrayed the location of the ritual.

Mary. He hoped he wasn't too late. He wasn't even sure what he would do, but he had to move quickly, decisively. If that meant going in and blasting away, then he would. In his mind, given what he'd seen them capable of doing, he would gun them down in cold blood, even if they were unarmed.

"Help me carry those crates and the gas can, Father."

Something of a plan was forming in his mind. He would get Mary out of the cave, then shoot and burn as many of them as he could. Seal the entrance in a blaze of fire. If the cave wasn't deep, maybe the fire would suck all the air out, choke them to death.

Maybe.

Now it was time to act.

He was out, searching his flanks when the creature leapt on the Jeep. It came shrieking at him, flying on top of him, something wearing a deer's head. Whether they were real claws or not, they came slashing for his throat as he toppled to the hard-packed soil with the thing on top of him. Somehow Jantzen hauled out the Colt, jammed it in the naked flesh of the Satanist's stomach and squeezed the trigger, twice. The gun blasts were muffled somewhat as the slugs blew out the Satanist's back in a spray of gore. Flinging the twitching corpse off him, Jantzen found Father McMartin standing next to him. Fear and disbelief shadowed the priest's face.

The chanting had grown louder, more intense.

"Come! Come!"

"Father, snap out of it! I need you strong!"

Jantzen took a crate, hoisted it on his shoulder.

Finally the priest moved, hauled out the other crate. "Yes, yes."

Shotgun in hand, Jantzen asked, "Can you carry, drag, whatever, the gas can?"

"I think so. Yes."

"Do it. Let's hurry, Father!"

It was a grueling, agonizingly time-consuming hike to the mouth of the cave. Only fear and adrenaline kept Jantzen moving.

At least they were still chanting. Sick bastards.

He peered around the corner. The praying

sounded as if it came from twenty, thirty yards away, from just over a ledge that probably overlooked the cave's floor.

"We are preparing her, oh, Lord of Darkness... see her fear..."

Jantzen handed the priest the Colt. "Take it, Father. Stay here. Use it if you have to. I'm counting on you. Take the can, slosh the gas over the front of this entrance. Take each jug and put them about three feet apart just inside. Half on one side, half on the other."

"What are you going to do, Mark?"

He saw the priest was becoming terrified. Something that bordered on despair or desperation showed on McMartin's face.

"I'm going to get Mary. Stay here and wait until I get back. I know there are still some of them out there behind us. Watch your back."

Jantzen hefted the other crate on his shoulder. Then he moved into the cave, eyes peeled, finger curled around the shotgun's trigger. If anything moved for him, it was dead.

In some way he didn't even comprehend, Jantzen knew he was possessed. But at that moment, cold as he felt, he had never known a more pure and enlightened sensation.

He came over the ledge, rising, looking down, bringing the shotgun to bear on the circle of demons.

At first he felt outrage, seeing his wife naked, trussed up. Then he saw some crimson substance, most likely blood, on her stomach. His head swam in terror.

"Mary!"

"Mark! Mark!"

She was alive. They had only doused her in some ceremonial gore.

Jantzen recognized the back of the head of the stark white dome of the bald demon. He was wearing a ram's mask. He held a large knife. His black eyes seemed to shine with anticipation of bloodletting.

Jantzen spotted a rocky incline that led to the floor of the cave. Descending, he tried to take in the horror of what he found. Masks of animals with cold, dead eyes of humans stared back at him. They turned slowly toward him, silent things, grinning lips. The women were naked. In all, he counted thirteen Satanists in the circle around his wife. They had painted the same black circle he had seen before, with the upside-down crucifix at the top.

"Cut her free!" Jantzen ordered.

"It doesn't have to be this way, Mark."

"It's over," Jantzen told Michael. "Cut her free and give her her clothes or I'll start shooting."

"You cannot escape us. You cannot leave here."

"Watch."

"It isn't that easy," the demon said. "The circle has been destined before our time to be completed. Only now do I see it must be sealed in the blood of your anger."

"The only thing I'm angry about is what you did to me and my family in Atlanta. It won't happen again."

"But it must."

"Cut her loose right now, or you're the first one to go."

The bald demon gave the order to let her go. But something felt wrong to Jantzen. It was something in their looks, their silence.

A Satanist in a wolf's mask took a knife. If it made any sudden move other than cutting the ropes around his wife's hands and ankles, Jantzen would blow its head off, and he warned just that.

Mary scrambled free, grabbed her discarded clothes, dressed. Moments later, Jantzen took her in one arm.

"Have they hurt you in any way?"

Trembling, she shook her head, blurted, "No."

Then it happened. He had let his guard down long enough for the attack from behind and above to descend on him. He heard his wife scream his name, then, at the last possible instant, spotted the thing in what looked like a bat mask falling straight from the ceiling.

Jantzen was hammered to the floor by the full weight of his attacker slamming him in the back. Somehow he held onto the shotgun, rolled and fired point-blank into the bat face. Blew its head clean off.

Racking the slide, Jantzen was on his feet as the Satanists screamed and cursed and scattered for the farthest, deepest parts of the cave. It didn't appear there was another way out, but it was obvious to Jantzen they were seeking cover behind boulders or low-lying walls of rock.

A bullet whined off stone beside Jantzen. He triggered the shotgun into the wildly dispersing Satanists.

Grabbing Mary by the arm, he pulled her back up the incline.

Gunfire ricocheted off stone below him.

In the chaos below he couldn't determine where the firing was coming from, or even how many guns they brandished. But it didn't matter.

Flicking the Zippo, he torched the first strip. He took the jug and hurled it toward a trio of male Satanists charging for the incline. It blew, spewing gas, flaming wingtips consuming them. Shrieking filled the cave.

"Move!" Jantzen ordered his wife, lighting the strips on the rest of the jugs, eight in all, with deft, swift movements. He picked up the crate, all strips lit, and threw with all his strength.

Down there, the Satanists were darting everywhere, bumping and slamming into each other, knocking each other down.

Someone—he thought he recognized the voice of the bald leader—bellowed, *"Noooooo!"*

Then a fireball exploded, brilliant boiling waves of flames eating up more Satanists. Human torches flailed, screamed.

Then Jantzen heard a startled yell, followed by an angry snarling sound.

A gunshot.

The sound of his Colt.

Reaching his wife, he took Mary by the arm.

Rounding the corner, Jantzen saw the thing with flashing teeth bury its fangs into Father McMartin's throat. His mind screamed even as he saw it, even as he knew it was too late. The priest struggled beneath it, but his gun hand was held to the ground. Another shadow form dropped into the mouth of the cave.

Jantzen triggered the shotgun and blew the head off of the one with the fangs with the blood of the priest on them. He jacked the action and triggered a blast that disemboweled the other Satanist and blew it over the edge of the hill.

"Father!"

Heart sinking, Jantzen knelt by the priest, but he could see the extent of the wound. The Satanist had ripped Father McMartin's throat out. Grief and rage tore through Jantzen.

Then unearthly screaming and cursing from the bowels of the cave snared his attention. Turning, he saw them boiling up over the ledge, as if scaling the wall like human spiders. He glimpsed the horror in his wife's eyes and screamed, "Stay behind me and do exactly what I tell you!"

The creatures crawled across the floor, crabbing toward him. No ram's head. Perhaps the leader of these monsters was already burning alive below.

The stench of roasting flesh and gasoline pierced Jantzen's nose. Four, maybe five shadows were coming at him.

He pulled his wife by the arm, scooped up the Colt. "Take it, and use it if anything comes at us!"

She gave a shaky nod. Jantzen reached down, dragged the unmoving form of the priest from the mouth of the cave.

He heard their vile curses, screaming at them that there was no escape.

"Come. Come."

Jantzen flicked the Zippo. In the dancing flame, he saw that Father McMartin had placed five jugs on one side, five on the other side, several feet deep inside the entrance.

"Come. Come back. We need you!"

Jantzen tossed the lighter. He darted, Mary in his arm, down the ledge as flames whooshed to life. There was a series of muffled explosions, followed by one long chorus of unending shrieking.

With his last reserves of strength and will, Jantzen draped Father McMartin over his shoulder in a fireman's carry.

The shrieking went on and on, echoing, some maddening din that seemed to carve his brain in half. He looked back, stumbling down the ledge. A flaming scarecrow burst through the roiling firewall, pitched over the edge and tumbled in freefall.

Jantzen searched the night, shotgun low by his side, and told his wife to drive, don't stop, don't look back. Mary hopped in the Cherokee. Gently, Jantzen laid the priest across the backseat. He hadn't wanted it to end like this, but Father McMartin would never know how he had helped save their lives.

Or maybe, he thought, the priest did know.

The engine roared to life.

With heartfelt sorrow, Jantzen closed the priest's eyes.

With one last look at the mouth of the cave he found nothing moving.

The shrieking died.

Mary hit the gas, reversed the Jeep out of there.

Jantzen kept watch for anything that rushed or even dropped on the Jeep.

He found nothing but a cloud of dust in their wake.

Chapter Thirty

They drove through the night, north up I-35. In a few more hours they would be home, but Jantzen had to wonder if they would be safe. He became troubled, dark, and couldn't understand why.

Solemn, haunted, Mary kept her eyes on the road. Staring at Mary, Jantzen was concerned how the whole nightmarish experience would affect his wife.

"Are you okay?" he asked.

She nodded.

"Are you sure?"

"I...I think so. I'm still...in shock. Mark, this isn't over, is it? I mean, there will be legal trouble."

"We'll need a lawyer. It's a mess, but we can get it worked out. It's going to take time."

She reached over and took his hand. She seemed

to be on the verge of tears. "It doesn't matter. We'll face it together. You saved my life, Mark."

"I couldn't have done it, I don't think, without... Father McMartin."

Grief tore through her eyes. "Yes. I don't... What are we going to do now? What do we do about Father McMartin?"

"I need to call Colonel Wiley. I think he can help. But I'll have to come clean. Mary, there's some things that happened while you were gone. I killed Buddy Simpson. He was one of them. Find a place and pull over."

He told her everything. About Simpson. The bank robbery. The cow's head. At first she looked shaken, mortified. Then she said she was just glad it was over. She was exhausted by the entire nightmarish ordeal.

They talked about Father McMartin, and he told her why the priest had involved himself. Without the priest's help, having been drugged, Jantzen told Mary he wasn't sure if either one of them would still be alive. For a good forty-five minutes they sat parked in the rest area near the Texas-Oklahoma border.

He was surprised at the strength and courage his wife showed.

They held each other for some time. He told his wife he would take over the driving.

"I just want to go home, Mark, where it's safe again."

"I couldn't agree more. I don't know what will happen to us, but as long as we face it together, we'll be all right."

She smiled, a sad, warm smile, but Jantzen read a message of hope in the look.

"I believe that," she said. "Now more than ever."

It was four-thirty in the morning when they arrived home.

Jantzen turned on the lamp by the couch, then brought Father McMartin's body into the living room and covered him with a blanket.

"Why don't you go lie down?"

Mary nodded. She was ready to collapse. She went into their bedroom. He went outside. He looked around, searching the darkness, the highway. Everything felt too still, too quiet. He took the box of .12 gauge shells, loaded the shotgun, then slapped a fresh clip into the Colt, chambered rounds in the handgun and shotgun. Again he scoured the night for a full minute. And again he was troubled, instinctively felt something was still wrong.

With his back turned to the house, Mark Jantzen didn't see two shadows boil up out of the night beside the front porch. Silent and swift, the shadows entered the front door.

Jantzen tucked the Colt in the waistband in the back of his pants.

Back inside, at the couch, Jantzen called the State Police barracks. Colonel Wiley was still on duty.

"Jantzen, where the hell are you?"

"I'm home. Look, it's a long story—"

"I'll bet it is. Where have you been?"

"It's not important now. We need to talk."

"Do you know Stephens is dead?"

"What?"

"His deputy went to his home at about five this evening. Report of a gunshot by a neighbor. Stephens blew his head off with a shotgun. We found Satanic paraphernalia all over the man's trailer. What I'm thinking is that you know something, and you're holding back."

"I have a lot to tell you, Colonel."

"Jantzen, don't jack me around. I haven't been home in two days, with all that's been happening. Fact is I've been right here the past eight hours, trying to call you. I've even been to your house, looking for you. You know why?"

"Colonel, how long will it take you to get here?"

"I can be there within the hour. No, sit tight, I've got a man in the area. You're right about one thing—you've got a lot of explaining to do, because my gut tells me you've been jerking me around."

Numb with disbelief, Jantzen laid the phone down. Stephens had committed suicide? Or had he? Had he even been part of the cult? Or covering up? Bribed?

Something blurred in the corner of his eye. Something huge was flying at him from his blind side while another large figure peeled off and melted into the bedroom.

Jantzen reacted, jumping to his feet, but the huge figure slashed him in the jaw, exploding stars in his eyes. Jantzen toppled over the couch but not before the image of Jonas snarling in his face took shape in his mind.

"Mark!"

He looked up, saw the malevolent grinning face of Jonas. He glimpsed his wife struggling in the arms of the bald demon. Terrified, knowing he had to do something fast or they were both dead, Jantzen pulled the Colt .45.

"You thought you could kill me or Jonas!"

He had another glimpse of the bald demon. Now the Satanist leader truly looked inhuman. Somehow he had survived the fire, had escaped the inferno in the cave, but the left side of his face was horribly burned. It was now a partial but living demon's mask of blackened-purple flesh. He was bringing up a knife when he slung Mary into the china cabinet. She cried out as glass shattered and she hit the floor.

"You killed my whole clan, but not us!"

At point-blank range, Jantzen triggered the Colt, two, then three times into Jonas's chest. Still the Satanist, even as bullets gouged holes in his chest and blood sprayed, charged Jantzen. Before he knew it, Jantzen was lifted into the air and flung like a rag doll, crashing down through the coffee table, pulping it to shards and splinters. Desperately clinging to consciousness, hearing the bald demon snarl, "Come here, bitch!" Jantzen lifted the Colt, saw Jonas staggering for him, and began to empty the clip into Jonas.

Jonas twitched and jerked, growled and cursed. Jantzen's final round cored into the Satanist's head and dropped him just as Jonas loomed in his sight.

Jantzen swept up the shotgun. The demon was descending on Mary, knife raised.

Bellowing in outrage, Jantzen triggered the shotgun, the buckshot tearing into the demon's back. A hideous scream erupted from Michael's mouth, his face contorting in rage and agony. The impact of the blast twisted him around and Jantzen cannoned another round, tunneled open his chest. He jacked the action and blew the thing's face off, then followed up with a final decapitating blast.

Jantzen rushed to his wife. She was shaking violently, near hysterics. He held her.

"Mary! Mary, it's all right, they're dead, they can't hurt you."

She wept.

"Take me out of here, Mark, please!"

He picked her up in his arms. As he carried her outside he saw the first of several police cruisers rolling down the driveway.

Jantzen tossed the shotgun away. He let his wife weep, loud and hard, in the crook of his neck.